THE LAST MERMAID PRINCESS

LILY LEWIS

ANAPHORA LITERARY PRESS

QUANAH, TEXAS

ANAPHORA LITERARY PRESS
1108 W 3rd Street
Quanah, TX 79252
https://anaphoraliterary.com

Book design by Anna Faktorovich, Ph.D.

Published in 2018 by Anaphora Literary Press

The Last Mermaid Princess
Lily Lewis—1st edition.

Library of Congress Control Number: 2018947710

Library Cataloging Information

Lewis, Lily, author.
   The last mermaid princess / Lily Lewis
   202 p. ; 9 in.
   ISBN 978-1-68114-433-7 (softcover : alk. paper)
   ISBN 978-1-68114-434-4 (hardcover : alk. paper)
   ISBN 978-1-68114-435-1 (e-book)
1. Fiction—Literary. 2. Fiction—Women.
3. Fiction—Asian American.
PN3311-3503: Literature: Prose fiction
813: American fiction in English

THE LAST MERMAID PRINCESS

LILY LEWIS

CONTENTS

Introduction

We all have a little voice that whispers things we would prefer not to hear. It compels us to stay on the right path and do the right thing. And while most people have a pretty good grasp on the rules of play, many tell themselves tiny little lies to justify their bad decisions and continue in the wrong direction. But make no mistake, life has a funny way of exacting a price, a price that may be impossible to pay.

The heart betrays us, time and again. And knowing with the head is not the same as knowing with the heart, so we close our eyes and swan dive into the abyss. I have plunged into the deep end, foolishly denying it all the way down. Yet, one must invariably take ownership of the destruction they have caused, and with that admission of culpability, they may begin the long way back.

This pseudo-autobiographical story chronicles the life of Lily and her attempts to understand the world and her place in it. The triumphs and failures she encounters resonate in every human because Lily represents the human condition and the inherent flaws in everyone. In one sense, she is an alter-ego manifested in a fictional character whose behavior, words, thoughts, and personal history intentionally represent those of the author. In another sense, she is the embodiment of all people in all places at all times.

The mermaid princess comes from ancient text of the Ramayana, written in Sanskrit over 2,000 years ago. In the Thai folklore adaptation, Suvannamaccha is the daughter of the Demon King who defies her father in order to help the Monkey God, Hanuman, on his hero's journey. Thailand's myth and magic along with powerful water imagery are recurring themes in Lily's life. The deep, blue sea is a metaphor for the powerful and timeless source of all things that speaks to each person through the ages.

Disclaimer

After the passage of a number of years and in order to protect the identities of both the innocent and the guilty, I have determined that the contents of this narrative are approximately 90% truth. With my penchant for embellished tales, the other 10% is partial or complete fabrication which may be construed as alternative facts.

Acknowledgements

For my children and their children
and the ones who have tried to love me.

I attempted to be the best I could be,
and I loved you the only way I knew how.

Prologue

I am sixty years old and for the life of me, I cannot imagine sixty-one. I have always had a plan. A short-term plan for the day or week, and a long-term plan for a three year or five year or even ten year stretch of time. I sit in the circle at my weekly co-dependents anonymous meeting, "Hello, my name is Lily, and I am a proud member of the worldwide family of Al-Anon." I repeat the one day at a time mantra with no real understanding of how to actually get through *just one* day with no thought of the next. A few days later, I fumble with little post-it notes where I have scribbled thoughts and feelings from the week and turn to my therapist and say, "If I have to imagine it before I can make it happen, then I cannot imagine anything more. It's as if my whole life is in the rearview mirror, and I'm just coasting along Thelma and Louise style right up to the cliff's edge."

There is always silence after I make a pronouncement such as this, and she is really good at hitting the pause button. It's as if she's waiting for me to hear my own words and suddenly have some epiphany or light bulb moment that will enable me to move forward. We just look at each other, and I wonder if I should focus on her face or look away or change the subject or what. Her therapy dog, Maddie with the horrible breath, groans and shifts positions on the couch beside me.

For the longest time, I believed I was a smart and talented individual who was completely devoted to my children. It was only after they were grown and gone that I came to realize I had been making myself feel whole through my exploitative relationship with them. My inability to craft my own identity was simply too formidable to overcome. In spite of it all, I loved them and did everything I could to give them health and happiness.

Things like that are doomed to fail—and fail, I did. After years of attempting to be the dutiful mother, I stumbled in ways that revealed how flawed I had been all along. I think the heart and the body are inextricably linked so that if there is sickness in one, there will be sickness in the other. Now, sadness has squeezed my heart, blinded my eyes, and twisted my bones.

Make no mistake, we all get what we deserve, and I deserve every bit of the endless ennui that fill my days. I like to think of my suffering as atonement for my sins, retribution for my crimes against the ones I love. I have found ways to cut and bleed without ever lifting a blade.

Now miles separate us, thousands of miles, and visits are relegated to a week in the summer. How does one let go of the people that mean the most to them and define who they have always been? I realize that I have very little identity apart from them and no idea how to create one. The thought of having everyone close so I could actually participate in their lives has been impossible to fully abandon. So here I am. Waiting. Believing there might be a chance they will return.

We always talked of going West. Finding our place beside the big blue. Dancing barefoot in the sand under a silent moon with the infinite power of the surf roaring in our ears. We felt it calling in silent moments. Stirring deep within, drawing us closer.

I'd like to share something meaningful that I have harvested from the mad seasons, but I can't give you any answers. I can't tell you how to have a happy ending, but we do learn from the mistakes of others, so maybe you can learn from mine. If my story can serve as a cautionary tale to help others see something from a different perspective or avoid some similar fate, then that would be a terribly good thing, indeed.

Maybe I just need a little more time to figure out how to navigate these unchartered waters. I never learned to swim, and that has impeded my ability to flow with the tides. If I could just learn to float or tread water, that would be a good start. But I flail about and gasp for air; pause and giggle at the absurdity of the whole spectacle, then continue the thrashing and splashing. I don't want to drown . . . I really don't. At least most days I don't. I just keep trying to see the shore and get to solid ground.

So, let me tell you how it all came to pass—my first taste of shame at the tender age of five and the years of guilt that sang to me with full-throated urgency, demanding attention, refusing to be silenced. At least I'm not so consumed by self-loathing or regret that I can't find some humor in it all. Sometimes the absolute madness makes for moments of breathless laughter and fearless abandon. I have accepted what I am, both good and bad. Maybe, if I tell you this story, I can start to see sixty-one.

Chapter 1

Banana Man Song
Harry Belafonte 1961

I have always been a strange girl with wild crayons. The reason I color outside the lines is actually quite clear. My book is damaged and torn, so I can't see all of the pictures clearly. And I think parts of it may be in a different language, something I don't understand very well. Also, I'm pretty sure I was absent when they went over the rules and instructions. Excuses, excuses. There are so many things that explain why it is so messy, but if you look a little closer, it radiates a savage, surrealistic beauty.

At an early age, I realized that the world from which I came was very different from the reality of life in the High Plains of the Texas Panhandle. My house, a red brick on Royal Road, was quite typical of 1960's suburbia; however, one step inside was a ticket to a different destination far, far away.

Amarillo, Texas was smack dab in the middle of the Bible Belt, and it was there I found myself at age five, traveling from halfway across the world. I used to go into the backyard with a spoon to see if I could dig my way back to the mysterious place of my birth. I thought I might find people there who looked like me, but I never got very far before I was discovered and had the spoon snatched away from me along with any hope of escape.

Even though the repression of the 60's knew no boundaries, this conservative mecca was a world of its own. It was all so simple. Boys had guns, and girls had Easy Bake ovens. Everything was clearly defined, no moral ambiguity or gray areas just yet. Just right and wrong, good and bad, and Sunday "church and chicken" with grandma.

I never saw other people who were dark like me and my dad. They were all white and shiny and smelled like soap. I wondered where all the people of color were because they certainly were not at our neighborhood Piggly Wiggly Supermarket or JC Penny's.

I had not developed my social awareness yet, so I did not understand the stares and disapproving faces, especially when my dad was with us. But even as a young child, I remembered the words. Words whispered with ugly faces contorted by anger. I did not know what they meant, but I knew it was something bad. Something that made my dad lower his eyes to the ground and my mother stand stiffly with steely resolve. I felt confused, bewildered, isolated. Like a baby animal separated from the herd. I was alienated, left to find my way in the dangerous Texan jungle. I was forced to navigate the waters of childhood alone, forever on the outside looking in.

These were my Wonder Years.

My house was always dark and different, all wallpaper and wood. Tiny velvet pagodas and gold foil lilies covered the walls as if my mother were trying to transport a little bit of the Orient into our living room. Tapestries and rice paper etchings of temple walls depicted stories of myth and magic. Beautiful, sad princesses draped in opulent sarongs and intricate headpieces, held captive by hideous monkey Gods, possessed stoic grace as they sat erect, bare breasts poised on languid bodies. Ancient Gods whose futile quest for love was always doomed to fail. Maybe that was the fairy-tale ending that was imprinted or scripted for me, the one I tried to recreate in my own life.

My house was filled with elephants of wood and brass and marble, all sizes and shapes. I arranged them so the daddy would be in front with the family trailing behind him until the last little baby completed the caravan. They had real ivory tusks that some street artist had meticulously carved and proudly displayed on bamboo tables near the waterfront in Bangkok's crowded marketplace. Bright colored wooden snakes were scattered about, and a real stuffed crocodile graced the table to complete this domestic jungle. My parents trekked to Thailand every few years and brought back beautiful Thai silks and the soft dark gold I came to love. The jewelry was exquisitely exotic. My favorite was the princess ring that was fashioned to resemble the ornamental head-piece worn by the temple dancers.

I think guilt prompted my mother to seek some kind of karmic balance by replacing what she had stolen from my father, but the feeble gestures could never fix what had been broken. All the trinkets and tapestries could not bring his home to America, nor could he return to his native country. He could make token visits whenever he had time off from work as a civil engineer, but he was never really home there after he left that life to begin one with my mother. His Asian wife and her three dark children with sad eyes haunted my mother for the rest of her life. It almost seemed like his other family simply vanished as if consumed by a fog. His other children, his first children, were lost in some faraway land, never to be reconciled or forgotten.

I sat on the twilight sofa and ran my long mocha fingers over the velvety patterns on the wallpaper hoping to decipher some secret, but nothing was ever revealed. I listened to my father speak strange and beautiful words that were rich and smooth as river rock. Sitting nearby, I felt like I was in a faraway country where no one could understand my plain words. When my father was not speaking Thai to a select few, he was silent as if the English words were too troublesome to manufacture. I could not speak like my father, so I was never heard. I thought that if I said something, it would be too ugly and would ruin the flow of the liquid language that spilled forth like the waterfalls at Chanthaburi Beach.

There was always steam on the windows from the rice pots perpetually simmering and a sweet spice in the air, heavy and moist. Dinner was always so hot my nose dripped with sweat, but I was continually offered more and more pepper. Little green peppers in soy sauce and lime with red chili and sugar. They smelled bitter and hot and made my eyes sting. If I ate them, my lips would burn, and my mouth would feel numb for a while. Spicy curries, noodles, dumplings, rice with fish, squid or tongue. My mother learned quickly that my father would never eat American food. I wasn't sure what that meant, but I saw commercials for Swanson's TV dinners with a little piece of something called meatloaf and some green beans and mashed potatoes. The most interesting thing about this so-called American food was the little apple pie tucked in the middle of the tin foil tray. I wanted to try it so I would know what all the other kids were eating in their homes. But our menu was never what the other kids at school ate at their dinner tables, and it was many years later before I had the chance to try my first Swanson's TV dinner. The tasteless lumps of food were disappointing except for that little clump of gooey, sticky apple pie. It was only two or three bites, but it was surprisingly good. The mystery meat with something called "tater tots" were unremarkable and hopefully not indicative of what white people enjoyed. Only after years of frozen dinners and chicken pot pies did I come to appreciate my parent's culinary skills and the exotic curries, noodles, soups, and stir-fry I enjoyed every single night.

Sometimes my dad brought home fresh coconuts, and we stabbed them with a screwdriver, first one hole, then another, to get to the watery blue milk inside. It looked like it should have been sweeter, but it was oddly mild. Dad made a creamy Jello-y dessert with it, something strange with two layers- one clear, one milky white. It was a treat we didn't get all too often, but I still remember how cold and sweet and smooth it felt in my mouth.

A low table stretched across the living room where we all sat on the floor when we had company. I think they hungered for more than a little Thai food. They wanted the whole experience replete with chopsticks and Asian music. Coming to our house was like a vacation to the Far East. We always played the obliging hosts to their curiosity. My dad was all charisma and charm, while my mother would rattle on in the background with no one really acknowledging her presence. She was not the featured attraction. Most of the guests were my dad's golf buddies or co-workers at The Texas Highway Department. My dad sang his childhood Thai songs, then switched to Dean Martin or Tony Beannett. He played the guitar and violin for hours, taking requests and getting appreciative applause after each performance.

"Oh, my papa, to me he was so wonderful," he crooned with that rich Frank Sinatra voice and heavy Thai accent. It was enchanting. Then he always finished with *Three Coins in the Fountain.* Guests could never get enough. I, too, could never get enough. I pretended he was singing just for me.

Unforgettable
Nat King Cole 1956

Life seldom goes the way you try to take it, and my father never anticipated meeting someone like JoAnn Thompson. They discovered one another at the Diamond Horseshoe Dance Parlor near the small Texas town of Clarendon. It was a moderately upscale ballroom, considering the location, with lights that looked like little stars floating above. They were both great dancers and knew all the steps to the Rumba, Cha-Cha, Waltz, and Tango. After a six-day whirlwind courtship, they were married. It wasn't long before he completed his studies and announced that he would be returning to Thailand and that it would be best if my mother remained in Texas.

Somewhere in all of this, the little issue of the wife and three young children in Bangkok was revealed, and after that, the rest is history. My mother followed him 8,850 miles, and they all lived unhappily in this foreign land for the next two and a half years. I bet his family was flabbergasted to see what my dad brought home for a souvenir from the States. When all was said and done, my mother won her exotic Oriental Prince.

My father was handsome in a beautifully exotic way; his eyes were large and luminescent light black water, always moist with glinting light in them. He had full lips which covered his overbite, a classic Asian nose that was flat with little flufflers on the sides, and jet-black hair he touched often with his slender, graceful hands and long delicate fingers that made him look like he was dancing with them to some Thai song playing silently in his head.

I can understand why my mother followed him around the world and back. She couldn't let him go. Sometimes things are like that, and you can't just cut your losses and walk away. This was one of those times. She traveled in the belly of a freight ship for five weeks to find him in a place she had only seen on a map. Across the tumultuous seas through storms and peril, only to endure the indignities of sharing him with his other wife.

Supah was a petite little Thai flower who was both obedient and reserved. When she married my father, she married into a family of wealth and social position. My grandfather's job as a diplomat for the Thai government afforded him many privileges, and he had high expectations for his many children. Terminal degrees were standard, followed by a stint of civil service of some kind, culminating in a solid career that was prestigious and honorable.

My mother had been raised on a farm in what appeared to be little more than a chicken coop. Her family was not highly educated, held no high office, and knew little of service or the life of a diplomat. She did not have the skill set that would enable her to be at ease on my grandfather's estate, yet she remained. Day after day, wearing them down, manipulating, strategizing, pleading, and making certain that everyone knew she was not going back to Texas empty handed. To illustrate the lengths she would go to achieve her goal, she conceded to sharing my dad with his other wife. My grandfather was the first to introduce them.

"Supah is you sister now. You come to lib here wid us, you must be family. Kiss your sister to show you will accept your place," he said as he cast his eyes toward the door where the small woman stood wrapped in a colorful sarong with gold and beads around her ankles.

My mother walked right over, leaned in, kissed her on the cheek, then turned to look at my grandfather with a smile.

"Bedy goood. You learn. Tonite you sleep togedder," he said as he strolled away with hands clasped behind his back.

And they all slept together, cooked together, cleaned together, and shopped together for over a year while my mother gradually worked her way in and to a position where she had some leverage. She befriended his three young children and cozied up to the elders. Always looking for opportunities and pondering the next strategic move: public shame and scandal, legal action and lawsuits, an unplanned pregnancy perhaps, maybe murder. It seemed clear that the unexpected pregnancy was the best option to get the results she desired. And with that, I was conceived in a Thai harem on the outskirts of Bangkok.

As time passed, my father had to choose, and his family made it clear what the choice should be. He would be disinherited and banished from his home if he abandoned his family and chose my mother. In retrospect, I guess he must have loved her. Maybe that kind of love makes you forsake all others, and you simply cannot let go of it.

All this drama only served to illustrate the fierce and fiery nature that my mother possessed. Or perhaps it possessed her. Charlie, as everyone called my father, was like oxygen to her. She hated him for all that he put her through, but she loved him in an obsessive-compulsive way that only those who knew her could understand.

I'm Sorry I Made You Cry
Connie Francis 1958

When they settled in Amarillo, Texas in 1958, they were probably the only bi-racial mixed couple in the whole city of 68,000 people. For the Texas Panhandle, Amarillo was the largest town besides Lubbock which was a couple of hours south. Built on cattle and oil, the area consisted largely of conservative white Baptists and a few other well-populated denominations. But suffice to say, it was place where the something called the "blue law" shut down everything on Sunday so everybody had to be at church and church functions.

Before the impetuously hasty marriage, my dad had been a foreign exchange student at Texas Tech University in Lubbock where he was finishing his graduate degree in civil engineering. Amarillo and Lubbock were sister cities, pick-up driving, gun-toting, wild west twin cities, smack dab in the middle of the Bible thumpin' Belt. People always say Texans are so hospitable and the friendliest folks around, but that was never my experience. They all seemed common as cornbread and old as dirt, not to mention judgmental and close-minded. A mixed-race couple in Texas was about as welcome as an outhouse breeze.

Having a half-breed bastard baby only made things worse. By the time my father had divorced his Thai family and legally remarried my mother, I was six years old. My fundamentalist Christian grandparents wanted my parents to have a church wedding, so they married in a little chapel in Tucumcari, New Mexico because it was illegal for a mixed-race couple to marry in Texas. Fortunately, New Mexico allowed interracial marriage long before the 1967 Supreme Court case that changed federal laws. I was the flower girl at their wedding, but all I can remember now is the pair of ugly black patent shoes that hurt my feet.

People came up to my mother at the local Piggly Wiggly and asked if her little boy was adopted. They were always taken aback to discover I was a little girl, and I was my mother's biological child. I guess she was so white, and I was so foreign looking, they just couldn't wrap their minds around how something like that could happen. There were laws against these kinds of things.

Integration had not even fully happened, and my father was a rather dark-skinned Oriental, so he could have easily been mistaken for a Negro. These were the politically correct terms in the 50's. To say they experienced discrimination was an understatement. Their first years were fraught with daily encounters with the gun totin', pick-up truck drivin,' church goin' folks of "Amarilla" as is was so often called. They immediately came up with a nickname for my dad because they could not possibly manage the pronunciation of his real name, and the only Asian people they could think of were from the movies namely Charlie Chan. So my dad became "Charlie," and the name followed him to the grave.

My mom decided that things would go better for us all if I were a few shades closer to her marshmallow white. Given her gift of improvisation, she decided the best way to get me to that snowy shade was a little bit of Blue Cheer detergent and a jigger of bleach. Once a week, I basted in the bathtub until I was pruney and pale. It never really worked. People at the mall and the grocery store still stared with a look of disgust and whispered about the dirty little brown kid with the starchy white lady.

Red Rover, Red Rover
Olsen Park Elementary School 1962

Elementary school was like its own little microcosm replete with different types of people, only in miniature. That's what I was told, but it was not true. I was the only caramel face in an ocean of vanilla. And as everyone knows, people can be cruel, especially children. The other children in the school seemed different from me, but for some reason, I could never put my finger on the exact reason why I stood apart so much. I only knew that I was always the little long-haired girl with the name nobody could say. I sat in class with my attention drawn to my fingers as I pulled at the skin on the sides of my nails. Not bold enough to bite, I would pick, pick, pick until I bled. That just about sums up my entire early childhood experience. Chronically torn and bloody.

It was the first day of school in 1962, and Miss Winkle was my 1st grade teacher. She was tall and thin with short, dark hair and very white skin. I wondered what she did to be so white. I liked her because she spoke softly most of the time unlike the loud, shrill, flat sounds that bellowed out of the mouths of my fellow classmates. Thinking back, I'm not sure if it was their redneck hillbilly words or their thick Texas accents that grated on me the most.

Soon it was time for lunch, and Miss Winkle smiled as students shuffled to line up at the door.

"Lily, which line do you belong in, honey?" she asked.

I had not been listening to instructions. I had been lost in her face.

"Come over to this line if you're Catholic and go over to that line by the door if you're Protestant," she repeated.

I just stood there, staring at my pink, tattered fingers.

"Lily, sweetie, you need to get in a line. We're ready to go, everybody is ready to eat, and you are making us late," she explained with a hint of impatience in her voice.

I didn't know what to do. I had no idea what the difference was between Catholic and Protestant and whatever she said about fish and Fridays, and I was embarrassed that everybody else seemed to know but me. I had never heard those words before. Maybe I didn't understand much of the language my father spoke, but I didn't understand much of this language either. So I did what any other six year old in a pickle would do. I chose the line with the least hostile looking people. I chose the fish line.

Every Friday that year I ate with the Catholics, and since I was fairly fed up with fish by the time school was out for the summer, when 2nd grade rolled around, I got into the Protestant meat eaters line.

"You can't be over here. You're in the wrong line; go over there," shouted a freckled, red haired girl when I first made the move to switch teams. She was just not having it.

"Teeeeecher, Lily is in the wrong line. Make her go over to the other side," whined a snot-crusted boy with dirty fingernails and yellow teeth that looked like corn.

"Young lady. Hey, you! Girl with the long hair. I can't pronounce your name...it's foreign, isn't it? Oriental maybe? They call you, Lily? Are you in the right place? Are you Protestant? You can't just change lines if you're supposed to be in the other one," exclaimed my new, abrasive 2nd grade teacher who always stood too close and spoke too loudly. Her breath smelled like my wet poodle. She also taught PE and was rumored to paddle people on their birthday until they cried. Horror of horrors, I was terrified of her. I longed for sweet, soft Miss Winkle and didn't know what to do, so I just stood there trying to summon a little bit of Jackie Kennedy or Audrey Hepburn but ended up coming off more like a cardboard cut-out or statue.

"Okay, just go on then. But I'm going to check with your mother to see if you are where you are supposed to be. Someone your age should know!"

Regretfully, she did indeed inquire with my mother who probably gave the speech about being in an inter-racial marriage with a Buddhist. He was probably the only Buddhist in Texas in 1963, so that certainly didn't help me fit in. The teacher simply avoided me after that and let me get into whatever lunch-line I chose, but she did look at me occasionally as if I were dirty or had some kind of cooties or something. It wasn't until much later that I figured out the secret that everybody else already knew. There was no 'right' line for me, and there was no seat at the table.

A Change is Gonna Come
Sam Cooke 1963

When I reflect on my mother, attempt to recreate her face or summon a memory of her now that years have passed since her death, I am saddened by the misery in her face. Always trying so hard to be something else, make some impression. She was not an authentic person; everything was always for show, and she was consumed by what others thought about her. People were not kind or welcoming to her because she just tried too hard and was so visibly "plastic" as people loved to say when I was growing up. She could never fully make amends for who she married at a time when that kind of thing simply was not done. She became an instant pariah.

I believe that she never experienced one single moment of genuine joy in her whole life. My parents fought often. Most of the time, I did a pretty good job of becoming invisible during their fights. But I could hear them, and although I didn't understand a lot of what was being said, I understood enough to know that my mom thought my dad did bad things. It was a central theme of their fights.

"I know you regret coming here, so why don't you just go back to them? I know you love her more than you ever loved me. I know you want to be with your kids," my mom would repeat over and over again. I could hear his response, but it was brief and quiet, and I think that just made her even more upset. Her guilt seemed to be eating her up from the inside out. The wretched condition of her soul seeped from her pores, from every inch of her being until her outward appearance was as twisted and gnarled as her tormented soul.

One late Sunday afternoon after what seemed like a whole day filled with arguing, it escalated, and my mom started throwing things around. This went on for a bit and then suddenly my father appeared in my room and asked me to sit down on the edge of the bed.

"I'm ask you question and I want you tell me da truth. Tell what you think," my dad said in his soft, mellow voice.

"Your mudder and I not get arong beddy well. We not lub each udder like it is suppose to. She had so many problem, she not well," he went on. It was unusual that he was talking to me when it was usually no more than a few words here and there.

"I tink it migh be bedder if we not stay togeder. It migh be bedder for you not hab da fighting all da time. Is no good for anybody," he said while looking at the floor and studying the blue shag carpet.

"What you tink about dat? You tink that migh be bedder?"

I was eight. I don't know why he thought I would know what to do or what was best or anything like that.

"So where would you go? Where would I go?" I asked since those were really the obvious questions that concerned me.

"I go back to my family in Thailand. You can stay wid your mom. If I not here making her feel upset, she probably be okay and be take care ob you bedder," he said as if he wanted me to agree and give him permission to leave.

I didn't have a response. I felt like crying but tears would not come out. I felt sick inside like my tummy was on a swing being pushed too high, and I needed to put my feet on the ground and jump off. My could feel my heart beating and felt like someone was squeezing me so tightly I couldn't breathe. I looked at my bare feet in the ocean colored shag carpet and dug in with my toes to hang on. Sometimes I felt like that was the only thing that tethered me to the ground.

Then suddenly the most miraculous thing happened. My face felt warm and I felt like I needed to sneeze, then I stood up and buckets of hot blood started shooting out of my nose. Not a trickle but a gusher. I lifted my hands to my face because I saw the red all over my arms and hands before my brain fully understood what was happening. I had never had any kind of nosebleed before, so I simply could not process what was happening. My shirt was drenched within seconds, and it was still streaming out onto the carpet like someone turned on a water hose. My dad grabbed a pillow and grabbed my head and pressed the pillow against my face. I thought I might be dying or that he had decided to kill me or something, but I just looked up at the ceiling and gasped for breath through parts of the pillow that weren't pressed against my face.

My mother, who had locked herself into her bedroom to "pretend pack" a suitcase for a "pretend trip" away that never happened, came into the room and started crying louder and louder until she was just sobbing and gasping and choking and wailing and she wasn't even the one who was spurting gushes of blood all over the place.

After wet towels were brought in and I had cotton balls stuffed up my nose, we all sat down slowly on the bloody bed like it was the scene of a mass murder or something like that. After a while, my dad said, "Don't worry Lily. We stay togedder if dat what you want. We do it for you. Is dat what you want us to do?"

I looked at him, soaked in my blood—on his shirt, his pants, all over his flip-flop feet and looking like he wanted me to be the one to make everything okay. Then I looked at my mom, blood splattered across her arms and hands, and then across the room with the blood-soaked carpet and bed.

"Yes."

"What you say? I didn't hear you," my dad coaxed.

"Yes. Stay with us," I replied with a trembling weakness and lightheadedness.

And with that, the deal was sealed. In that moment, there was recognition in my dad's face. An epiphany. He suddenly awoke to what he already knew and feared all along. He couldn't leave me with my mother. We would fail to thrive and die a horrible death without him.

We were all baptized in rivers of my blood that Sunday. This was the life he would have, and I was the reason he had no other choice.

Chapter 2

High Hopes
Doris Day 1964

*E*ven though we had two little white poodles, I always thought the best pet would be a monkey. I implored my mother to get one year after year, but I do not think she ever actually acknowledged my request. She simply said, "They are mean and dirty, and they poop everywhere so forget about it." But I kept hoping she would wake up one day and change her mind. That actually happened quite a lot.

My inspiration probably came from the rice etching of the Thai Monkey God and the Mermaid Princess that hung on the kitchen wall behind my dad's chair. Maybe he identified with the Monkey God in some way. I think I did, too. We both felt betrayed by my mother.

I have always heard that children adapt some childhood fairy tale into a life script. For me, I had no stories of Cinderella or Snow White. My mother had purged our house of anything that wasn't from Thailand including the food, the music, the furniture, and even the exotic wallpaper. So my fairy tales were not the ones all the other kids at school heard. I identified with Suvannamaccha, the mermaid princess. The story goes like this:

The monkey God, Hanuman, was building a bridge to help the King when he discovered that the mermaids who lived underwater were hampering him. When the King's wife Sita was kidnapped, he enlisted Hanuman's aid in rescuing her. Hanuman learned that Sita was being held captive on the island of Lanka, so he collected his band of Vanaras and they began throwing huge boulders into the sea to make a foundation for the causeway that would enable them to rescue her.

After a few days, they notice something is wrong. Each day they threw rocks into the sea and the next day they were gone. They discovered a large number of mermaids underwater. As they watched, a new rock was tossed in. The mermaids living underwater took the rocks and carried them away. Hanuman looked for their leader so her could speak to her and discover why they were doing such a thing. He saw a lovely mermaid supervising the others but when he swam towards her, she skillfully evaded him.

Hanuman realized he was falling in love with the creature. He changed his tactics and began to silently woo her. She responded to him and soon they were together at the bottom of the sea. Hanuman asked the mermaid why she is stealing the rocks. She told him that she is Suvannamacchaa, daughter of Ravana (the demon who had abducted Sita). When her father Ravana saw Hanuman's Vanaras building a causeway, he instructed Suvannamaccha to stop it.

Hanuman told the mermaid why he was building the causeway. He told her of the abduction of Sita, the battle between King Rama and her father Ravana, how they started to build a bridge, and in consequence how he was ordered to finish the causeway within seven days or pay with his life.

Suvannamaccha turned to Hanuman and her eyes were filled with love. No more, she said, would she prevent Hanuman from completing his mission. Her mermaids underwater would, in fact, return all the stolen rocks to the causeway.

They parted as lovers part, but it was not to be the end for them. Hanuman had left a seed with Suvannamaccha, and soon she gave birth to their son. Now they would always be part of one another, never to be separated.

I was enchanted by Thai myths and folktales such as these. Another favorite was *Sun Ngokong* who possessed great strength. He could lift a 17,550 pound staff called *Ruyi Jingu Bang,* with ease. He was also extremely fast, able to travel 13,468 miles in one somersault. *Sun Ngokong* knew 72 transformations which allowed him to transform into various animals and objects. Each of his hairs possessed magical properties, capable of being transformed into clones of the Monkey King himself, and/or into various weapons, animals, and other objects. He knew spells to command wind, part water, conjure protective circles against demons, and freeze humans, demons, and gods alike. He defied Hell's attempt to collect his soul. Instead of reincarnating, he wiped his name out of *the Book of Life and Death* along with the names of all monkeys known to him. Now if that isn't awesome, then I didn't know what would be!

The lessons were about virtue, trust, honor, pride, and forgiveness. They exalted love among families and towards society. These universal themes recognized the infallibility of human nature and showed people how to control their minds in order to gain inner peace. Being such an enchanting story, I filled my notebooks with pictures of the Monkey God, his mermaid princess, and his monkey friends, costuming each with golden suits and ankle bracelets with precious jewels and elaborate headpieces. It was a wonderful escape that helped me see that there were strange, exotic things in this world that no one else in Amarillo, Texas knew about but me. That explained why I was not like the others. I had to be alone, solitary, hiding in lush jungles or swimming under the deep blue sea. I was waiting on my own Hanuman, the white monkey god, to defeat all of the evil demons and rescue me.

My Heart Belongs to Daddy
Cole Porter 1965

"Lilly, it's time to go. Get in the car," mother said as she nervously straightened the pillows on my bed. "It's time to go to the airport to pick up Paddie. She'll be here in an hour, and your father is in the car waiting!"

Paddie was the American name my dad chose for his other daughter because no one could say or would want to say her real name, Padachuan Sithvongsaray Chaidee.

"Okay, let me put my journals away," I mumbled softly, then shuffled out to the car and slipped into the back seat. It was about thirty miles to the airport, and I always became car sick after about ten minutes in the car.

"Let me look at you," my mother said as she inspected me from her seat next to my father. "We'll have to fix your hair when we get there, and you need some powder on your nose because you look all shiny and oily."

"What difference did it make", I thought to myself as we pulled out of the driveway. My half-sister had just traveled halfway around the world and had never seen me before, so I doubted that she would care if my nose was a little greasy. I was only twelve and what twelve-year-old wasn't already horrified by her own appearance? My nose was huge, a monstrosity in fact. I wanted my dad's flat nose with the little puffs on the sides, but instead, I had my mother's beak, and I hated it. My mother was an idiot if she thought a little powder was going to fix anything.

When I first saw my sister, I was shocked that she was so brown and looked a little like Diana Ross. Then I remembered her mom was Thai, not some really, really white lady who couldn't tan if her life depended on it. She had a blue dress with a crisp short jacket over it and looked like she had read a lot of American fashion magazines with pictures of Jacqueline Kennedy, Connie Francis, and Sandra Dee. Even her black hair was all big and poofy with little flips at the end and a little tiny bow front center, like the ones mother puts on our poodles. I had expected a fourteen-year-old wearing colorful Thai silk with long, black hair like mine and maybe a flower behind one ear. Maybe even a lily.

Immediately she began speaking Thai to my father and his face came to life. I couldn't believe it was him. He never looked that happy around me or my mother, but now, he was luminescent. I stood over to the side and was pretty near invisible to everyone except my mother who kept whispering to me, coaching me on what to say, telling me to stand up straighter, and holding me in front of her like a trophy or a shield.

"Stand up straight. Go over there and say something to her. Brush your hair back. It's falling in your eyes. Stand up. You're slouching. Be nice. Look friendly," she repeated mechanically as she stood stiffly and grasped my arms tightly. I kept thinking she should leave me alone and go over there and do those things herself. What was I? An ambassador of Goodwill? Proof that we weren't monsters as my sister had inevitably been told? At least now, my mother was invisible too, but she didn't even know it yet.

Awkward months passed by and my mother learned to use Paddie as a vehicle to get brownie points from my dad. They seldom spoke except to argue, and she needed something to make it better. So Paddie got parties. She was the first new foreign novelty at school, and everyone loved her. She would gather 30 or 40 classmates from High Plains High and cram them into our little house. It brought more excitement than I could remember.

The girls clustered, and then went in groups of three or four, back and forth to the bathroom, to Paddie's room, to the kitchen, and back. They played the age-old "he said she said" and "so-and-so wants to know if so-and-so likes them" game. Screams and giggles or tears and drama would follow. They would play records and dance the Twist, the Pony, and the Mash Potato, and slow dance to *Soldier Boy* or *Love*

Letters in the Sand.

My mother used food coloring to dye our poodles festive colors like red and green at Christmas and pink and blue on Easter. Paddie's friends were so amused and acted like they thought that was just so grand. One time I remember my mother baking Morton's mini cinnamon sugar donuts in the oven and serving them on a platter to Paddie's friends. She was popular, but these warm treats were even more of a hit. My mother was careful to arrange them oh so perfectly. This time, when she set out the mountain of goodies, there was a scream, then another, and soon mass panic. A little brown mouse popped his head up through a donut, and then before you knew it, girls were screeching on chair tops and boys were on their hands and knees with cups for capture and books for bashing. What a rollicking good time!

Paddie was so embarrassed, that she vowed never to have another shindig. In Thailand, someone might have shish-kabobed the poor fellow on a bed of salted peanuts, but luckily, he escaped and neither he nor any of his furry friends garnished our food again.

Not only was our house filled with furry little rodents, but it was also covered in ants. I thought the mice were cute, but the bogs were another story altogether. I liked playing with them outside. I would put little sticks, stones, and other obstacles in their way and watch as they would go around them. Clever little buggers. I poured water near their highly trafficked ant highways, but they also found ways to avoid the puddles. It was so interesting to observe. I wanted to be as smart and determined as the ants, to just keep going no matter what got in my way and overcome all obstacles.

But inside the house, ants were not so great. That was supposed to be my domain. I did not want to worry about them crawling on me when I slept or falling into my food or getting lost in my ear or nose while I was sitting in my room doing my homework. So naturally, I did what any child would do when they felt threatened by intruders. I went to war.

I tried a number of things and they all failed. I stuffed toilet paper in the cracks in the window where they got in. I sprinkled laundry detergent along the windowsill as a barrier. I stuck aluminum foil against the windows to seal it. Yet, somehow, they always got in. I would sit in my safe spot, my overstuffed blue chair, and watch them parade up and down the wall as if to say, "Ha, ha! You failed. We will not be stopped."

I felt helpless.

So in response, I think my overall feelings of powerlessness fueled my resolve, and I launched a physical assault. Even though my dad said it was against our religion to kill anything, I decided that it must be done because they were taking over!

Armed with my best shoe, I began smacking the little soldiers in the ant army. They came through the window in groups of about six to eight, so it was pretty easy to hit them and take out the whole group in two or three whacks of the shoe. When one group was dispatched to their maker, the next group arrived. The wall was a mess of splattered ant guts, but I was not stopping until I had killed every last one of them. This went on for quite awhile, and then it happened.

Something so horrifying that I had nightmares for years!

After the bing, bang, boom of the shoe on the next team of ants, something happened. Suddenly, a group of about twenty ants came through the window and were followed by another group of maybe thirty or forty. In a manner of seconds, the groups blended into one massive attack with hundreds of ants streaming down the wall. I couldn't approach them with the shoe. There were too many. It might turn into one of those *Twilight Zone* episodes when the guy is covered in bugs or frogs or alien blood-sucking leeches.

I was terrified.

Unable to call out for help with the scream firmly stuck in the back of my throat, I climbed on top of my bed and watched in horror as they poured in by the thousands. I a matter of seconds, they began breaking up and swirling in circular patterns, then as quickly as they came, they were gone.

The retreat was swift and well coordinated so that no one was left behind. It was a mass exodus. I don't remember if either of my parents asked what all the commotion was, but I do know that the swarm was in some way connected to all the murdering that was going on.

The next day, I went to the library to try to get a book about ants in order to understand what had happened and how to protect myself from future attacks. The librarian followed me around and after thorough questioning, concluded that I had simply killed the wrong ant. After explaining how the drones all protect the queen, I knew that the war was over. They all looked the same, so how could I know which one was the leader in order to spare her life and save myself? According to the helpful library staff, I came to realize that they had all come for her body to give her some kind of honorary queen bug funeral. Ants were even smarter than I imagined.

I decided that I had no choice but to peacefully cohabitat alongside these clever creatures. Except for a few bites from one who strayed from the path every now and then, nothing like the Battle of the Wall ever happened again. They pretty much stayed on their side of my room, and I stayed on mine. None of us wanted any trouble.

Moonlight Bay
Bing Crosby 1966

The police were regular guests at my house, and it seemed like they came more when the weather was warmer or when there was a full moon. I have heard that hot places like Arizona have higher rates of murder and other violent crimes. Maybe my mom got all stirred up because she was hot. My dad made frequent visits to the backyard where he would turn on the water hose and spray the evaporative air conditioner pads to cool off the house and especially to cool off my mom.

She liked to carry knives around and show them to you in furtive, sneaky little glimpses with a crazy glitter in her eyes. Sometimes she would lift up her pant leg or even her dress to show that she had a knife stuck in her shoe or sock or even rolled up in her girdle. She just showed you it was there and then carefully replaced her clothing.

When she lost control, I mean really lost it, we all knew the police would soon be on their way. My sister and I would go out to the backyard and sit on the swings or disappear across the street to Karen and John's house to watch TV and hide out. I never went alone, I would just try to be invisible, but while my sister lived with us, it was our go to place. Karen and John were sort of "mod" since she wore white go-go boots, and he had a leather vest with fringe and a few beads. It was the 60's and the hippie thing in Amarillo got off to a slow start, but they were a little bit ahead of the curve. They knew something bad was going down at my house because the police would show up at some point and then everyone on the block knew JoAnn and Charlie were at it again.

I remember one particularly bad episode when my mom went

crazier than usual. She had already pulled out the knives, waved them around at everybody, and even feebly tossed a few in my dad's direction. He cursed at her and tried to grasp her by the wrist. He told her to stop acting crazy in front of the kids. He said he would just leave if she did not calm down.

She did what anybody in that situation would do. There had to be a sacrifice, a murder. She sat down on our living room sofa, grabbed a knife, and made one violent stab into the back of the couch. Next, she proceeded to grab the material and rip and tug until large pieces of the sofa tore off. Then she plunged both hands inside the couch and pulled out stuffing and threw it in the air so it looked like it was snowing. By the time she was finished, the sofa was bare to the springs with tapestry and cotton polyester in piles, mountains of debris all over the room. The final act was to grab a large mirror off the wall and hurl it towards the television while screaming something about not getting any attention and that my dad would have to listen if he had no TV. Thank God he was quick to block the mirror because it was headed right for the screen with a sideways force like a death Frisbee or a missile. It would surely have shattered the screen and then no more *Beverly Hillbillies* and *The Monkees* for me.

Police descended on our house, handcuffed my mother, and put her in the back of the police car. They talked to my dad for a while, said something about observing her in the hospital, but she promised to settle down and after almost an hour, she was quietly picking up our sofa pieces and stuffing it all in paper grocery bags without a word.

My dad came in the room with me and my sister, locked the door behind him, and took the twin bed next to mine without saying a word. Silence filled the room, and after a while, we heard my mom talking to someone, but we knew no one was there.

A Whiter Shade of Pale
Procol Harum 1967

Every few months, my dad would take us to Ding How for the closest thing to Thai food that Amarillo had to offer. All of the Thai officers who were my dad's friends wanted something with rice, so we headed to the boulevard, Amarillo Boulevard, to eat something familiar. It didn't taste like the Thai food we ate every day at home.

This food had weird names and gelatinous lumps of unidentifiable goo. After they had all knocked back a few beers or polished off the bottle of scotch my dad brought in his coat pocket, they would have eaten anything and enjoyed it. The room was smoky, loud, and decorated with Chinese themed red and gold things all over the place.

My favorite thing about the whole experience was the little red, plastic basket filled with rye bread and little squares of cold butter wrapped in silver foil. We never had bread at home, only rice and noodles, so this was a rare treat. I sat there for hours eating one slice after another, slowly and carefully smearing the creamy butter all over it, hiding it in my lap, and breaking off little pieces to secretly pop into my mouth. Over two or three hours, I probably consumed seven or eight pieces of the soft, delicious bread.

My mother was too busy trying to look beautiful and be charming to notice what was going on. I knew she really loved attention. Since my dad was always at work or at the golf course, she never got the attention she craved. One time, we started a secret affair with the guy who worked at the gas station a few blocks from our house. She would get all dressed up, and we would walk down to Sinclair's where she would flirt and flatter to her heart's content. On the walk home, we always stopped for a Sprite, and then she would tell me how he thought I was so adorable and would like to be my daddy. Then she would go on about how nice and kind and tall he was.

"Do you like him? Would you rather have him for your daddy?" she would babble on as we walked.

"Jake likes me and is nicer than your father. He could go back to his family. That's where his heart is. Then we could all live happily like a normal family with Jake," she continued.

I kept walking as I studied the different kinds of doors on each house. Some were really fancy while others were merely screen doors.

"I think I might be in love with Jake. Do you think you could like him?"

So as I sat in my little red plastic chair at Ding How on the boulevard, I watched her flirting with all my dad's friends from the air base and then shooting these Bette Davis looks at my dad. They were all drunk by now, and I was stuffed with bread and butter, so nobody really noticed her. I guess she was invisible. Actually, I didn't mind going unnoticed. It was usually best that way.

Bad Moon Rising
Credence Clearwater Revival 1968

On a fateful summer day in June, my mother and I walked to Western Plaza Mall to get autographs from a couple rock bands, the Grass Roots and The Turtles. I don't remember whose idea it was, but considering my mother's vicarious nature, it was probably hers. She always enjoyed experiencing the things she missed when she was growing up in the chicken coop out in the boonies. She was probably exaggerating, but you could never tell. Maybe she was really raised beside poultry. I do know for certain that her childhood home was no more than a little sign by the side of the road which read: Lelia Lake, Population 42. I was her opportunity for a second chance to have the kind of experiences she had been denied, so she stole from me. The means always justifies the end, right? And JoAnn would do whatever it took to get her way. She certainly proved that time and again. She usually saved the histrionics for my dad.

She often said, "I have given my life to you, sacrificed and stayed with a man I don't even love, all for you. The world has condemned me for marrying a brown-skinned man, but I tolerate the prejudice and abuse for you. I know he regrets coming here to this country and leaving his family. You are the only reason he stays with us. How do you think that makes me feel? I am a human, too. Why don't you appreciate me? Why don't you like me? Neither one of you care if I live or die."

After diatribes like that, I thought she might lift her hand to her forehead and swoon like the dramatic ladies in the old movies, but it didn't happen.

I never knew what to say. My child brain could not even fully comprehend her question. How could she say that about a man she had followed halfway around the world? A man she had torn away from a wife and three children? Surely, she loved him. What could have gone wrong, I wondered. She drank from me all the life juice I possessed until I was a dry hole. Sucked out the life fluids. Took my blood and replaced it with poison. Basically, a sweet, sickly parasite with no mercy for her host. I should have thanked her if she had taken my blood, washed me clean, purged my soul, but it wasn't like that. She only baptized me in her rivers of madness.

Barbie Me was dressed in clothes way beyond my eleven years. I remember how she put makeup on my little girl face, and told me that I was royalty like my grandfather who lived in a palace in Thailand. I was enchanted by all of the stories about my exotic ancestry. There were stories of harems, giant cobras that walked upright like a man, torrential monsoons, roasted rats on beds of peanuts, shamans who walked on hot coals, and the sweet decay of the rotting jungle.

Gradually, I discovered there were only small threads of truth in the stories; she had such a penchant for embellishment. Nevertheless, these tales helped explain why I was so different from everybody else and why I didn't walk in step with the others. I was a Royal Thai Princess displaced in a small Texas town.

The trip to the mall that day in July was a fatal one. My innocence escaped me that summer. There was a boy. Stories with that beginning always end badly. There was a boy who was all charm like a salesman eager to make a sale. Standing just a little too close, smiling just a little too big, confident and crazy. No wonder he and my mother became such allies. They shared the same disease. My grandma said my mom had mad cow disease from walking around barefooted in cow patties on the farm, but I knew she was kidding. I was pretty sure it was some kind of madness but not from wading around in a shit-field.

Somehow my mother played matchmaker, and the proverbial prince showed up the next day to claim his princess. His skin was the color of a caramel latte like mine, but we had different geography all together. He seemed taller and older with thick black hair, big white teeth, and a stupidly charming air about him. Most people would say he was handsome in a cheap or sleazy way. Later he taught me to *habla poquito espanol,* but only dirty little words and phrases. No white stallion or shining armor, just a predator canvassing for a fresh piece of flesh. New meat. A juicy little girl to devour.

As the summer progressed, so did his visits to my house. After several weeks passed, I experienced my first kiss. It was actually more like an invasion. And it was only the first of many ways I was violated. I resigned myself to the idea that it was supposed to be that way, so why protest? We stood in my living room and although my house was small, I felt like I was alone with this man; my mother was always absent but lurking nearby. Actually, it wouldn't surprise me if she had been peeking around the corner, satisfying some sick voyeuristic tendency.

In retrospect, I regret that I didn't have the conventional first kiss: the awkward first glances, racing pulse, tentative touching of hands. It should have been tender, something meaningful and worth remembering for years to come with a smile, lips barely brushing, then meeting for a brief, sweet moment. I hadn't even had time to begin anticipating it or romanticizing it. I was still a child. Not even a teenager yet. I still played make-believe, climbed trees, and believed in Magic.

Suddenly, it was over in one aggressive assault. A hot wet tongue probing unmercifully. Sloppy. Unwelcome. Relentless. I felt like I was violated, but didn't know why. It was like a fragile piece of crystal had been slammed to the ground and beauty shattered forever. There should have been something sweet to cherish always, but I only remember the little bubbles of his spit gushing into my mouth and the sensation of something slick and foreign sucking on my tongue.

One of the worst things about it was that he didn't even get my name right. He called me Libby or sometimes Lucy, and my name was Lily. Although this was not a huge transgression, it was enough to de-personalize the whole experience like it was some anonymous transgression towards me. The whole thing was not meant to be like that. It was years too soon and centuries beyond what my prepubescent mind could fathom. I had just finished sixth grade and would be going to junior high in a few weeks. Surely everyone else had experienced something similar, I thought. It must be the way things work. When elementary school ended, a stranger was invited to bring the child into the world of adults.

I didn't really think about it beyond that and had no real idea at the time about how things should work, but somewhere inside my intuitive self, I knew there was something very wrong and inappropriate about all of it. I just didn't know how wrong at the time.

I remember the first time I felt shame like that. I was five and didn't even know the word yet, but I kept the feeling and experienced it over and over through the years. My dad threw parties on the weekends for the Thai officers from the Air Force base. He had been a pilot in the Thai airforce, so they had a lot to talk about I guess. They played Thai music and kept several ice chests full of beer. The room was always so filled with smoke, it was hard to see.

My mother dressed me up like a little doll. While I don't remember the tiny plaid skirt or pretty white sweater with little pearl buttons, I do remember the thick white tights and what the seams felt like as they rubbed against my toes. Years later, I found pictures that brought back memories of that night, sitting on the man's lap with a clueless grin, him with one arm around me and the other holding a cigarette. I was suddenly transported to that moment and those scratchy leggings.

The memories came in snapshot moments of crystal clear clarity that surprised me. The man asking talking in a low voice with a heavy Thai accent I could barely understand. He bounced me up and down and held my hands as I dangled backwards and giggled until I was dizzy.

Then I remembered how he rubbed me and petted me like you would pet one of our poodles. I remembered him touching me in places that made my tummy feel tingly and like butterflies.

"You like that? Feel good?" he asked as he put his hand inside my scratchy white tights.

Then there was my mother. Standing in front of us and looking angry in her glamorous party clothes and perfect hair. She always dressed like a movie star and wore a lot of makeup and red lipstick and sparkly jewelry. I didn't think she was really beautiful, just a little bit fancy.

"Lily!" she said in an angry voice as she grabbed me by the arm and dragged me off the nice man's lap.

"What are you doing? You are a very bad girl. You have done a bad thing to let him touch you in your naughty places. Shame on you! I don't want to see you getting close to any of these men. They're drinking and you're just making trouble for them. Go sit on the sofa and don't move until everyone leaves," she demanded as she held me by the shoulders and got right up close to my face.

I didn't really understand what I had done wrong. What naughty place was she talking about? My preschool brain raced to understand, and I wondered if it could be the same thing as my boowoo. When I was two or three, my grandma's robe fell open as she got out of bed, and I thought the hairy clump of fur I saw on her was a little puppy. As I learned to name things, I called all dogs boowoos since that was the barking noise they made. My mom said that it was not an animal but something all grownups had when they got older. None of it made sense. The man was nice and gave me pony rides on his knee and made me laugh with tickle hugs. My parents never hugged me. I liked it. But he had petted my boowoo place, and now I felt ashamed and embarrassed that I had done something bad. I figured out that nobody is supposed to ever touch each other, especially in the bad place, and that I was not a nice girl for letting him do that.

And now that this guy from the mall was in my house and touching me and putting his hands on me like the nice man did, I felt ashamed all over again. Funny thing, I still didn't understand why.

Ohio
Crosby, Stills, Nash, & Young 1969

1969 changed a lot of lives. It was one of the most significant years in history, and for me it was monumental. While young people a few years older were packing into rock festivals and tuning out and turning on, I watched a lot of bad TV. My favorite shows were *I Dream of Jeannie* and *Bewitched*—both inane dribble that transported me to some other destination far beyond the confines of my house on Royal Road.

While Mick Jagger was strutting and preening, and Robert Plant was becoming a proverbial God, the kids at Ashford Junior High we went to see *Tommy* and *Planet of the Apes* over and over again. Some were already making out while others fidgeted nervously between trips to the restroom for crucial updates. A year had passed since my first kiss, and I tried to dismiss it completely like it never happened.

My seventh-grade crush was Patrick Beanning. He was my Robert Plant and Jim Morrison all rolled into one big blonde sweetheart with puffy lips and soft eyes, my knight and shining silver braces. Thirty-five years later, he has retained that untarnished armor in my memory. It's nice to have that idea of a man of honor, even if no one has been so perfect in real life.

Patrick wore little John Lennon glasses and was the epitome of cool. There was something so gentle about him; even his voice was like milk chocolate melting slowly. Kissing him made things get all swirly, and I was always dizzy afterwards. This was how it was supposed to be. Coming of age with awkward grace and giddiness.

His house was almost directly across from the school. It was a white two-story home that looked like the pictures of mansions they put on the covers of the magazines about decorating. There were big pillars in front and chandeliers in the entryway. He had friends over for parties and such, and I was awkwardly fascinated by it all. A large tree house complimented his massive, beautifully landscaped backyard. That became everyone's favorite make-out spot, and I'm pretty sure there were other shenanigans that happened there as well.

Nobody is thinking about serious stuff when they are passing into adolescence. They only giggle and gossip and begin to entertain the idea that there might be something great in all that boy-girl stuff. Some pairing takes place, and a crush on Monday is often over by Friday. All I know is that Patrick made me feel like I could burst with excitement, and for the first time, I fell in love with the idea of love.

I was beginning to have hope that I was going to be a part of the group. A girl like all the other girls. They would cluster together, and I'll always stand on the fringe and listen to who liked who and who was going out with who. I was soon disappointed to hear that Patrick liked some other girl, and I was old news. Junior high was like that. Flavor of the week. Puppy love. My time in step with the masses quickly came to an end. Now I was outside the circle again. I always felt like I was standing apart and eavesdropping. Everyone else seemed to be experiencing life at a different pace and as Thoreau once remarked, I walked to the beat of a different drummer.

Nothing lasts forever, including 7th grade. When summer arrived, Patrick went away to camp, and mother thought that I should meet new people. Augie, the nineteen-year-old Latin lothario who robbed me of my first kiss the summer before, had fortunately been drafted to the war shortly thereafter. Uncle Sam needed a few good men, but good was too much to hope for so he settled for men like Augie.

Later, I would agonize that I was not active in the anti-war movement. I regretted that I had not been one of the protesters for peace and glorified all those who spoke out against our involvement in Vietnam, but I was too young to understand anything at the time. I did not understand the politics of such an immoral war and the atrocities that were committed in the name of democracy and freedom. It was reprehensible, but all I knew at the time was that I was glad there was a war because it got this creepy older guy away from me.

He was stationed in San Diego and continued to send letters

begging for pictures to show his bunk buddies. My mother answered all his letters, encouraging him. I hoped he would disappear in the jungles of the war I saw on TV. I imagined him falling out of the sky from helicopters or bleeding out in some rice paddy as he grinned mindlessly, letting his last breath float up like smoke into a starless sky. If I began to feel guilty for lingering over such grim machinations, I reminded myself that he had the heart of a rapist, and I felt like diving into a tub of Blue Cheer detergent whenever I thought about him putting his clumsy paws on me.

It was my mother who obliged him with the pictures for his locker. Strange that military types would have lockers like school children, but where else to put your stuff in a dormitory style living situation? She put me in a bright red flowered bikini and asked my cousin Gary with the Polaroid camera if he would snap some pictures of me spread out on a chenille bedspread wearing little more than a smile. Actually, it was a white bikini with spashes of big red flowers, but it just seemed kind of creepy, and I felt like I needed to cover everything up. I thought it was strange that I felt so awkward while the others didn't notice anything odd at all, so I just went along. Gary sure seemed to be having a good time. My mom talked and talked and coached and coaxed until an hour later we had created something she called genuine 'cheesecake'.

To top it off she said, "If you put a lipstick kiss on the envelope, he will never forget you." Like that's what I was going for. She demonstrated a few times, and I remember thinking she should just go ahead and do it herself. After some protestations, to get it all over with, I reluctantly puckered up and unwittingly tossed another log into the proverbial fire.

I was a twelve-year-old pin up girl.

The Long and Winding Road
The Beatles 1970

June 5, 1970 was the beginning of my theatre experience. After only a week, the only acting I had learned to do was acting like I was older than I really was. The kids were a bunch of rich brats. Their moms had dumped them on the local community theater as an alternate babysitter while they went to therapy or Jazzercise or to spent naughty time with their boyfriends. They were a rowdy group, and they all smoked. It didn't take me long to figure out that I better just go along with it. After all, that was something I did well. Just accepting stuff and going along to keep the peace.

I remember clutching a red pack of Marlboros and trying to figure out how to get them open. Tricky task. Finally, after ripping off the whole top and tossing all the silver foil on the sidewalk, I put one in my mouth; it stuck to my lips and hurt a little when I pulled it off because it was such a windy West Texas day. It stuck kind of like wet fingers on ice cubes. I was glad no one saw that, and I licked my lips a few times before I tried again. This time it was wet and slippery, and I struck a match. The wind blew it out promptly as if some higher power didn't want me to light up.

After about five minutes and nearly a whole pack of matches, it held the flame. I didn't really quite grasp the whole inhaling process, so I just puffed a little and blew it out, then choked and coughed a bit, but it wasn't too bad.

A few days later after I had been practicing the cool look, a girl in the drama class said, "Hey Lily, stop nigger-lippin that smoke." I wasn't too sure what she was talking about. "Where did you learn to smoke like that? You're not even inhaling. It's not a cigar, you freak. You're just faking it."

Well, go figure. Faking it? The nerve. How would you even do that? If nothing else, I was determined, and before long I was a regular pro-smoker. I learned to flick it when I was done and had even mastered the basic concept of blowing smoke rings. My throat was raw, and I still gagged and sputtered a little, but it was coming along just fine.

Billy was a sixteen-year-old sophomore from my school and played the role of Captain Hook and our production of *Peter Pan* that summer.

"Hey, Lily. Looking good," he'd say or "Shiver me timbers, you're the prettiest tree I ever did see," using his special pirate voice. His friend Randy would taunt him and say, "Billy, wanna climb that tree don't you? Got a woody for the woody?"

I didn't know what they were talking about, so I just smiled. My skirt was short enough, and my hair was long enough to get away with all kinds of things with just a curl of the lip or a bat of the eye. My mother loved to dress me up in provocative ways, put make-up all over my face, and send me out into the world looking like a very fashionable prostitute. Maybe she was just crazy to get her kicks like that, but I guarantee it got results. Everywhere I went, I got attention. Guys would drop what they were doing to come over and talk to the thirteen-year-old who looked like she was twenty. All the boys at summer camp got pretty worked up whenever I entered the room. The part I didn't understand is that it made most girls really hate me for some reason.

I was lucky enough to have two roles in the summer production. I was one of the Indians that danced around Tiger Lily, so at least I danced and had cool fringe and beads on my costume. There was a chorus of younger Indians, but I was paired with another girl about my age, and we danced on either side of Tiger Lily. I had wanted her role since the character used part of my name, but they wanted someone older. My other role in the play was that of a tree.

I spent several weeks making my tree using chicken wire to fashion a trunk and papier mache with green toilet paper for leaves. I would get inside and stick my arms out the sides like branches and waddle out onto the stage. Unfortunately, I couldn't see where I was going very well, so I was a little scared when I had to walk by the edge of the stage in front of the curtains between acts. I could just see myself taking a dive off the edge, then rolling around on the floor, unable to get up. I guess I was all too charming with my fancy foliage and cute little trunk, so it goes without saying that Billy was smitten.

He took me to see a movie called *Anne of a Thousand Days*. It was my first date where a boy picked me up in his car and took me out. I was thirteen and a little excited that I was the only girl I knew who was allowed to do something like that. Something about him reminded me of Patrick, and that made him appealing to me. He played Frisbee and liked to listen to The Beatles, so I thought he might be cool. He also let me clean his wire-rimmed glasses with my shirt which was endearing in a cheesy, adolescent kind of way. On the way home, we went to Dino's drive in for a couple of cherry limes with extra cherries. We listened to Eric Burdon and the Animals while holding hands. It was like a real date. I was light headed by the time I got home. Maybe it was infatuation, but more likely an allergic reaction to either the aftershave or the leathery aroma of his fringed jacket. I never could tolerate perfume or anything fresh off of a dead cow. He walked me to the door and kissed me on the cheek, and I was intoxicated with the possibilities.

By the end of July, we were hanging out all the time. I told him

I was sixteen, too. Of course, Mother welcomed this suitor as she did all of them. The way she acted, how could he have guessed I was still a child by most definitions? Thirteen is that awkward time when you look old enough, but you are definitely *not* old enough.

It was the last week of rehearsals before *Peter Pan* opened, and theater camp would be over for that summer. He told me he had a great idea he thought I would like. So, we jumped in his car and drove to the edge of the city and up a dirt road to a hill where we could see the skyline in the distance, and we started to make out as we had done several times before.

He said, "Have you ever been with a guy before?"

Staying cool, I replied, "Sure." His hands went lower.

"I mean, have you ever gone all the way?"

I didn't know what he meant, but I felt like I should say yes so that he wouldn't think I was a baby or a fake or a freak—every thirteen-year-old girl's worst nightmare. Nobody had ever explained what sex was, and in 1970, sometimes you had to find out the hard way.

"Let's get in the back seat so we'll have more room."

Things were moving at light speed. I didn't know what would happen next, but I was trying to not act surprised or anything. I was cool. I had on a tiny blue skirt that stayed on, but he was tugging at my panties. My heart was racing, and I started to get scared about what he was going to do next.

"What are you doing?" I asked with my hands on his shoulders, holding him back as he pressed in close.

"Don't worry. I'm not going to hurt you. Just relax."

I leaned back as my panties dangled off one ankle, and my head was pushed into the door at an awkward angle. He was lying on top of me now with the buttons on his jeans all open, fumbling with something I couldn't see.

He hesitated, "Are you sure you've done this before?"

At this point, I wanted to climb back over into the safety of the front seat.

My face was on fire, and I felt dizzy. I wasn't sure what was going to happen next, but I thought it might not be a good idea. He wasn't even waiting for me to answer.

"I will stop if it hurts, okay?"

Something warm and hard was pushing up against me. He was

having some difficulty because I was scared, confused, and I didn't know what to do. Then it happened. Something unlike anything I could ever have imagined. It started making its way deeper. It wasn't too bad at first, and then it felt like something inside me made me want to pee. It pushed in harder and faster until something finally gave way and the burning pain felt like it would tear me in half. I was hurt. And I'm talking throbbing hurt, and after what seemed like the longest short time ever, he got off of me and sat beside me all sweaty and red faced. He wouldn't look at me.

"Are you okay?"

It was too late for that question. Something wet was trickling out between my legs. I touched it and saw that it was pink. I was swollen and bleeding, and I could feel my heart beating down there. I wasn't sure what had just happened. Had I just gone all the way? I wasn't sure if maybe there was something more or if that was it. I was too embarrassed to ask. Raw, inside and out, I grabbed my panties and scrambled into the front seat.

"We better get out of here," he said while fumbling for an 8-track tape of The Beatles.

"How about a cherry lime? The soda fountain at the pharmacy has that flaky, soft ice that melts in your mouth, and it's right across the street from theatre camp. Let's go there."

I couldn't think about cherry limes. His voice was distant and his words were swirling around me like bees. *The Long and Winding Road* floated out of the window as we sped away, clouds of dirt in the rearview mirror.

Paint it Black
Rolling Stones 1971

Wild Kingdom came on Sundays at 5 o'clock. They would feature a different animal every week. Sometimes they would do specials on a specific topic like poisonous snakes of North America. My favorite was about the mothers who eat their young.

Within days of the backseat encounter during theatre camp, my mother was suspect. Within a week, the whole ugly experience was revealed. I tried very hard not to think about it, and Billy avoided me after that like he had broken something and felt guilty.

I was sitting in my big blue chair drawing pictures of Audrey Hepburn wearing a myriad of sophisticated ensembles when my mother broke the silence.

"I found stains on your underwear. What exactly did you do with that boy? Did you let him do things to you?"

I was still uncertain about how far I had actually gone, so I didn't know what to say. When I thought of her inspecting my underwear, I was humiliated. My mother never heard me anyway. She only listened to her own voice.

"What did you do? I need to know. You might be pregnant or have a disease."

Two things that had never crossed my mind. Surely what we did wasn't "sex". There had to be more to it than that. But now my heart was racing, and I was beginning to feel like one of the hunted animals on *Walt Disney's Wild Kingdom*. The questions were like gunfire.

Suddenly, I felt ashamed. Whatever it was that I let him do to me that day, it must have been really bad.

"Did you have sex with that boy?"

"I don't know."

"What do you mean you don't know? How can you not know?"

"I mean I don't know."

"Did he penetrate you?"

"What does that even mean? I don't understand what you are asking me. I don't know what you're saying," I stammered as I tried to turn away and make her disappear. 7th graders never talked about things like that. They only talked about things like, "Did you get to second base? Did you let him feel you up? Have you made out yet?"

This was different. I hadn't even seen anything that he had in his pants. I wasn't even sure what he did to me. Now it made me feel humiliated to hear my mother talking in such an ugly and embarrassing way.

"Answer me!"

I nodded and whispered, "I guess so."

If my mother had been one of those carnivorous baby-eating animals, I'm sure she would have devoured me at that moment. She lunged out of her chair and grabbed my arms, squeezing them tightly.

"You little whore!"

I had heard this word at school but was never sure what people did to deserve being called that name. Now I know. You let a boy put his thing in you.

"You are ruined for life. You're probably pregnant. Nobody will ever love you now. You're just a trashy, no good slut. Nobody will ever want you now. You might as well just die!"

So I did.

A mother has a strange power over her daughter. She can bless her or curse her. My mother's words that day were like an evil curse. Her condemnations were a pronouncement of my fate. I believed her. I had lost all value as a human being. It was a self-fulfilling prophecy. Nobody would ever love me.

School began in a few weeks and the kids returned with stories of their vacations to Florida, their week at Grandma's house, summer camp, and maybe a few had even gotten to second base. I was in a different dimension. I had gone in all the way, and now I was worthless.

Patrick started going to the movies with a little blonde girl who had just gotten her breasts over the summer. They passed notes in class and cast furtive glances when the teacher turned her back. How I wish that were me who was smiling bashfully at this beautiful boy. But I was a whore, and whores don't get to smile like that with anybody.

By October, Augie had been discharged from the service because of some problem with his eyes. Later he confessed that he had stared into the sun to blind himself so he could come home. Crazy people do crazy things like that I guess.

My mother welcomed him with open arms. They would sit in the kitchen and discuss what a bad girl I had been, and how I needed to be straightened out. I think they both got some perverse pleasure out of talking about how naughty I had been, and he was more than happy to help out. He straightened me out almost every weekend in the back of his camper truck in the parking lot behind the Dairy Queen. His best friend George worked there and gave us free cherry limes when we were done. No Beatles music though. No music at all. Only heavy breathing punctuated by an occasional noise that sounded almost like he was in pain. Pretty soon I learned to make the same breathy noises because I figured that was part of the whole thing, and I didn't want to be weird or anything.

The seven years between my thirteen and his twenty made him more of a man friend than a boyfriend. I just went along because I would do just about anything to get out of the house and away from my mother's scathing stares. All that black makeup made her look like an evil witch trying to kill me with her eyes. Sometimes I imagined death rays shooting out of them in my direction. I made sure to never look directly at her for this reason, just to be sure. And after all, she had recruited him to save me. To straighten me out. I think he tried to bang the badness right out of me.

At first, it really hurt. When I first got a good look at what he was taking out of his pants and waving around at me, I thought it was something gross that surely was not connected to his body. It was the first time I had ever actually seen one of those things, and it looked like he might be able to just pop it off and put it away in the tool box or something. We had not even studied the human body at school in health class or anything like that. The diagrams that were in the books were of the *inside* of the body: ovaries, fallopian tubes, urethras. Certainly, no pictures of any of the dangly stuff on the outside of a body. I guess they knew it was too gross to show us or thought we might be so freaked out by it that we would never want to get married, take our clothes off, and do all the sex stuff to make a baby.

He told me to touch it. It was brown and looked like one of those wrinkly dogs with the skin that falls over their eyes. He made sure that I learned all the words for all the parts, and I was ashamed that I had been so stupid before. I had known nothing. I can honestly say I wasn't all that curious either and thought it was all pretty weird, but we would spend hours in that camper. Regardless of what he did to me, I never felt the fuzzy feeling inside like I did when I kissed Patrick Beanning. I would just lie there and try to imagine why he loved doing this so much. I would rather be inside the Dairy Queen eating ice cream or drawing pictures of the bums who came in there for the five-cent coffee and to get out of the cold. That was a lot more interesting to me.

When I got home after a late night out, my mother was eager to hear about my evening. I hated talking to her, and when she asked creepy questions, I felt like a bug trying to escape a giant can of raid. She drilled me more mercilessly than Augie did; it was brutal and incessant. It did make me wonder why she was so curious, and something told me that other mothers would never ask their daughters these kinds of questions.

"Is he large? Compare it to something. Is it bigger than a large banana or cucumber? Show me with your hands, just hold them out and show me," she goaded.

"I don't know, mother. Please just stop. Why do you need to know this? I really don't want to talk about it."

"You're no good. You've never been any good. You're just dirty. You might as well just tell me everything. You are not allowed to have secrets. I want to know exactly what he did to you."

I hated her for making me feel so filthy. She gave me no other choice; it was simply the way it was. I couldn't possibly hope for happiness or romance or beauty. I seldom thought of those things anymore. She made it painfully clear that I had done something so terrible that there was no way to ever escape it. I was ruined in a most profane way so that I no longer had any value. I wasn't sure what that meant, but I knew it had something to do with ruining my future and any dreams of happily ever afters.

That year I stopped drawing pictures of the elegant and graceful Audrey Hepburn wrapped in delicate pearls and silk.

Amazing Grace
Judy Collins 1971

Grandma and Grandpa came over on Saturday afternoons. Gramps sat in the kitchen and played dominoes with me while grandma would follow my mother through the house arguing and would eventually end up crying by the bamboo lamp in the living room. Dad was always gone, usually at the golf course or with his friends in a world where I had no place.

Gramps was the kind of man with gentle eyes. He wore big black boots, probably a remnant of his farm days. He had a grey windbreaker and a felt hat that he would take off and roll around in his hands. He always brought me a fresh dollar bill when he came to visit. No used, crumpled ones, but always a crispy new one. He would straighten it out between his fingers, over and over before finally handing it to me.

Sometimes they brought the Neapolitan ice cream in a little square cardboard box. It would be soft and drippy, and mother would fuss about it saying she didn't like to keep sweets in the house. When they left, she would put it in the sink and run water over it until it disappeared. She made me feel like that ice cream. Unwelcome. Melting. Helplessly flowing down the drain. Disappearing in streaks of color.

Grams didn't just bring sweet treats on Sunday afternoons; she brought her own personal friend, Jesus. When my mother made her cry, she would rock back and forth and sing hymns from a deep place inside her and talk about how her friend would never fail to be there for her. If I ever tried to approach her to tell her one of the dirty little secrets of that house, she would burst into prayer and shout praises to her God.

"The Lord will take away all of your tears. Just believe it. Just put it on Jesus, and he will lift you up and take away all of your burdens," Grams would proclaim with absolute certainty.

I always wondered why it didn't seem to work for her. My mother never missed an opportunity to torment my grandmother for the sins of the past. She would wail and whine about how her mother tried to abort her, never wanted her, never loved her. There would be screaming and tears, and my mother never backed off. She kept coming at her again and again until my grandma just broke down. Why didn't she use God's armor and her personal companion who could perform miracles to protect herself from my mother's vicious attacks?

When I was sick, grandma would bring out her Jesus jar. Her pastor had blessed the contents that turned regular cooking oil into special Jesus juice that could heal anything. Her fingers were dripping with the oil as put her hands on me and start hollering strange words and working herself into a frenzy. Gramps would fidget with the oil and mumble in the background. Mother would disappear as if they had somehow managed to banish the evil sickness from the house which was her madness, not my measles or chicken-pox.

There would be talk of miracles and grandma would say how Jesus would answer all prayers, we only need to ask. There was always talk of Heaven that dominated the day.

"There will be streets of gold and mansions for everybody. Lots of singing and worshiping like one big joyous revival, praise the Lord!"

Her gaze was far into the distance like she could just see the angels and hear their sweet voices. She never seemed to look at me or make eye contact during these healing sessions, but I was used to it because my mother never saw me either. I was truly invisible to pretty much everybody, and that really wasn't such a bad thing under the circumstances.

"We'll all be together again, and Mama will be there. I can't wait to see Mama again. And your uncle Otis and Aunt Lucille and all the cousins and nephews. My brother Francis, oh sweet Jesus my Lord and savior. They're all going to be there and will be one big happy family again just like when I was a little girl on the farm," she would go on as she raised her hands and closed her eyes.

She went on and on for what seemed like a really long time, caught up in the rapture of the Rapture while I was thinking about things she had said. Mansions for everyone? What about people who prefer teepees or igloos or caves? Singing hymns? I hated those songs and singing in church. What about all my dad's relatives in Thailand who were Buddhists? Where were they all going to go? And the getting reunited with all of your family part. Who would my dad be with if God forgave him for believing in Buddha, his other wife or my mother? Or maybe even both of them? I was sure that was a family reunion my mother would not care to repeat! I had so many questions and not one single answer that I could believe. Soon all the talk sounded as foreign to my ears as my father's native tongue.

The truth was that I did not want to be re-united with anyone that I had ever known. The thought of spending eternity with my miserable and pitiable mother or my unapproachable and distant father was not something that sounded good to me. If I had to be reunited with everyone, then there had to be a caveat, a special clause written in the deal that says they must all be healthy, healed, and happy. They must have shiny, smiling faces and there must be lots of laughter and dancing and joyful moments. If they can't be the best version of themselves, then I wanted no part of it. Just let me cease to exist and go to sleep forever. That would certainly beat the alternative of extended suffering where nobody ever gets what they want. That would be everlasting misery. No thanks.

There was a time when I would try to do what my grandmother said. I prayed and prayed, sometimes for over an hour. I would close my eyes and press my hands together and implore God to fix my family and make them happy. I tried to imagine a huge guy with a long white robe and really friendly face who would hear my words and close his eyes and nod and then, "Poof," everything would be okay. My mom would be healed from whatever was wrong with her, and she would suddenly be like those moms on television who bake cookies and say the right things and never ask questions that make you just want to die. My dad would come home, and we would take a walk, and he would talk to me and enjoy my company and tell me how proud of me he was because I was so smart. Kids at school would play with me and come over and sit at my table at lunch and smile and laugh and tell funny jokes.

God never failed me, but religion did.

Sometimes I would get down on my knees beside my bed like the children on TV did when they went to bed and said their prayers, and I would just say the same things over and over in case he didn't hear me or was distracted or sleeping or out of the office. That would explain why a lot of people suffer so much and never get any prayers answered.

I prayed, "Please, dear God, make my family be okay and please, dear God and Jesus, help me to be like everybody else and have a good life. I'm sorry for being a bad person. Help me know how to be good. Thank you for listening." I repeated it over and over maybe fifty or sixty times.

But my mother continued to sweep me out the door with Augie and childhoods later when I returned, she asked the same sick questions. So what conclusion could I reach? God must think I am as disgusting and worthless as my mother did. I didn't deserve his help. He probably only helped people like the pretty blonde girl who only held hands with Patrick Beanning. Not girls like me. Girls that made bruises up and down their thighs because the pain made them feel something. Girls that chewed their fingers bloody and tore the skin off their lips until they bled. Girls that wanted to ruin the bodies that others wanted to use. Girls that were so numb they were dead inside. These girls were damaged throw-aways. I was one of those girls.

I saw a lot that year. More than young eyes should ever see. Augie had a motorcycle and liked to go down Jefferson Street which was the main drag in town, and pick fights with anyone who looked at him the wrong way. The lowlifes he called friends also liked to fight, and so I tagged along to many of these blood-fests. They used bottles and bats, chains and brass knuckles, and roamed the streets in packs like wild dogs. Like animals, they would circle close, cock their head sideways, move in like they were smelling each other, then someone would throw the first punch, and it was on. It was horrible to watch, but there I was like always, no matter where I was or who was with me. Standing on the edge, close enough to see but far enough to be only a spectator. I thought they were monsters but never said a word.

"Pinche pendejo is lookin' over here like he wants to start somethin'. Chingate, cabron. What's your problem, ese? Want some of this?" Augie stands up and starts to posture and move towards some kid sitting low behind the wheel of a big yellow shitmobile, head tilted back and to one side like my grams when she is trying to read small print on a label.

He slaps at his chest and looks aggressive kind of like the big gorillas on the animal shows that come on tv. The guy sees a chance for escape and cuts his wheel sharply to the left as he quickly drives away. I watch it all passively as I play with the beads on the fringe of my purse.

"Let's go. I got a cold one waitin' on me with my name on it," he says excitedly as we head over to meet up with the gang.

His biker friends probably had a collective IQ of a peanut, but they certainly didn't lack enthusiasm. I remember a guy they called Little Billy. He was so loyal yet such a thug that he couldn't stop himself from talking crap to people, so a fight would always be brewing. He would get a little to drink, then start stirring up something. It was so predictable. Then when the police, or pigs as they called them, showed up, everyone would split up and then meet back at the Tally Ho Drive In for cheeseburgers and chili fries. They would beat their chests like the monkeys in the jungle and piss all over their territory like dogs. I sat there and studied them, trying to imagine what kind of dog they would be. Maybe a pit-bull or a wiener dog. I always liked to imagine what kind of animal a person might be. There was a guy at the grocery store that looked like a crippled cockroach. There was a lady who worked at the library who looked like a giant bird. And this one girl in my class had a hamster face and hairy body just like all the pet hamsters and guinea pigs she had for pets.

Augie's world was filled with colorful characters, but what they all had in common was that they were the lowest form of life on the planet. Nothing was ever wholesome or refined, just abject poverty, ignorance, and animal urges that compelled them to face another day. I thought that grown-ups deserve this misery because of terrible choice and natural consequences of the bad decisions, but it was the children who were truly the ones that were a true tragedy.

I remember two victims who stand out as the most horrific. One was Bong Baby. He was a little guy not even two years old. His parents were both addicts of some unfortunate variety, and we went to the house a few times to bring drugs or get drugs for some of Augie's biker buddies to sell. This little fellow would always be buck naked except for a soiled diaper, even in the depths of winter. When we sat down, everyone would pass around a bong. Augie and I would abstain because he said drugs were bad while he handed me a beer. Then the entertainment began. Bong baby would come up and put his mouth on the long pipe and take a big hit just to make the water bubble, sort of like kids who blow bubbles in their chocolate milk. Then he would run in circles and make crazy animal noises for a while before collapsing to the floor and humping his great big, filthy, crusty teddy bear. Dad would say, "Hey, buddy, come on back and make the bubbles go again."

Then the mom said, "Leave him be. He's gotta get his rocks off. Look everybody, ain't that the cutest thing? Him just going to town on his teddy."

Bong Baby wasn't the worst thing I ever saw. Big-Headed Baby was even more appalling.

Big-Headed Baby had a single mom in her thirties who was a stripper at a tittie bar by the airport. She also had a nasty coke habit, so her emotional disposition certainly left a lot to be desired. I had never seen a mother with a baby she absolutely loathed before. She hated this child and everything about it. It was ugly, with a disproportionately large head that made it even worse. I recall how she carried it on her hip like you would carry a 20 lb. bag of dog food. She kept trying to give it a baby bottle filled with Dr. Pepper, but the baby just wouldn't have it. She kept cramming it in his ugly face, then yelling at it and slapping its bare feet and legs, and then jerking it around by its rubbery little arms. It was maybe 18 months old but oversized and awkward with little hands that tried to cover its face and stop her hands from hitting it.

Finally, she reached over to get her cigarette, and it projectile vomited across the room unlike anything I had ever seen. She grabbed it and held it in front of her, cursing it, shaking it, and screaming more obscenities before throwing it on the couch where it bounced, then rolled off onto the floor. It made no sound as it lay on the ground, rigid, with an open mouth twisted in complete and utter agony and a look of terror in its eyes. I just sat there in horror, in shock at what I was witnessing. It made me feel sick. I so desperately had to get out of this hellhole; I went outside and waited in the car, lighting a cigarette with trembling hands and feeling like I was going to throw up, too.

Nobody even mentioned the violence and abuse when they finally climbed in to leave. Were they blind? That was a helpless baby at the mercy of a madwoman. She was probably going to kill it at some point, and they were all complicit. I wanted to tell someone, but I knew it was pointless and there was no rescue or happy ending for people like this. If it had been someone on the other side of town, it might be a different story, but then again, they were guilty, too—of worse things than this. I was only thirteen, so what did I know?

I watched Augie beat people until he was covered with blood, then would take off his shirt and fight some more. When it was over, we would go somewhere so he could get fresh clothes and wash up. The dried blood would turn the same burnt sienna color of his skin, so it was hard to tell how much he was covered in it. I guess all this made him feel like a manly man, the ruler of his roost, the alpha male. There would be some chest thumping, then he would always be ready to eat or screw. I was completely disgusted. They were savages.

My life had become so false to me that I couldn't remember who I used to be or was supposed to be. Maybe I was never anybody in the first place, and that was the real problem. I never really had an identity of my own anyway. I always had a penchant for adapting and assimilating the personalities of those around me. I was like a sponge that just soaked up the essence of everyone else. I was a chameleon who changed colors depending on where I was and who was with me. But I could never be Augie, and I could never be my mother. I was not composed of the same material and could not be like them. Those two people were both anathema to me.

Love Hurts
Nazareth 1971

My sister and I never really developed any close relationship. Part of it was probably the age difference, part the cultural dissonance, and mostly because my mother stole her father. She seemed to barely tolerate me, but I wanted her to be the person I could actually relate to since all the other relationships I had with everyone else were broken for one reason or another. When I put myself in her shoes, I didn't blame her. I get it. But I needed someone, anyone who was reasonably sane, unmotivated by guilt, selfishness, or madness, and unaffected by the color of my skin.

"Paddie, are you busy? Paddie, can I come in?" I asked as I peeked into the door.

"What do you want?" she said without turning down her music or lowering her *Teen Beat* magazine.

"Can I come in a minute? I need to ask you something," I replied.

"Okay just for a minute. I'm sort of busy."

I opened the door slowly and closed it quickly behind me. "Paddie, are you leaving? Are you going somewhere?"

"Who told you that?" she demanded as she lined up her multicolored hair bows that clipped on the top of her bangs in front of her bouffant hairdo. She wore white pedal pushers, Ked sneakers, and a blue blouse that had a white sailor collar.

"I don't know. Is it true?" I was always the last to know anything, and I was determined to find out before it happened this time.

"I'm going to stay with some people I met at church. I've been here almost three years, and your mother and I do not get along. It will be better for everyone I think," she said as she kept arranging her fingernail polish.

"Umm," I muttered as I stood there with her back to me. "I like you being here Paddie," I replied.

"Thanks, really, but I only came here to go to high school and attend college in the United States, then I planned on going back home anyway. I wanted to get to know my dad, but my mom is alone, and I think I'll just go back when I graduate next year. I can go to college in Bangkok," she said as she brushed a vibrant pink across her nails.

"You can avoid my mother the way I do. Just don't talk to her, don't look at her," I offered, trying to offer a solution.

"Why do you even care? You are never home. We never talk or do anything. You are always at school, at dance class, or with some boy. You won't even know I'm gone," she said as she turned and sat on the edge of the bed.

"I know you're here. It makes me feel better to know you're here," I said.

"I don't understand that. You like it that I'm here sometimes so nobody notices that you're not here. You are only fourteen. I was your age when I first came here, and I was just a kid. You are just a kid too, but you do things that I don't even do, and I'm eighteen," she said as she started putting her things away.

"Paddie, I just can't be here without you. Not in this house. Not with my Mother. It makes me feel like I can't breathe when I'm alone with her. I know she does things and says things to you, but just stay away from her like I do," I said, feeling the urgency and hopelessness of the situation.

"I have to go Lily. Listen. Things were said. Your mother accused me of some really crazy things involving Dad. I can't pretend she didn't say those things, and I don't believe she won't say them again. She needs help. I've heard her accuse you of things, too. It's sick. And think about this, even if I don't go now, in six or seven months when I finish school, I'm either leaving for college or going back home. So think about that. It was only a matter of time. I was never going to be here forever. I'm going to do something now to make things better and easier, but just remember this: everybody leaves. You will leave too in a few years," she said as she got up and stood by the door, opening it to show me my exit.

My cue to leave.

I thought to myself, everybody leaves. Everybody leaves.

Then I looked at her and realized that I didn't even really know this girl. We just never connected. We were from different worlds, and our lives were light years apart. We both had the same challenges, foreigners in a foreign land and a dysfunctional home, but the thing that made the biggest difference was the way we handled what was served up to us on this poo-poo platter. It seemed like she just knew how to get through it all and rise to the top like a delicious cream. She was Miss Howdy Doody Spirit winner at school. She went to church every Sunday with friends who drove up to get her but never came in. She wore a padded bra and perfume and put hairspray in her hair. She was popular and sociable and the only thing we had in common was sitting in the living room watching our dad sit in his chair after a long day at work or a long day at the golf course watching *Bonanza*.

Unfortunately, I did not know how to rise above what was happening to me. I was helpless, powerless. Any time I tried to climb out of the muddy pit that I had fallen into, someone grabbed me by the ankles or held onto my arms so I couldn't escape. They dragged me back down and held me under water until I stopped fighting and submitted.

I should have been happy for Paddie for having the opportunity to get away before something super bad happenned. There was no point fighting it or putting up a struggle, so I did the only thing I could do. I got up, walked out of her room and said, "Goodbye Paddie. Take care of yourself."

Firebird
Stravinsky 1971

I was surprised to discover how many serious dancers actually smoke cigarettes. Somehow, my perceptions of the ballerinas on TV told me that dancers had to be real health freaks or something. Boy was I wrong. The ones who didn't smoke a pack a day, smoked pot, or had some really unhealthy eating disorder with a secret food fetish. Anything to stay thin.

Everyone had to wear black leotards with pink tights. The couple who ran the dance studio argued a lot, and that certainly felt normal. I felt right at home. I had found people like my own people, only with something valuable to teach me. I became deeply invested in the whole process. Dance class had been twice a week until now. Soon I was there four days a week.

The studio owners, Neil and Camilla, were the living embodiment of dance. It lived in every cell and exuded from every pore. They were the closest thing to culture in our little cow town. I don't think the community ever appreciated the miracles they produced and lives they changed, but I did. I knew the transformative power of dance and so did others. Perry, Sarah, Vikki, Kathy, and Matt were all disciples of dance. Each of us carried our own share of troubles, but in the studio, we were free.

The studio was humid and warm with all the sweaty bodies, and there was the familiar fog on the windows. When I left dance class, I bundled up with a scarf and wrap to keep the wind off since I was wet with perspiration. When I got home, I would wring out my clothes in the bathroom sink to see what looked like cupfuls of my labors pouring out of my clothes. I would wash my face and get a big glass of water, then get lost in my big blue chair. I drew dancers in mid-air draped in spectacular costumes. When I wasn't in the dance studio, I was filling my sketchbooks with pages of dance.

My mother often interrupted me with a bowl of chopped up fruit, all peeled and diced nicely or a plate or sliced vegetables like bell peppers and zucchini. Strange that she would do that, but I think I decided that it must be what mothers do. Chop up stuff. I lived on fruit yogurt V-8 vegetable juice, cheese, Triscuits, bell peppers, and the nightly little bowl of spicy Thai food. It kept me skinny. At 5 foot 9 inches, I weighed only 118-120 pounds. Even though I was taller than the other dancers, I looked the part with the classic long neck, square shoulders, perfect posture, and slightly turned out feet.

For me, dancing was something that lifted me above all the ugliness of my life and gave me a sense of beauty. I could be someone else. More elegant, less troubled. I was smoke, ether, fog in the empty air; it transported me. When we did that, I moved like I was under water, so fluid.

Ironically, I never learned to swim. I was terrified of the feeling when my head went under the water. It was loud in my ears and squeezed all of my breath away. It requires a kind of surrender, and I could not afford to lose control of the little that I could control. Funny how water can be buoyant and lift you up to keep you afloat or drag you and drown you with its suffocating strength.

When we went to the beach, I always stood stiffly looking out to sea. When the waves retreated and made their attempts to pull me out into the endless blue, I fought it with my rigid stance. Somehow, being grounded to the earth made me feel like I was real and connected to something, something bigger than me and my life. I watched the water rushing around my feet, my long brown toes curling to grasp the wet sand as it implored me to move deeper. Sometimes I imagined going under, surrendering to a silent secret sea of colorful fish and dolphins. Maybe I could dance with mermaids with glittery flowing scarves and a sparkling fishy fin that trailed behind me heavily. My long, dark hair spread out like smoke in the water. The lightness of being lifted me as I twirled and used my strength to push against the power of the sea. I was a mermaid for a moment and in perfect harmony with the rhythms of the waves.

Dancing was the closest thing a human could do to be like a flowing mermaid under the sea. It was a magical transformation and glorious escape. There was power and strength in the movements and a lightness of being that transported you to an imaginary place full of joy and grace.

I danced in my sleep, too. It was so real, the feeling of jumping and turning, only it was higher and lasted longer and was in slow motion frames. I could feel motion and movement as I stretched out my long legs and lifted myself into the air. I jumped from sleep with a jolt and suddenly awakened because I had landed too hard or missed a step and kept falling and falling forever. When I finally hit the floor, the resin and dust exploded into clouds around me as I lay there trying to recover my composure. The show must go on, I thought. There was an infinite numbing silence, but I could hear the breathing of a thousand people in the audience and feel a thousand heartbeats throbbing in my head. I felt them all watching me as I studied the battered wooden floor of the old stage in the recital hall, paralyzed, sweat dripping into my eyes until I could not see to see.

American Pie
Don McClean 1971

It wasn't long after Paddie left before I became an adolescent pregnant poster child for a childhood gone wrong. It's probably number one on the list of what not to do if you are a middle school tween-ager. It didn't seem real at the time, and it has maintained a veil of secrecy and shame ever since. I was a middle-class adolescent who was on the honor roll and seriously pursuing ballet and violin. School began as usual for my 8th grade year, but by October there were conversations about how to address this atrocity. Funny how nobody ever mentioned birth control even though they knew what was going on. I certainly had no idea about what it meant and barely knew what intercourse was. Augie, consumed with little more than his own animal impulses, was never one to be safe or sorry. Looking back, I'm surprised that it didn't happen months before. A series of insane events followed, but that wasn't unusual.

Augie moved into my grandparents' house. The adopted son they always wanted and never had or something like that. My mother decided to load us into the car one day and drive us to Oklahoma where fourteen-year-olds could marry twenty-one-year olds with their mom's permission. I turned fourteen in December, so we were on our way the first week of January. My dad didn't even know about it until several months later, but I guess my mother had enough enthusiasm for everyone. I cannot imagine what she thought we had to gain by this little field trip, and my grandmother rode shotgun as co-conspirator. It was sort of a cross between a hillbilly wedding and a pre-arranged third world arrangement where you marry your chosen mate when you're only ten.

I had never thought about marriage or what it was supposed to be. When you're fourteen, that's not something you think about. I was accustomed to thinking about my pimples or my homework or how to do a sharper pirouette in dance class. It was like a pretend thing where we would all laugh about it later and say, "Wow, that was scary. Just kidding. Now go back to dance class or go back to school." But nobody was laughing.

And there I was, standing in front of some old guy with bad posture and really bad breath preparing to say things I was sure I did not understand or even want to understand. The man who performed the ceremony had these ashy white hands that made him look like he was dead and embalmed already. His big, baldhead also had a corpse like appearance. While I was contemplating the length of his nose hairs, beside me was this big, dumb, hormonally challenged Mexican with no morals, honor, or sense of anything except his body and what it wanted. He was handsome in a trailer park kind of way. But it wasn't supposed to be like this. I felt disgusted when he smiled at me like we were the same because we weren't the same at all. And when he touched me in public, I was so embarrassed because I knew he was slimy, beaneath me, a dark and dirty secret.

According to the plan that I lost somewhere along the way, I was supposed to go to New York and dance jazz and ballet and have big bouquets of roses brought to me after the show. I was suddenly aware that I was a child. I looked at him and wondered who this was, why it wasn't years later and the magnificent Patrick Beanning, famous director and producer, standing beside me in a fancy tuxedo, and wondering where God was at this moment in time. Why did I not deserve those things, and why had God turned his back on me? He must have been busy with my grandma because he sure wasn't there with me. Not that day, not any day. I don't think that God ever actually failed me. I still talked to him sometimes. Little whispers in the dark or conversations with him in my head as I tried to sleep. But while I still hoped that

God might hear me, religion never did. And when I turned in that direction for help from the church or the people who were there every Sunday, there was none. In spite of all of that disappointment, I still had the idea of someday walking down a long asile in a massive church with tall ceilings to a beautiful altar covered in flowers, drenched in radiant light streaming in from stained glass windows, beautiful music playing, and a sparkly white dress covered in glittering lace and pearls and rhinestones. God would be there with us as we spoke soft and sacred words to each other.

It was just a fantasy. A silly, childish dream. God was nowhere to be found on that bleak day. He must have been on vacation. There was nothing holy about the words exchanged. In fact, none of it even seemed real. It was like a distant scene from some far away faded photograph or slow playing film in back and white.

Afterwards we went to Dairy Queen for ice cream. Everybody got something, but I felt sick. It was a long, silent ride back to Amarillo, and I was nauseous the whole way. When we got back, Augie was dropped off at my grandmother's house, and I went home to my room, to my big blue chair to sit alone like nothing had happened, like I had not just been robbed of any dreams for a future worth having. In the face of that grey day, there was a resignation, a stoic numbness. I accepted the situation because I lived in crazy town in a house without hope.

Chapter 3

Go Tell It on the Mountain 1971

Sometimes I think you know when something is wrong even if you don't have anyone to tell you or show you what is right. I knew there was something fundamentally wrong with my family and the whole setup, but stoic by nature, I didn't see the point of questioning something I couldn't change or control. What can a child actually do to compel the people around them to do what they should? Nobody would have believed me anyway, so I resigned myself to my unfortunate fate and went through the motions of being a normal adolescent although normal never even visited my house.

Years later, my therapists said I must have had PTSD which caused a dissociative state and chronic depression. I'm sure that is all true, but at the time, all I knew was that I had to do whatever I could to survive. One of the things that was required was a complete shutdown of all feelings and emotions. I had been practicing that for years when my parents would fight and drag me into it. Something just flipped off like a switch, and it was like I became an observer, a spectator—not really alive or participating in my own body.

At night, I lay in my little twin bed with the pink blanket with little pink roses on it and felt my body shape shifting. I felt myself shrinking until I was like a twig or toothpick. I thought I might just disappear since I was so small. I could feel my bones shriveling up and my skin sucking close like plastic you lay over hot food. Then the next minute, I felt myself growing to be the size of the room. My body was so enormous and stretched that I could feel my skin tearing and pulling. It scared me to feel like I might just burst like a water balloon. I wondered if everybody felt like this sometimes. But as always, I never said a word and suffered in silence. It never helped to say anything to anyone. The response was always, always bad regardless of which one you might have reached out to. Just bad in different ways.

Rationalization was another label affixed to my childhood struggles when, years later, I recounted the events to an empathetic soul who I paid $100 an hour to hear my horror. So I told myself that my family culture and geography were the reasons why my life was so unusual. All the exotic stories of my father's country made me think it was possible that in some places it might be acceptable to do things differently. So I told myself that I was just different. Maybe in the wrong country. Maybe on the wrong planet.

On Sundays, my grams and gramps brought Augie, and picked me up from my house to go to the Pentecostal Holiness Church of the Living Waters. It was a small, wooden building not much bigger than a modest house. I don't think Augie believed any of it; he just knew that if he went along there would be a big Sunday dinner afterwards with me for dessert.

The preacher was unlike anything I had ever seen. He put on quite a show which was very different from the quiet, meditative Buddhist stuff my dad and sister did. This guy was maybe fifty and sort of fat. He reminded me of a pig in shiny shoes. He threw his arms about with wild gesticulations and got louder and started to sweat and spit and turn red when he spoke. He strutted and pranced about and put a display worthy of an Oscar.

"Praise God! Hallelujah, brothers and sisters!" He got animated and threw his big arms around in his jacket that was too tight for him. I thought he looked like the used car salesman on TV with the brightly colored suits and big rings on his stubby fingers.

"Hallelujah, praise the Lord!"

Toward the end there would be a big climax, and the people would jump up and shout. There were maybe a dozen rows that wrapped around like a horseshoe and every single one of the people were standing and making noise for Jesus.

"Praise God! Jesus, Jesus, Jesus, Sweet Jesus my Lord and Savior! Glory to God!"

Some would cry and shake and drop to the floor and keep shaking. Others would clap and holler and throw their head back in some feverish Jesus induced hysteria. All the women had big tall hair, and I wondered how they slept, had sex, or played sports and still managed to keep it so neat.

When church was finally over and everyone had worn themselves out, Augie slid into the back seat of the white Oldsmobile with me on the way to Gram and Gramps house and then slid his hand up my dress and into my pantyhose. He would finger me all the way home and say, "Hey Granny. Are we going to have some of your special fried chicken for lunch today? Some finger licking good chicken?" and he would snicker like he had said something clever.

She never heard him because she was with her personal Jesus, pouring out her gospel hymns and soulful jubilation, still pretty worked up from the message we had just received in the little white church. Most Sundays, she continued singing and clapping all the way home, recounting how Brother Bob was filled with the Holy Ghost and preached a wonderful message.

I just sat there and ignored it all because all I could think about was how my grandfather kept his foot on the brake. Wherever we went, there was a subtle lurching back and forth going on as he rode the brake which created the most nauseating motion sickness imaginable. Add to that any pregnancy queasiness, and you can imagine. Augie could do whatever he wanted to me, and it's like I couldn't even feel it or acknowledge that it was happening because I had to focus on not throwing up all over the bibles and blankets in the backseat of the car.

After lunch we retreated into Augie's room at my grandparents' house, and they went into their room for a little Sunday afternoon nap. My grandmother worked off all that energy with a nice romp with my Gramps which we could hear with each disturbing squeak of the mattress and muffled moan from my Grams. It sort of sounded like praying. While all that awkward business was going on, Augie laid me on my side as I got thicker around the middle with my baby bump and did his thing for what seemed like forever. Again, I would let my mind drift to thoughts about the beach, dance class, a song I liked, or just about anything to transport me from that room and away from what was happening to me. I had a special ability to disconnect and float out of my physical body. Sometimes I thought it was like the transcendental meditation my Thai family did. But let's get real, this was no spiritual or meditative experience. It was an escape, and I could do it on command.

There was a tree outside the window with branches that sounded like bony skeleton fingers scraping against the window. I had a bad feeling about the noise and thought something evil was lurking outside that window, just trying to get in and get me. I believed in ghosts and demons and magic and was pretty sure these evil things were always nearby, watching me, waiting in the closet, or hiding under the bed. Sometimes my grams would say through the door, "Augie honey, you're not hurting her, are you? Mind that baby."

He would grin his vapid grin and say, "Okay granny. I'm being careful."

I was sickened. I couldn't understand why he couldn't get enough of the recreational ways he used my body even though I really wasn't even present in the moment. I never allowed myself to experience any sensation at all and imagined it was like making love with a zombie. Who are we kidding? None of this was about love, but houghts like that made me smile sometimes, and I guess he thought I was smiling about what he was doing, but he was wrong. I had been shutting down and tuning out all my life to escape the terrors of my house, so this was pretty easy except for once in a while something inside my tummy tickled so bad like something was rolling around inside of me that I wanted to scream or pee or cry, but luckily, it didn't last long.

Finally, in the late afternoon, I would go back to my house sometime before suppertime and retreat to the security of my big blue chair. It was a comfort to be in my spot with my books and journals and drawing pads and away from all the people who either wanted to take my soul or my body.

We are Siamese If You Please
Peggy Lee 1971

What did a girl like me dream about? I first saw Nancy Kwan on television in a musical called *Flower Drum Song* sometime in the mid-60s. I was enchanted. Here was an actress who was part Asian and part Caucasian like me. She had the same eyes, the same hair, the same skin. Maybe I couldn't ever be Audrey Hepburn with her swan neck and delicate pearls, but maybe I could be the stylishly brown Miss Kwan.

I dreamed I lived in Hollywood in a house with big windows that overlooked the endless blue of the Pacific. I had little fluffy dogs that sat on little fluffy pillows all day and maids and maybe a butler to prepare exquisite meals that were as beautiful as they were delicious. All the vegetables would be hand carved like flowers, and there would be miniature ice sculptures and candles at dinner each evening. I would have big fountains and green all through my tropical paradise. They would even put the little paper umbrellas in my Ovaltine and have ice cubes shaped like little fish swimming in my sodas. There might be a little stream flowing through the inside of my house and out to the sea. The floor in my room would be glass and somehow suspended over the ocean floor so I could watch the fluorescent jellyfish, manta rays, and dolphins swim Beaneath me as I floated to sleep.

Yes, I would live in luxury and drive a fast car to the studios where everyone would greet me with warmth and admiration. I would tie a long red scarf around my ink black long hair and wear dark sunglasses. No Isadora Duncan endings as I sped like mercury down the highway. Just grace and beauty and elegance. Poise personified.

When I finished with that little fantasy, I would move on to my secret agent world, agent Double-0 Oh No, an international femme fatale and Defender of Truth and Justice. My lipstick doubled as a transmitter and deadly poison for some unfortunate fool. My shoes converted into knives that shot out of the toes. I wasn't a Bond girl; I was the female Bond himself. Why not? I had watched Emma Peele for years and loved her life as a spy. I always wondered why she needed the stuffy British sidekick. I guess I had the heart and soul of a feminist long before I discovered the word to ascribe to it.

There would be amazing fight scenes utilizing all those years of dance training of course. Wearing nothing but black and cool black sunglasses, I would sip martinis and smoke extra-long cigarettes and speak with a French accent, *je t'aime, mon cher. Je ne coup pompa?* Then I would slink into my black DeLorean and disappear in a streak of pure speed.

When Hollywood and spy games became droll, the third scenario was that of Master of Magic. A popular sitcom at the time was *Bewitched*, the story of a witch with a twitch. I had her powers, so with one wiggle I could transform people into just about anything you can imagine. That allowed me to do all kinds of fun things like pop into Paris one minute, then move to vapor and on to Venice the next. I would travel the globe and digest all of its wonder. As a world traveler, I would feast on the local cuisine, be multilingual, soak up the culture, see all the famous churches and museums, and witness the world's greatest ballets all while wearing breathtaking wide-brimmed hats. Every day would be a consummate experience. All of the art in the world would surround me and transport me to a place of grace and beauty. My imagination carried me far away, beyond the reach of crazy sorrow and despair.

Killing Me Softly
Roberta Flack 1971

I will never know if the things my mother did, the crimes she committed against me, were maliciously intentional or simply accidents caused by her complete inability to function within the parameters of conventional society, home, and hearth. I suppose it doesn't really matter. What happened happened, and it really doesn't matter why.

In the sixth month of my pregnancy, I caught a nasty stomach bug. I threw up, then had diarrhea, then threw up again. The baby had only recently begun to move, and I was freaked out that something was inside my body swimming around like that.

I was sitting in my blue chair beside my homebound instructor that the school had arranged since a visibly pregnant fourteen-year-old could not possibly go to school with other children. Even teachers who became pregnant had to retreat into the privacy of their homes to grow their brood and re-emerge when skinny and flat again. These "leave of absences" were mandatory in the 70's when all females had to wear dresses to school and of course the pantyhose that were so revolutionary and requisite. Heaven forbid that young people might see such things as round bellies and respond with frantic abandon of all moral imperatives!

I sat there with a book propped up on my swollen bulge when something fluttered, then stretched out what might have been a foot or an arm. "Holy guacamole," I thought and turned with an incredulous face filled with awe towards Miss Betty. She was an older woman, maybe forty-five or fifty, who undoubtedly was appalled by my condition at such a young age. I thought she probably went to a church like my grandmother's where everyone smelled like rose water and ate a lot of potato salad. Her reaction was one that paralleled mine—joy and horror, disbelief and sadness, all sprinkled with a bit of confusion.

But now I was puking my guts out and my mom called Dr. Pritchett to get something to help me. Dr. Pritchett was a rather grim fellow whose wife had slit her wrists in the bathtub a few years earlier. He never smiled and always looked like he had just been jumped by thugs and beaten within an inch of his life. He was our family practitioner and friend of my grandmother's whom he revered as a good, holy woman. She started a prayer chain after his wife killed herself, and Dr. Pritchett seemed very grateful. Small town folks need to stick together and pray for each other a lot.

The prescribed remedy was some suppositories that Avondale pharmacy was happy to deliver for a small fee. I don't know what happened next, but my mom brought in the medicine and said she was going to coat them in Vaseline and that I could do it or she could do it, but one of us was going to have to shove these greasy globs of wax up my butt. She handed me the first one. I slid my hands under the blanket and rolled over a little, keeping one leg to the side. Awkward, I thought as I pushed the cold mass around the vicinity of its destination, finally feeling it suddenly slip in. My fever was so high, I thought it would melt immediately and just run back out.

Then my mom held out the second one. I looked at her standing there, Beant over a little like the deformity within had manifested itself outside her and twisted her body up to match how tangled she was on the inside. I hated her a little as I said, "One was enough. I'm okay. Why do I need another one?"

"Just take it. It's what the doctor ordered. You are dehydrated. Just take it."

Reluctantly, and grossed out by the first suppository, but feeling delirious with fever and nausea beyond description, I took it.

I fell asleep almost immediately after and languished there in feverish dreams for what seemed like days. When I woke, my fever had broken, and both me and the bed were wet with fever sweats. After changing into dry pajamas, I was able to have a cracker, a spoonful of jello, and a few sips of Sprite. As I was sucking on a waxed paper Beandy straw, my Grandmother entered my room.

She had come over to lay hands on me and had been anointing me with oils and praying while I was sleeping. When I opened my eyes, she began singing praises and speaking in tongues. She was dancing around my bedroom and speaking the foreign language of Jesus so that it looked like quite a party. This went on for maybe ten minutes before she settled down. I wondered if she would go home and get frisky with grandpa since that usually happened after church on Sunday afternoons after getting all worked up and everything.

I had forgotten that I had something inside of me. Actually, I forgot about it quite often and rarely contemplated that life until it would move, and then I was forced to acknowledge it for a moment. It seemed unreal like something that was never going to come out and be a real person or anything. I started to wonder if it this thing in me had been sick, too. I had been really sick for a couple of days, and I could not remember when I had last felt it move.

Sorry Seems to Be the Hardest Word
Elton John 1971

When I went to see Dr. Pritchett, it had been nearly two weeks since my stomach virus. What happened next is a blur, but I remember never fully processing the idea that something had gone wrong and the thing inside of me might not be okay.

I had never fully embraced the reality of being a mother. It was such a remote, disconnected, fantastical prospect. I never imagined a real flesh and blood baby that might be part of my life. I never imagined what its name might be or what it might eat or wear or play. It was never more than a weird dream or maybe more of a surreal nightmare.

When I was told it might be dead inside me, all I could think of was, "How are we going to get it out?"

I tried to remember what it had felt like when it was still moving. I thought it was kind of like a charley horse cramp in my leg or foot or maybe it was like being tickled. It was like it never happened, yet I looked down and there was this huge stomach that I couldn't figure out how that was part of me. I had some kind of dissociative experience I guess because it really seemed like it was someone else's body that just held me hostage for a little while, abducting me and hijacking my body... my life. The reality of having a dead baby inside did not seem real either. By the time they decided to induce labor, it had been dead inside me for almost a month. I could tell everyone had on their worried faces, but I was just relieved that all this was going to be over soon.

I do recall with vivid horror the reality of the thirty-one hours in that drab and dark hospital room where I suffered agonizing pain as they tried to get it out. I remember the burning agony of labor pains that were induced with different chemicals with no result. I do recall the smell of blood and amniotic fluid and how much I wanted it to stop hurting. I recall the doctor standing nearby and talking in a low voice about what to try next since things were not progressing. I remember how he never met my eyes with his or attempted conversation, always telling nurses what to do and exiting quickly. I guess I was still invisible.

Most of all, I remember overhearing that the baby's feet were going to come out first, so they decided to tie a weight around its feet to pull it out slowly. I guess it was tough to get a five-pound dead body out of a little girl who weighed no more than 115 pounds, so they had to be creative. They got a small, white lotion bottle and used it as a weight, and tied the other end of the string to the tiny corpse inside me. Hours passed. Screams of anguish punctuated the emptiness of the room with every contraction while the crying and whimpering never ended. And through all of it, I remained alone. My mother was the only one who kept coming in and out. She didn't stay for more than a minute, maybe just checking to see if I was still alive, then she would disappear again. In almost every situation, she would find a way to make things worse, but I wanted somebody, anybody, to stay and tell me how much longer the agony would continue, do something to make it stop. I was embarrassed by the things they were doing to me, all the poking and prodding and sickening smells. I didn't want anyone to see me in such a wretched condition, but it went on hour after hour after relentless hour. I thought, "If I die, that's okay. I don't care. It will stop hurting."

And finally, after over thirty-seven hours of unending torture, I felt a slippery mass slide out into a bedpan and heard the heavy sound it made when it fell. Like the waste typically carried in such a metal pan, they quickly took it away without letting me see it and gave me drugs to knock me out.

Hours later, I awoke in a bright room like the horrors of the night before had never happened. There was a new mother on the other side of the curtain and all the chatter and cooing that accompanies such moments. But no one was there with me. No visitors, no flowers, no nurses or social workers, no apologies. I did not know what had actually happened until I returned home two days later. My mother told me what I had been too afraid to ask or even think about. She told me that "it" was a little boy that had died inside me, she held out her hands to show me how big he was, described his big mouth that held a hint of a smile, spoke all the unspeakable details. She finished by telling me that they were getting a little coffin for him with soft white satin and having a little funeral service at the graveside. At that point, I should have been devastated or disappointed or sad or something.

I felt nothing. It wasn't even real.

During the hours that followed when I was left alone in the hospital, I remember going into rooms up and down the hall, telling the new mothers that my baby was fine but sleeping in the nursery and that my husband was so excited and happy to be a father. I was a great teller of lies, and I am not sure what compelled me to tell these stories to all these people. But I did, and they believed it for all I know.

Little did I know so much of me had died with my baby. Nothing about it seemed real, everything was in a fog. I did not go to the cemetery the day of the burial, but when his little body went into the cold, March ground, bits and pieces of Lily went into the ground with him.

Augie was destroyed by the loss of his firstborn son. I guess that's a really big deal to most guys. There was no going forward together after something like that. It just sucked all the fun out for him because every time he looked at me now, he was reminded that he had a son, a son he named Shane, a son forever sleeping in a little white-satin lined coffin. He lost his swagger and smile somewhere in all this and shortly came to realize that the only thing he could do in such a situation was flee the scene of the crime. He soon left Amarillo and moved to an Indian reservation in Oklahoma. He'd always been infatuated with Native American culture and decided to re-invent himself as one of them—feathers and war paint and moccasins and all. White people are often guilty of cultural appropriation in insensitive, politically incorrect ways, but this was different. He was going to actually become one and assimilate into the culture completely. So ended the most disturbing chapter of my life at that point.

I just wanted to forget all about all of it. Augie with his big stupid smile, Augie's baby boy with a big smile on his perfectly dead little face, and all the crazy supporting actors in this God-less tragedy with their useless, condescending smiles. I wanted them to all stop smiling their vapid, empty smiles and let their faces shatter into a thousand unrecognizable pieces, so I could stop seeing them look at me. They were always watching my every move now, all the while smiling like demons and disappearing like ghosts.

White Rabbit
Jefferson Airplane 1971

After all the baby business during my 8th grade year, the middle school I attended allowed me to skip all of 9th and go on up to the high school as long as I promised to attend summer school to restore the credits from that year. Truth is, they didn't want me there, putting the wholesome kids at risk. I'm not sure what they thought I might do to corrupt them, give them cooties? My grades had always been solid A's, so someone with my academic ability could easy take the fast track.

I continued to dance a couple of days a week, but it was the music that became increasingly important to me. Whether it was Joni Mitchell or Janis Joplin or Jethro Tull or Eric Clapton, I was hooked on rock and roll. Mornings begin with a cough drop, a cigarette, and a big dose of Black Sabbath or Led Zeppelin. I was empty, completely empty, and music was the only thing that filled me up at least a little bit for a little while.

I also discovered that drugs were the perfect thing to make me feel like I might be able to get through the day. Self-medicating was easy in the 70's since drugs flowed like water. Homeroom was first period, but I never made it there. As soon as I got to school, friends with pockets full of pipes, pot, and other paraphernalia found me, and we drove around the school listening to Iron Butterfly and Steppenwolf and smoking a fat one. Nothing was more important to these people then getting high and getting into quality music. Nothing else mattered, not even sex. That was cool with me. I never got anything out of it except getting bruised and battered, so I'd rather be getting stoned than getting laid.

Everyone I hung out with either played in a band or dated someone who played in a band. We would get so wasted that I could stand up and sing the whole soundtrack from *Tommy* and nobody seemed to care that I couldn't carry a note. *See me, feel me, fix me, kill me.* That's what was great about these people. They may have been a bunch of dickhead losers, but they had kind hearts and smiled a lot about nothing in particular. They could be amused with their own drool. I liked that. They may have lied and stolen from their own mothers to get twenty bucks for a five-finger bag of weed, but what the hell. They shared it with their friends and made me laugh when I had nothing else to laugh about. We played a lot of foosball at the bowling alley across the street from my school since it was a popular hangout for all the stoners. I was a walking contradiction who stood apart from the others. It wasn't my desert boots or moccasins with faded jeans with patches all over them—"Keep on Truckin,'" magic mushrooms and an upside down American flag. I think it had something to do with the ballet leotard that I had on many days because I went straight to dance class after school Monday through Friday. I just slipped off my hippie threads and into a pair of pink tights and leg warmers in the car on the way to the dance studio which was less than two miles from the school. I usually did a "wake and bake" while listening to Janis Joplin or Jethro Tull, and then I'd smoke again during homeroom and again at lunch. Sometimes I dropped acid—a half a tab of orange sunshine or purple barrel and tripped through the morning. And occasionally, I'd do white crosses and redbirds to manage my ups and downs and control my high. By the time 3:35 rolled around, I was usually straight enough to go to dance from 4:00-6:00, and then I'd come home and study or read for an hour or so before going to bed. That was my routine throughout high school. I didn't remember much until the afternoons, but I did remember being pretty wasted in class and still making straight A's and the National Honor Society.

Somehow in spite of the fact I was high for the majority of my secondary school experience, I did manage to get to all of my real classes and maintained stellar grades. That's how I kept my parents off my case. I showed them my report card, stayed in my room and did homework on school nights, then split on Friday and didn't return until Sunday. It was amazing how many other kids had parents who never asked questions either. They didn't want to know.

I guess my parents figured if I could make those kinds of grades, I must not be too far gone. They used the extra time alone to try to kill each other, so I wasn't missing out on quality family time. And of course, as any responsible parent would do, my mother took me to Planned Parenthood and had me fitted with an IUD just in case I got so drunk or wasted someone might jump my bones. We sure didn't want our little Lily to get knocked up a second time, now did we? So, I guess I was ready for high school.

I became the youngest 10th grade student at Tascosa High School and fresh meat for the older students.

In Amarillo, folks like to name their kids Randy, Billy, Jimmy, Donny, Bobby, and names that sound like good ole' boys from Texas—names that sound good with a Bob or Joe as a middle name. The most popular leaders of the school were athletes and members of all the clubs like Key Club and Student Council, not scholars or brainy types like Latin Club or fruity types like Drama Club. They were the arrogant alpha males of the school and ruled with a vicious condescension towards those who weren't part of their group.

Everybody knew that I had been up to something shameful the year I was out. A 9th grader named Cheri and I were both removed from class as soon as our pregnancies were confirmed. Nobody ever saw her again, but here I was…back from the dead.

The boys decided they would have some fun. One of them asked me to hang out and said they would pick me up around 6:00 pm. It was exciting to think this older guy who was such a big deal at school would ask me out, so I agreed. When he came to get me, there were three other guys in the car and a bag full of cherry vodka and other libations. I had never really drank alcohol before, but he said we were all going to party and have some fun. They kept pouring the drinks, mostly vodka with a little Coca-Cola, one after another. I thought they were drinking with me, but later I realized they were staying sober for what they had planned next. After a couple of hours, I remember feeling dizzy and sick to my stomach. The room was swirling and everything was moving even when I was sitting still.

"I'm feeling weird. Can you take me home now?" I asked as I tried to stand up.

"Don't you worry, baby. We're gonna take good care of you," he said while the others all laughed as they pulled off my boots. In the 70's, nobody knew what the term "consent" meant, and these guys certainly weren't Rhodes Scholars.

"I don't feel very good," I said as I staggered to the bathroom. Next thing I remember, they had caught me in the driveway by the side of the house.

"She was trying to get away or something," one of them said as they rushed over and surrounded me, ushering me back inside. I remember falling and scraping both knees and being dragged back into the house. After that, it was mostly a blur. I faded in and out of consciousness and couldn't move. It was like I was paralyzed. I knew I was on a bed, and

I knew I was naked. I didn't know how I got there, but I remember voices, laughing, and the sound of a Polaroid camera.

When I commanded enough sobriety to regain control of my body, I sat up and heard a girl's voice say, "Get that little Chink out of here. Get rid of your Gook whore, right now!"

A guy I had never seen before helped me to the bathroom and set my clothes on the counter.

"Are you going to be okay?" he asked with a concerned look.

I couldn't even process what had just happened. Maybe I was still drunk or maybe I had been drugged. Either way, it was all a fog. I was cold and embarrassed and felt raw, inside and out.

"You're bleeding. I'll get some paper towels. Be right back," he said as he stepped out and closed the door behind him.

I saw blood on my legs and couldn't tell if it was from my banged up knees or from somewhere else. There was a vague memory of falling down in the driveway and hitting rocks or bricks with both knees, but I wasn't sure. Everything was stiff and sore and hurt too much to know what really happened. Maybe I was hit by a car, I thought as I fumbled with my things. I swept back the long hair that fell below my waist, feeling sticky clumps of tangles that made it impossible to manage and pushed back the sickly face of humiliation that was creeping up on me. The burning pain made me panic a little to think about what had happened when I passed out. It was like witnessing a murder scene or something and slowly realizing that I was the victim, but I didn't die. I was too dazed and in shock to process any of it, so I just stood there staring at the floor and trying to get make sense of the pile of clothes in front of me.

The perpetrators had gone by now and tasked this nerdy guy with thick glasses to deliver the remains of their victim back to her house. I think he was the water-boy for the basketball team, so they abused him, too. He was pretty low on the food chain and lacking the tremendous testosterone they apparently possessed.

"I'm sorry about what happened in there," he said as I patted the wet paper towels up and down my legs. My whole body was sore and ached as I stepped into my panties and put on my clothes. I felt embarrassed and humiliated, maybe even a little surprised that I had survived the night at all.

"Are your parents going to be mad? It's almost 2:30 am. Are they wondering where you are? You think they could call the police?" he went on, partly out of concern and partly out of fear. I guess he was worried that there might be consequences like criminal charges, outraged parents with guns, big brothers coming to exact revenge.

But there was no one. And funny thing, I had no one to even tell. My broken mother would only blame me and dear dad was always out of reach. If you can't tell your own family, who can you tell? Pitiful victims can rarely raise their trembling voices enough to be heard, and the angry defiant ones are shamelessly and ruthlessly attacked and demonized. The good ole boy network would stand by each other to the end. They were bulletproof, untouchable, invincible. I was just some easy target and worthless little tramp who was frequently wasted, so it was my fault for tempting them and being in that situation in the first place. Boys will be boys.

"They don't care," I finally managed to say after being unable to do anything but nod at first. I was completely empty and felt like I might just float through the ceiling or melt through the floor.

Here I was, naked and bleeding and covered with God knows what in front of someone I had never seen before. He looked like a boy scout and seemed very uncomfortable, like all of this had gone way past his 'okay with it' limit. Clearly, he did not think it was okay. Yet here we were, in this together. He was hardly a rescuer, just the nerd who got tapped to be the clean up boy. Maybe every team has someone with a bit of morality to clean up their messes in the locker room and the bedroom.

I made it home and never told anyone about it. But it was never really over. I heard talk of nasty pictures circulating and the boys who did it continued to rape me daily with insults and catcalls. They barked and howled when I walked by, whispered obscenities in class, and asked me if I liked it and wanted more. Their girlfriends looked at me like I was dirty even though some of them were there that night and complicit right down to their pink hair bows and French tips. Knee deep in their knee socks for knowing and keeping the secret to protect their boyfriends' prized letter jackets that they wore with such pride.

Like everything in life, I just took it and kept going like nothing happened at all, summoning a little of that Thai stoicism and fatalistic resignation. When it became too much to handle, I could always take a little something to make it all fade to nothing. I maintained a "comfortably numb" anesthetized condition much like the Pink Floyd song of the same name. But the boy's club, the jock rapists, they taunted me daily with racial epithets like "chink" and "gook" and "yang", and then in the next breath called my dad a "nigger" and my mother a "nigger-lover". I always wondered how they thought I could be Asian and my dad African-American. Silly boys, that simply made no sense.

I kept an image as a "snapshot moment" that returned to me throughout the many years that followed. It was the picture of fat Billy who was one of the most arrogantly sadistic of them all. He was trying to run across the street to the parking lot at Tascosa. It was lunchtime and he was half running, half skipping in his cowboy boots and tugging at his pants as they slipped a little and his huge, blubbery-butt came spilling out of them, ass-crack and all. He saw me come outside of the building and started howling and barking and whooping and yelling, "Slop-dog," then making more obnoxious sounds to mock and shame me. The four or five jock rapists with him just grinned their smug grins and glanced my way. I remember thinking that he was a sorry, sack-of-jello shit who would have a sad, shallow life filled with a cruelty that only comes from truly loathing yourself. I had suffered in ways he could not ever wrap his ugly, pink pig head around. He was hideous and deformed both inside and out. I lit a cigarette as I walked toward the bowling alley where the stoners all played pinball and ate tater tots, and although I envisioned myself showing him the finger or waving and blowing a kiss, I just kept walking and never looked back.

The hardest part was not the way they continued to torture me. It was how I tortured myself if left alone too long with time to think about it. I was the foolish one. What kind of dimwit would fall for something like that? What was I thinking when I kept drinking every time they so graciously topped off my glass? I let it happen by putting myself in the situation where it happened. My skirt was too short. I should have just walked home while I could still walk at all since they wouldn't bring me. It was only about two or three miles from my house, obviously a walkable distance. One thing after another, I beat myself up. It was my fault.

Soon after, weekends consisted of one party after another with a wide assortment of unsavory characters. Tuna was one of the guys who always had piles of stash and cash he was eager to share and an eye for lost girls. If fish were the moniker motif, I thought his name should have been Shark instead of Tuna since he was clearly another type of predatory animal. Not alpha males with future MBAs but bottom dwellers waiting for scraps to come their way. His pale blue eyes were always terribly dilated so he looked like one of the cast of *The Rocky Horror Picture Show*. They were almost that cloudy greyish blue that dead eyes get right after their soul leaves their body. The first time I ever saw those eyes was on a dead dog by the side of the road, but that was not the last time I ever saw them. I think he did a lot of acid microdot and countless other designer drugs that fried his brain like the egg on the anti-drug commercials.

LSD was always a wild trip for me.

Sometimes, after I took a half of a hit and went to class, amazingly I wasn't mind-numbingly bored anymore. Like the majority of my peers, now I too was struggling to understand what the teacher was talking about. When I wasn't tripping, they would talk so slowly and seem so shallow. Now we were all on the same page, but for me, everything was more vivid and colorful with deeper dimensions.

I had always been on the fringe, on the outside of the circle, but now there were others with me because of the prevalence of drugs at school. It took some of the brightest and the best out of the game. We saw the truth. We witnessed the ranks of the stupid and mean kids climb to the top of the food chain because they could catch a ball or run fast. Everyone hailed them as heroes, as leaders, as role models for poor stoners like us, but I knew better. I knew they were without compassion, without empathy, without soul. They bullied and cheated and exploited and preyed upon the weak because they were hollow inside. They gobbled up little girls like me, then vilified them and tormented them for being victims. Other lost kids like me, anesthetized to make it all bearable, self-medicated to go home and face terrible families, we all knew their game. It wasn't arrogance but anger that made me act belligerently. It wasn't the drugs to blame but rather the inherent inequities and injustices, the never-ending abuse that we tolerated every single day. We had nothing to lose.

"Let me teach this class, coach so and so. I know what's up and can teach all the important stuff. Can I try? Come on... we all know you don't want to do this and would rather be out on the field," I would think to myself.

My stoner companion, Nina, who had been sexually abused

repeatedly by her mom's boyfriend, rocked back and forth quietly with a big grin on her sad face. I liked to see the ones who had no joy in their life or hope that anything would ever get better have a break from all that. She was a tiny girl with bleached, crimped hair who always wore excessive amounts of black mascara and liner smudged around green eyes that glittered with pain; at least they still held the light, unlike the dead eyes of the predator-jocks that were held in such high esteem by most of the student body and all of the teachers.

"Lily, please don't make it hard for the other students to learn. We all know you know the answer. Please let someone else try," they would always say.

"Why make them try? They don't want to learn anything," I thought to myself as I started to draw in my notebook for a distraction. I never drew beautiful dancers in fluffy tutus or movie stars in elegant gowns or mermaids with shimmering tails anymore. Now, I filled the pages with ghosts and demons and dead babies and drowned girls with holes where their eyes should have been.

"None of these people care about knowing anything or learning something; just give them a mercy grade and let's move on already," I would mutter as my head spun and the floor moved like a billion ants under my feet. "I might need to take some of those pills Jeff gave me this morning because I'm still feeling stuff, and I'm not totally numb yet. My bones hurt, my brain hurts, and my skin hurts like I'm being stuck with prickly pins and needles. I really need to get to that comfortably numb place like the Pink Floyd song," I thought to myself.

I pitied most of them for being so ordinary. So vanilla. So clueless. Some of them pitied me I'm sure, although I really didn't think about it at the time. They must have thought that I was an arrogant loser. I guess that was about right, but I didn't give a flying rat's ass anymore. They were entertainment for me, like some other species in the jungle. The wild, wild jungle.

One weekend, I was out in the country with a group of my fellow revelers. I hesitate to call them friends since all we ever did was get high, talk about getting high next time, and reminiscing about our best highs in the past. It was more of a club, a support network if you will, of substance abusers. Anyway, here we were, sitting in the car watching the "flying submarine races", also known as getting wasted and watching the cars speed over the overpass on the freeway usually with King Crimson or Emerson, Lake, and Palmer blasting from the speakers until the car shook.

There were red and blue lights behind us and marijuana, seeds, stems, and rolling papers scattered around in the dark. Molly, the curly haired, big bosomed girl sitting next to me was the daughter of a local minister who was having an affair with her mom's sister. She had discovered it over a year ago and was lying to her mother daily to cover for her good ole dad and do damage control in the only way a fifteen-year-old knew how. We all had crazy stories. She was the first to signal the alarm.

"Holy shit! It's the pigs. Let's get out of here!" She screamed as she knocked over a can of grape soda into my lap.

So off we went, flying down the dirt road and onto the freeway, drugs and paraphernalia flying out the windows as we went. All I was thinking was, "What a waste. That was some really good stuff. I wonder if we can come back tomorrow when the sun comes up and find it before someone or something eats it? I wonder what that would do to the cows in the fields where we had ditched everything. "Then I giggled to myself, amused at the thought of a cow stumbling around shit-faced, stone-cold wrecked on our drugs.

The police station was really bright with those awful fluorescent lights that buzz and flicker and take away your buzz. My folks were summoned to retrieve me, and the only two who were eighteen were actually arrested. They never found the drugs, but I later heard they found a bunch of seeds that were suspicious, and it was enough to get probation for a couple of the folks involved.

I guess I was lucky that all this happened before our country began its War on Drugs. I just got a lecture from one of the policemen about the dangers of drugs and alcohol and how boys only gave it to girls so they would have sex with them. Is that right? Little did they know. There really wasn't that much sex going on, at least that I remembered. It required way too much energy better spent getting mellow, watching the ceiling melt and drip pink and lime green lava, munching on Cheetos, and getting down with some serious tunes. I could actually see the music when I was tripping. The best example is Queen's *Bohemian Rhapsody*. I could see the whole song play out like a Technicolor movie with choruses of dancers and fountains and a complete extravaganza. Pink Floyd and Emerson Lake and Palmer were also very visceral.

The drug years weren't all fun times. I smoked weed every single day for over four years and supplemented with speed, LSD, cheap wine, and a bit of psilocybin. Pillboxes filled with white crosses and black mollies, redbirds and yellow birds, dots of acid like Orange Sunshine and Purple Barrel. It wasn't long before I took a little more and got a little braver. One night on the way to I-Hop in the wee hours of the morning, we were driving down Western Street, one of the main streets that ran from one end of Amarillo to the other, and I suddenly needed to jump out of the moving car. I don't remember what I said, but I do remember that I felt I would explode if I didn't get out of that car. My skin felt like it was being peeled off of my body, so naturally, I panicked. I frantically clawed my way over the back seat of the car over at my buddies, and they were holding on to me by my desert boots until the driver pulled over into the Putt-Putt parking lot and restrained me by pushing me to the ground and sitting on top of me. Touchdown!

There were scary hallucinations like the giant blue spider that was really a water tower. It started moving toward me and pursuing me down the street until I ran blindly into a parked car and fell deliriously unconscious to the pavement. My people got freaked out and dumped me out at my house in the middle of the night. I was too trashed to find my way inside and curled up under a bush in the yard until the next morning. I can't remember how many times I woke up in my yard, not knowing how I got there. Sometimes I had even peed my pants during the night or woke up smelling like vomit. It probably wasn't mine since I rarely tossed my cookies or got the dry heaves. That's something to put on a resume, for sure.

I mostly felt safe with my drug infused friends because they were as screwed up as I was, so we all had a lot of sympathy for one another and did a lot of caretaking and parenting of each other. There was a kind of sacred brotherhood or sisterhood among us that was sealed by our allegiance to chemical dependency, so we tried as best we could to look out for one another in most cases. Kind of like a bunch of homeless people or victims of war. When you think of war as a possibility and you've never experienced anything like it, then naturally you would be terrified. But if you have lived in a war zone all of your life, witnessed the daily death and despair, and come to accept that a landmine could blow you to kingdom come with each step, then you don't really feel it anymore. It seems natural. You go on about your business, oblivious to the carnage surrounding you.

We had no fear of death; however, we did have varying degrees of PTSD before it was even a thing. In fact, we were beyond depression and our lifestyles confirmed that we all had a death wish in one way or another. If no one values you, how can you value your own life? We welcomed the release from this hell on earth that we all had to suffer. Live hard, die young. At least we would be remembered with our youth and beauty still intact. Where's the tragedy in that?

"Beam me up, Scotty."

House of the Rising Sun
The Animals 1972

Mother decided that she wanted to have me rehabilitated, so she sent me to the Xenith House of the New Dawn drug rehabilitation center. What a blast that was. It sounded more like a cult than the name of a halfway house. And what does "half-way house" imply? Halfway to what? How do you have half of a house? There were more drugs and better drugs there than anywhere else I have ever seen. And when we weren't high, we were getting off on hearing each other's stories about getting high.

It was a rainbow gathering of different colors and ages and stages of death who frequented the rehab facilities. We all had group therapy, art therapy, music therapy, and an assortment of other therapies to help us get sober and get interested in living our lives. Most patrons were teenagers with a few older folks who were as old as mid- twenties mixed in for good measure. I think twenty-one was supposed to be the cut off, but older guys blended in to get at the youngest girls who were always wasted and easy prey. The youngest kids were only eleven or twelve. There was a drug emperor they called Black Jesus. Well, he was indeed black, but the Jesus part was a whole other story. We would eat these hallucinogenic mushrooms, then go gather a group and head to his mama's house for some black people food. Greens, beans, chicken, ribs, corn bread, and other warm, easy stuff. It was pretty cool. People with gold teeth and gold pistols hidden in all the furniture. They talked really loud, and the mama loved skunk- weed dusted with some white powder that made your flesh fall off your bones and your whole face go numb. There were always gaunt looking dogs chained and pacing menacingly in the yard. Old men sat on the porch on furniture that would be inside most people's houses, and they would drink Mad Dog 20/20 or Colt 44 out of bottles in brown paper bags. Long yellow stained fingers cradled brown cigarettes, and some of the shriveled old ones with blue black lips would have no teeth but would go up to the women and say, "How about some sugar for your daddy? Put it right here," patting one hollow, sunken cheek.

The little sisters who couldn't have been much older than ten or eleven ran out to the boys 'cars and gave them hand jobs while the mama would say, "Young fool niggas. They ain't got no sense. They be killin theyselves one way or nuther. I guess they be ready to die. Ain't nuthin' for them here no how."

The boys pimp-walked into the house with their guns shoved down into the back of their waistbands and started cussin' at their sisters and their mommas and whoever was there. It seemed like there was always a room full of people watching TV or doing each other's hair or making food in the kitchen. There were always dirty children with snotty noses and nappy heads running around and skinny stray dogs and cats nosing around for scraps. I hated their big pimp cars more than anything else—all tricked out and covered in gold bling, with fur on the dashboard and crusty leather seats that were old and dusty and smelled like booze and cheap cigars.

Shortly after the failed attempt at a cure, my mother decided that Alcohol Anonymous would be the thing that would get me better. The House of New Dawn had not worked out so well, and she never sent me back after she came to get me and inadvertently opened the bathroom door to find one of the drug counselors and a thirteen-year-old drug whore named Becky balling their brains out. I guess he was "straightening her out." Great one-on-one therapy.

Some old guy named Frank was my sponsor and came to pick me up for my first meeting. He smelled like cheap cologne and was fat and balding. I hated his shoes. They were pointy and had tassels on them that didn't go with his cheap polyester leisure suit. He had big fat hands with dry rough stubby fingers. This was going to be amusing, I thought. I had popped a few reds and smoked a joint before he came, so I was ready for whatever they might try to do to save me. Sometimes they would have the "come to Jesus" talks that went on forever, and other times they opted for a more aggressive assault to scare you into submission that often included gory overdose and drunk driving accidents or tearful testimonials. Being sedated and a little buzzed made the gravity of the situation seem so much lighter. I was good to go and ready to rumble.

Boy, was I wrong. On the way to the meeting, Frank took a little detour to a secluded road behind the golf course. His old Impala was bumping along the road when I asked, "Where are we going? Is the meeting out here somewhere?"

He slowly stopped the car and turned to me.

"I think you're a real pretty girl. You got them big brown eyes and that long brown hair. I bet all the boys love that long hair, don't they? And they like them Chinese girls, too."

I was getting creeped out in a hurry by the way he was looking at me and wondered why he would think I was Chinese. *I bet he thought all people from Asia are Chinese. Ignorant hillbilly-goat.*

"You ever been with a man or you only been with boys? Your mother says you got lots of boyfriends and you just drive them all wild," he asked as he wiped his sticky forehead with a limp handkerchief.

I didn't know what to say. The drugs had kicked in and the whole thing seemed almost surreal. Who was this doofus? Surely he didn't think I was going to have sex with him or something. I was sixteen and he had to be at least sixty or seventy. He started putting his hands on me, touching my shoulders first, then sliding his fat paws down to grope at my breast.

"These little babies are so firm and perky. All your boyfriends like it when you don't wear no bra?" he said with little bits and bubbles of spit at the edges of his mouth.

"I bet them nipples is nice and brown like Hershey kisses," he continued with a ravenous glare.

It was starting to get dark, and I was starting to get worried.

"We better go. We're supposed to be at the meeting, aren't we? Don't you think they are going to wonder where we are?" I offered.

"Come on, darlin'. I know you've been with lots of guys. Your own mother says you're quite a little tramp, but I don't think so. I think you just know what you like. And you like this,'" he said as I noticed his pants were unzipped and his belt was hanging to one side. My brain scrambled to catch up. *Like what? Are you trying to show me your junk, but it's just too wrapped up in all your bunched up boxer shorts and fat, or is it just too tiny to see? Maybe I am so high I am imagining all of this. I do know what I like, Mr. AA Man. Pull a Hershey bar out of your britches. That's what I would really like right about now. The Hershey bar with the nuts.*

And with that, he was trying to stuff his clumsy hand into my jeans. I moved his hand away, disappointed that no chocolate had manifested.

"Don't. Just stop it, okay? We need to go now."

Frank was not going to be dissuaded so easily. His face was all red and sweaty, and he seemed to be glowing in the quickly approaching darkness.

"Don't or don't stop? I think you mean don't stop. Come on sweetie. I know you like this. You can't get enough. I've got something for you." After I moved his hand and repeatedly positioned it away, he started to get agitated so that his hot breath was fogging up the windows in the car that was pretty cold considering it was November. Just as I thought he was going to give up, I looked down, and there it was. He held his half-erect penis in his hand and was sort of pulling on it and trying to bring it to life.

"No. No, no I'm not," I stammered as I fumbled to open the door which was conveniently locked.

"Okay. Just touch it. Hold it for a minute and just let me put my mouth on you a little bit in places you like it. I know you taste sweet."

Well, that just about took the cake. I was out of there, one way or another. For a brief moment, I wondered if all the jock-alpha Randys and Jimmys at my school would become Frank as they got older. Of course, they would. Franky, the high school jock-alpha becomes Frank, the pedophile-AA sponsor. Once a monster, always a monster.

"Listen, Fred or Frank or whatever your name is. I'm a stoner, but I'm not some freak or something. If you don't start the car, I'm going to get out and walk home and tell everybody what you tried to do to me," I threatened as I plotted my escape.

"Nobody will believe a little tramp like you."

"Well, they might. You want to take that chance? I'll tell everything! I'll tell them I saw it and that you weren't cut. They will know I'm telling the truth then, won't they?" I said as I hoped that would be enough to end all this.

He looked at me like he was calculating the odds and maybe considering just taking me by force. The sudden silence made my ears hum. He was breathing hard. Another hungry look. Then he tucked it away and turned the key in the ignition, and I took out a cigarette and inhaled deeply as he sped down the road, my hands trembling a little bit, clouds of gravel and dirt behind us. No one said another word.

And that's how AA ended before I ever made it to the first meeting.

Fire and Rain
James Taylor 1973

By the end of 1973, my chemical companions had begun to drop one by one, and the whole world was in chaos. Deborah ran away to Houston with a boyfriend who locked her in a closet for days at a time and bit her all over her body until she was a bloody pulp. He only did it whenever he used heroin, but that seemed to happen more and more often. Molly's parents had her committed to The Pavilion, a mental facility where they gave her some of the mind-altering drugs that made her just sit there drooling and not even recognize us when we tried to visit. Some of us actually went to see her once but never went back a second time. They said she fried her brain on a really bad trip. She used whatever was handy—a paperclip or plastic spoon to carve out chunks in her arms. They had her tied up in restraints the last time I saw her. I think that's what they do to cutters and to people who hurt themselves in other ways. I guess she needed to remind herself that she was still here, still alive. Then she took scissors and chopped off chunks of her thick red curls all the way to her scalp. All of our friends witnessed this and simply said, "Bummer man," then went on like nothing ever happened, never missing a beat or pausing to mourn our fallen comrades. Drugs are so much more important than human beings or anything. It was those nasty humans that drove many of us to anesthetize ourselves in the first place.

I saw Billy and Patrick at school, but it was like they were not real people and the history between us was completely erased. We never spoke or acknowledged one another. I did wonder if Billy had screwed anymore thirteen-year-old virgins. And I wondered if Patrick knew what a golden god I still thought he was.

The arcade was shut down because of too many fights and drug deals. No more foosball tournaments for us. We would be too wasted to drive there anymore anyway, so those of us who were hardcore survivors partied on. Mostly, there was a bong, some chips and fast food junk, and bad TV shows. We tempted fate every day without a thought about any of the negative consequences and somehow managed to stay out of jail, out of the nuthouse, and comfortably out of our minds.

My mother was on probation now for shoplifting at the K-Mart discount store, so her guilt for getting caught seemed to keep her from messing with me so much. We were there doing some back to school shopping, and she decided to leave her shoes in the shoe department and walk out to the parking lot with some size 9 desert boots for me on her feet. Smooth move. She was a little woman with a size 5 shoe, so you can imagine how this must have looked to the security guards. I bet they were laughing their asses off.

"Maam, would you please step back into the store?"

It was pitiful to hear her try to talk her way out of it, then finally she started using me as her excuse.

"My daughter here just has me so upset I don't know what I'm doing. Look at her; does she look like a nice girl to you? She uses drugs and has sex with all kinds of people, and well, it just makes me crazy," she rambled on as they secured the handcuffs on her in the tiny little office in the back.

Thanks mom. Use the insanity plea and tell them I was the one who pushed you over the edge. Walking through the store to the police car was a trip. People staring at us as the cop walked us from the back to his patrol car parked out front. The ride in the police car was not my first, but it was the first time my mother had been arrested instead of me. I needed a cigarette, so when we got to the police station, I asked if they needed me, and I said no. I could call a family member to pick me up while they booked my mom. I had a couple of tightly rolled joints in my cigarette pack where I always kept them. Thank God the cops didn't search me too. I was out of the police station in seconds.

After walking a few blocks, I found a coffee shop that was mostly for the downtown crowd of businessmen during the day and the unsavory criminal element in the evenings. I opened the heavy glass door and headed directly to the bathroom to smoke some of the pot I had stashed in my cigarette pack. I locked the door and stood on the toilet so I could see out the window while I smoked. It was a small window with a handle that rolled open. I looked toward the parking lot where there was some scruffy looking guy grabbing a woman by the arm and forcing her into his car. She was cursing him and spitting at him, and he twisted her arm so she couldn't speak for the pain. Her clothes were too tight and her shoes looked cheap and dirty like the ones we had seen while shopping at K-Mart that afternoon. I remember black make-up streaming down her ugly face and a blood red mouth twisting in agony. Just passing images in a world of people equally as wretched, and I thought that they probably deserved each other.

She had a witness to all of her agony. That was more than I ever had.

A homeless guy was sitting on the ground next to the dumpster. He looked limp like he had no bones in his body and was almost folding up on himself. His gray, grizzly beard covered most of his face like a mask except for two sunken eyes that held no light. He watched the pair as they tugged and pushed and pulled on one another, a silent witness all the drama. I always saw homeless people because they were like me. Invisible. I knew what it was like to be a ghost. People look right through you. They can't see you. They can't hear the words you are saying to them. You're totally invisible.

A fat brown roach crawled along the wall from behind the toilet and moved up the wall beside me. I took a long hit, held my breath for a few seconds, then exhaled and thought to myself, "These people are all roaches. Big ones, little ones, fast ones, the ones, injured ones, sick ones. All roaches."

I took out my roach clip and held fire under the last of my weed, pursed my lips, and sucked the magic smoke deeply like it would somehow fill me with all that was missing inside. Sitting on the toilet with my head against the wall, I closed my eyes and felt nothing.

Chapter 4

Fool on the Hill
The Beatles 1975

My 17th birthday came and went, and spring was on her way. I loved spring because our yard was resplendent with purple iris, zinnias, wisteria, and lilac bushes. We had the best trees in the whole neighborhood. A towering weeping willow that drooped with the heavy weight of her sadness, a mimosa with tiny little leaves and fluffy pink blossoms, and tall poplar trees that reached to the heavens. I loved those trees. I talked to those trees. And one day I found something unexpected Beaneath one of those trees.

David Neely. I had met him in summer school the summer after my baby died, and he was the one who had first turned me on to the joys of marijuana. The first day we hung out together after class, we rode around in the city bus for hours giggling and pretending to be going somewhere.

"Look at this Lily," he said pointing to the little metal thing attached to the bottom seat in front of us.

"Bottom seat can be used as flotation device," he read out loud as we bumped along.

We both laughed so hard we couldn't breathe or see or stop. When I could get my words out I said, "Maybe it's in case of a flash flood. Is there a big water near here we could accidentally drive into?" And we burst into laughter until our bellies hurt.

"What will happen if I pulled this cord and then I don't get off?" I asked.

"No, don't do it… bad things will happen to us. It is a dangerous cord. Do not touch it. Don't even look at it," he said, then tilted his head and batted his big blue eyes at me a bunch of times like a girl trying to flirt.

His silliness was sublime. It made me feel so light and carefree. Hours passed before we finally pulled that cord.

When we smoked weed together, it was a delicious retreat from my prison of pain. The first time he offered me the clip with the roach on it, I put my lips on it and burned a nice-sized blister. He promised to teach me how to do it better, but summer school was over and just like that, he was gone like smoke. But I had a new friend, and her name was MaryJane.

I could thank David for introducing me to the wonders of marijuana almost three years earlier. I learned how to self-medicate and continued on that perilous road with more drugs to anesthetize my pain. Had I not been such a wreck, completely destroyed by the unfortunate events that I had managed to survive, I most likely would have stuck with a little cannabis and left the other substances alone. But I had been given a way to stop the suffering, so naturally I used it as much as I could.

I sat behind him that summer in summer school. He was there because he was a mediocre student who was not too bright and not too motivated, and I was there trying to make up credits so I could skip ahead and graduate early. I liked to lean in close to his long brown sandalwood smelling hair. He wore paisley with plaid and tie-dyed hats, and he was a moving psychedelic fashion fiasco. He was handsome, tall, very thin, and possessed the most magnificent blue eyes I had ever seen.

So much time had passed and now, here he was—sitting cross-legged like Buddha under my mimosa tree.

"Hi, Lily. How you doing?" he said with the tilt of the head that made his eyes seem to look up at me like Jesus. They were the bluest blue I had ever seen.

"How long have you been here? We've been gone all day and I hope you weren't here waiting too long or anything," I replied as I awkwardly fumbled for a cigarette from my bag.

"Not too long. How about something to drink? Water?"

"Oh, I'm sorry. Oh, just a minute. Oh, oh, let's wait till my mother gets busy with something. You know, she'll forget we're out here in a minute," I stammered.

"How have you been?" He asked as he reached for my cigarette and inhaled deeply. He had a large mouth with full lips and perfect teeth, not quite Mick Jagger or Steven Tyler big, but I liked the way the smoke moved out of his mouth. Being with him made me want to inhale a little longer, breathe more deeply.

"Okay. Busy. I'm still dancing. I've got a recital show in two weeks, and I'm in a play. A small part. Chorus actually. Just dancing and moving my lips. You know, I don't sing, but I do still dance."

"I thought we might hang out. Catch up. Tell stories to each other. It's been a while." As he spoke, he put emphasis on certain words that made me feel like a smile was starting somewhere inside, and I could taste him on the cigarettes we shared.

"Sure, I would like that," I said and leaned close to hug him. There was a vague hint of cannabis in his hair and something that reminded me of sandalwood incense. He was wearing paisley. He was great in paisley. I remember sitting behind him at school and thinking how groovy paisley looks on some people. Groovy. That was it. David was groovy. He swept his shoulder length, wheat colored hair behind his ears, and in a moment, everything was grand.

Weeks turned into a few months, and before long, I graduated from high school at midterm right after Christmas break and began at the local community college the same week. I was stoned senseless when I had my photo ID made. It was the first picture I had seen of myself in years, and it was painfully clear that I was wasted. Somehow, I still looked pretty amazing in my Yoko Ono white pantsuit and big floppy hat.

I had stopped doing all the other serious drugs by now. I think they were like a fever that had to run their course. They burned dangerously hot for a few years, then after numerous bad experiences, I think I just got tired. Weary was more like it. I just smoked a little in the morning, then again when I got home from classes. Whenever David and I were together, we smoked and listened to Joni Mitchell or played chess while feeding each other strings of cherry licorice or munching on Cheetos.

He was the produce guy at a local Safeway supermarket and not exactly academic material like me. I'm not sure what he did to the fruits and vegetables all day, but he had a lot of responsibility for an eighteen-year-old fresh out of high school. He didn't drive a car but rode his bicycle everywhere. There was something charming about a guy who prefers getting around with the wind in his hair. It gave him a kind of vulnerability or sensitivity or something. And if that weren't enough, he was a vegetarian before it was even trendy. It was from David that I first experienced the joys of Portobello mushrooms, sprouts, and tofu.

As for me, college wasn't even a choice. It was the only place I could be. It was like breathing. I just did it without thinking and excelled as always. Strange how it never mattered what a nightmare my life was, I still made the honor roll or dean's list. I guess I knew it was one of the few things I really did well, and I somehow needed to compensate for all the other shortcomings.

By the end of my first semester, I had the secured the lead in a classic Greek tragedy by Euripides. It was a great fit because I possessed a special ability to replicate authentic grief on stage. An evocative performance was a certainty, especially the scene where I shook my fist at the Gods that had mercilessly allowed invaders to pillage and plunder my city. It was replete with dead children, epic betrayals, and horrific violence. This was something I knew. I injected pathos into the role of Hecuba, Queen of Troy, with sorrow that was palpable. I will never forget how the audience wept.

Dance was also a time-consuming part of my college experience. I rehearsed every day and performed in recitals and productions every few months. Ms. Donafee was the first dance teacher I had ever studied under who wasn't my regular mentor, so I had to prove my worth all over again. For the first recital, I choreographed a nature trilogy with a fierce thunderstorm, a forest meadow filled with birds, and finally, soft rains. The costumes were designed to reflect the elements, and I still remember the feeling of sliding into the splits with arms holding a lightning stick high in the air. I danced with bare feet that remembered each inch of the dusty stage floor and dressed in flowing black and gray and white streaming chiffon that swirled around me as I jumped and turned and became the storm. I was powerful. I was stunning. I was in my element.

Between the plays and the dance productions, I studied to maintain a 4.0. When all that was said and done, with any extra time on my hands, I was with David.

We stayed together most weekends in the apartment he shared with his dad and his sister, Mary Ellen, who was only a year younger and the only girl in the family of twelve boys. They never had an issue with me staying over. We all crowded into the tiny kitchen to make nachos or guacamole and talk about the crazy people we knew. It was kind of like we were all a big family like brothers and sisters more than a couple. Oddly enough, we were more into the physicality of touch than actual intercourse. We usually just smoked a bowl and then connected fingertips or touched each other's faces. I often watched his big potato hands as they moved across my body. You could almost feel electricity in the air between us, and our hair would have so much static it circled our heads like a halo. Then we just went to sleep holding each other. He enjoyed Thai energy massage the most. I touched his arms ever so gently like a type of effleurage and then rubbed my hands together before circulating his energy that would leave his hair full of electricity and standing on end. My dad sometimes talked of aligning chakras and third eye sight, so I knew how to channel energy and cleanse it. That seemed to make him happy. I had the ability to feel dirty energy and be able to pull it toward my hands where it would stick so I could dispose of it.

As for me, I had always been such a cold and frigid person, so I could care less about any kind of gratification or comfort that did not come from food, dance, music, or drugs. To me, being satiated meant getting to eat whenever I wanted without guilt that I might not fit into my dance costume. I craved chocolate because I never got sweets at home, and it was such a decadent indulgence. Music could transport me to a better place, and I loved to visualize a dance extravaganza while listening to something like Queen. When nothing else worked, smoking a little herb could sure take the edge off an unusually brutal day.

We lay it on the mattress on the second- floor balcony of the apartment and talked silly and looked at the sky through his telescope. It was so quiet my ears seemed to vibrate, and I could hear the grass blowing in the wind. Cicadas hummed in the distance and sometimes we heard people talking and laughing down by the pool that was just outside the balcony. I could close my eyes and stroke his soft hair while studying his perfect skin and long eyelashes. He was beautiful. And I was beautiful, too. And life was beginning to look a little less ugly.

We often played with words. I like that, and he was much better at it than me. He called me Lily Boo and made a little song for me and sang softly in my ear, "LilyBoo, Flutterby, Butterfly, I love you, lovely LilyBoo."

The next nine or ten months were calm; I focused on school during the week and spent the weekends with David at his Tiffany Circle apartments. School was my safe place, my sanctuary. It was the one place where I felt good about myself, so what I could do? But good things never last, and before we knew it, there was a crisis at the door.

I missed my period.

Two weeks passed, then three, and of course my mother was right on it doing damage control. How ironic that a force of destruction as dangerous as my mother could perceive herself as a protector or rescuer. It was absurd. But there she was again, manipulating fate—my fate. She made me an appointment with Dr. Pritchett. There were rumors that he had suffered a breakdown recently because of his wife's suicide several years before but apparently he wasn't too far gone to see me.

He had been my mother's doctor for years and was the source of her little bag of pills. Thorazine, Valium, Phenobarbital, Librium, you name it. She was a veritable drug store, and he was her dealer. I wonder if he kept her medicated to help so she would stop being crazy or if he drugged her to keep her off his back. Either way, they had a special relationship.

I later wondered if she asked a special favor or if he took it upon himself to make the call, but either way, it was another loss for me.

"Lily, your mother says you haven't menstruated in nearly two months. Let's have a look," he said as he handed me a gown and adjusted the stirrups.

At first, it seemed like an ordinary exam. Uncomfortable and intrusive. Cold table and cold hands. All of the sudden, there was a sharp pain deep inside.

"Wow, that hurt. Uhmm, it really hurts; what's happening? Wait a minute," I said as I tried to sit up. There was no one else in the room. No nurse in sight, and my mother was gone as always.

"I am not here to have anything done, just a pregnancy test. That's all. What are you doing?" I stammered as I struggled to sit up and see what was going on between my legs. I knew something was not right.

"There. Sorry about that little pinch. It looks like everything's okay. You may have some heavy bleeding but don't be afraid. It's normal. Just get dressed now sweetie," he instructed as he pulled off the blue gloves and dropped them in the wastebasket.

"Why did that hurt? What did you do?" I asked with suspicion.

"You're just fine, get your things on and hop down," he replied as he closed the door behind him.

That evening I started to bleed. And he was right. It was heavy with clots and stringy things, and I was scared. My mother sent David home and told him I was "flooding" so badly they had to put bricks under my bed to elevate the end of it to keep me from losing so much blood. I'm sure he was horrified. He knew I might be carrying his baby and was happy, even excited. Now this. Later, he told me that he went home and cried.

That was the beginning of the end for us. After that, on the weekends when I spent the night at his apartment, I could feel him shaking his foot as he lay beside me, and I pretended to be asleep. If I reached for him, he would turn his back. Sometimes, he would be awake all night, probably asking himself if I had knowingly done something to cause this, if it was an accident, or if it was God's will. He had been a devout Catholic all his life, so of course God was always in the picture. He prayed for our dead baby and told me about dreams he had of the baby ghost of his son who should have been with us. So here I was, not even twenty and with two dead sons and no God to pray to. He could not possibly understand.

By the time the weekend was over, and I was headed back home to get ready for the week at school, we were relieved that we didn't have to make conversation or pretend everything was the same as before. We didn't talk silly and giggle or snuggle under the moon; the eyes like blue planets turned dark and looked very far away. No more peaceful moments. We never gazed at the night sky again.

Nights in White Satin
The Moody Blues 1974

Incandescent. I always wanted to be luminescent. Glowing. Shimmering. Hopelessly, romantically, a bearer of glittering light. Dreams are funny things. They sometimes fade so slowly that you don't even notice until one day you turn around, and they are gone. Vanished like ghosts in a fog.

David grew more distant with time, and I floated away before anyone noticed. One day after a couple of months had passed, he appeared at my door. It is my last picture of him, standing in the rain, soaking wet, skinny and frail, mouth gaping in despair, the big blue eyes now a cold gray that reflected the metallic sky. He begged me to try to come back and start over, give it one more try. But fate had spoken. I don't think he saw that I was just a spot on the horizon, and then I just disappeared and that was that.

When I landed, I found myself in the summer term of Biology I. It was the last class before I transferred to a four-year university. I was ready to be a junior in college. And I was ready for something else, too.

His name was Johnny. He wasn't pretty like David. He was wild and maybe a little dangerous. It wasn't his long, thick blonde hair that tumbled down his back or his scrawny sexy Mick Jagger swagger that drew me to him at first. Everyone said he looked like Woody Allen, and why would someone who looked like me want to be with a guy who looked like that? I think it must have been his arrogant *savior fare* and philosophical musings. He had sardonic wit and intensity—a cocky little rooster strutting his stuff and puffing out his brilliant feathers. I had found my own personal Jesus.

He was my lab partner that summer, and we were assigned to a pink little pig the size of a loaf of bread and given the formidable task of dissecting the poor thing. It was intoxicating to sit beside this intense energy and brilliant mind and absorb some of his radiant heat. I also really liked his pants. He sported a brown plaid pair that first caught my eyes, and there were these golden velvet ones he got at Colbert's department store in Wolflin Village. Don't ever underestimate what a great pair of pants can do for you.

I remembered seeing him once before, a few years earlier. A group of stoner friends were making rounds to sell some weed, and we went to a local "band house" to hear a practice session and do a little business, make a few transactions. The only thing I remember about that day was a mostly naked guy sitting at the drums wearing nothing but his tiny white Fruit of the Loom briefs, cigarette dangling from his mouth, waist length hair wrapped around him like a cloak, twirling those drumsticks and going into some John Bonham style drum solo that echoed in my chest and vibrated everyone in the room from head to toe. He was like that Muppet named Animal, a rock god with a wicked beat, a golden boy wild child force of nature.

My first date with him felt like the first real "date" I had ever had. When you think about the unconventionality of my past relationships, this was closer to normal. He arrived in a vehicle that was actually an old post office truck that was bought at auction and repainted, but the steering wheel was still on the right side. The wrong side. Surprise, surprise. How fitting that it would begin that way. A portend of future days.

We went to Medi Park by the Botanical Gardens and sat on a blanket by the lake. Within minutes he was playing his guitar and singing songs I had never heard before while I foraged through the little wicker basket full of cheese sandwiches and tiny candy bars. I threw pieces of crust to the ducks that gathered around us, lifting their chorus of voices, then lay down beside him with our faces to the blue sky to find the shapes in the clouds. Late summer never seemed so perfect after that day.

When the sun melted into the horizon like a liquid ball of fire, we left for the movies. Peter Sellers was my favorite actor and *The Pink Panther* was showing at the Western Plaza Cinema. I laughed until I was dizzy and then laughed some more. It knew it was the first time I had ever laughed with a boy. It was the first time I had ever spent time with a boy without being drunk or stoned. I was high on the feeling of joyful abandon. This was how it should have been all along. This is what I had been missing.

Sympathy for the Devil
Rolling Stones 1974

Like all knights in shining armor, Johnny lived in a castle. A tall cathedral built with stones and rock and a steep stairway that led to heaven. It was actually the little efficiency apartment behind his parents' house. They rented out the bottom unit and let their son stay upstairs, but at the time, I romanticized it until it became our little sanctuary and retreat, far from the maddening crowds.

When I was little, we often passed a house on the way to visit my grandmother. The whole thing was covered in stones and rocks and ivy that crept up the sides. I never said anything because nobody heard it anyway, but each time we passed it, I thought to myself, "I am going to live in a rock castle someday."

So like the princess I had always wanted to be, I ascended the steps almost every night through that fall and winter. The tall steps led to a small one room studio apartment with a sofa sleeper and a huge window that opened up and allowed passage to the roof which provided a glorious perch to sit and stare up at the sky under a canopy of stars. We wrapped ourselves in blankets and climbed out that window where we talked for hours about philosophy, psychology, and politics while watching the sun sink Beaneath the trees. He took breaks from the lessons to sing songs he had written about me and the world I lived in. His guitar was always nearby for those times that required a musical interlude. Then more dialogue that gradually opened the doors in my mind to a world of thought I never knew existed. He was smarter than me in many ways, and it was rare that I met anyone who could keep up with me intellectually. He showed me a new way of experiencing myself and the world around me. I was finally coming to life. Our friends were Kant and Nietzsche, Dostoyevsky and Tolstoy. I was not alone in the world.

I began to read. In the past, it was always linked to a grade, but now it had evolved into intellectual curiosity. Claude Steiner's *I'm Okay, You're Okay* and Eric Berne's *The Games People Play*. I read Plato's *Republic* and *The Cave* and couldn't wait to tell him what I thought about it, what it meant to me, what the "take away" was. We studied together for hours. I read his *Abnormal Psych* book for his psychology classes and he read Euripides for my theatre classes. And each day I came closer to understanding what had happened to me. I learned the words to ascribe to the dynamics around me. Dysfunctional, codependent, victims and martyrs, bi-polar, obsessive-compulsive, and so on.

"I think one of the impairments that you might want to work on that is an obstacle to your evolution could be your repressed or suppressed or just lack of genuine emotion. It's like you're a china doll or something. Just empty."

I was dumbfounded. Angry and immediately defensive.

"How can you say this to me? I feel stuff. Lots of stuff just like you."

"I disagree. You are like a zombie. Just numb or dead inside or something. Just think about it. Ask yourself what is genuine and what is false. Maybe you're just acting like a role in one of your plays. You know what it's supposed to look like, but there is nothing behind it. Just a façade," he said with those huge water blue eyes that could look through me to the bone.

I wanted to push him or grab him by the throat—anything to make him stop saying these hurtful words. I felt emotion for sure, I thought to myself. Emotions like exasperation.

Then the final blow. The one that took me out and made me a believer. The *coup de grace*.

"I am pretty sure that you don't even feel anything when we're in bed. Actually, you probably don't feel anything ever. You're like a perfect little China doll."

I flinched at the China reference since everyone knows that China isn't a word to cover anyone from the continent of Asia. He should've said Thai doll.

"It's like you are something not even real. I think you are fake and frigid," he asserted as he lit a cigarette and leaned back in his chair with a cocky tilt of the head.

Picture this. Atom bomb detonation in slow motion as I stand there too blown away to speak. Face flushing, heart fluttering. I feel panic and don't understand why.

I lit a cigarette and fumbled in my oversized bag to get my keys and get the hell out of Dodge. He had crossed the line. Two F words coming at me like missiles. The old one two punch. How do you know if you aren't feeling what you're supposed to be feeling if you've never felt anything at all? The painful realization that he was correct was slowly coming over me, and it made me feel like I was less than a person, inadequate, incomplete.

"Fake. Frigid," I mumbled under my breath as I approached my car. A cold wind shuffled the leaves on the street as I paused by my car. He stood silently behind me, knowing I would not leave, knowing I could never walk away.

I felt like jumping into a pool or plunging myself into any body of water even though I didn't know how to swim. But that day, I was pushed in. I didn't see it coming, but there I was. Thrashing about, flailing my arms like nobody's business. Trying desperately to keep my head above water and stay afloat. I was clearly in over my head and choking for air.

A dead girl doesn't really think about being dead, you know. You learn to go through all the motions and look quite animated. It was true that I was gone, and I didn't even remember when it happened. Of course, I felt nothing. If I did, it would drive me mad like my mother. After what had been done repeatedly to me by men, it was impossible to be in my own body when things went to that place.

It was a Gestalt awakening. A moment of recognition. A sudden awareness that I could not continue as I had before. That the ruse I had successfully orchestrated to convince everyone that I was a "real girl" was nothing more than a deception both of myself and others. I had no choice but to own it. Claim it. Admit it. And then to move forward to create and give birth to a new authentic version of myself. Maybe there was more to me than a pretty face. Maybe I could discover some kind of identity.

Helplessly Hoping
Crosby, Stills, Nash, and Young 1975

I got pregnant on New Year's Eve in Dumas, Texas. Johnny's band had a gig, and I tagged along to marvel at my Renaissance man. They played at the country club in this Podunk rural community about sixty miles north of Amarillo. It was all boots and hats and trucks and gun racks, but I liked to study people and sip on a cherry Collins or white Russian while they performed such standards as *Silver Wings* and a bunch of Eagles and Doobie Brothers songs.

Johnny pulled his hair back in a ponytail and wore a brown fedora, a button-down shirt with rolled up sleeves, and his black and white Converse sneakers. Not quite the wild man I remember from years before, but still a real character. He was so much more than a drummer in a rock 'n roll band. He was a songwriter and a poet, a philosopher and healer, a searcher and a genius.

I had acknowledged the pieces of me that were broken and had begun the arduous task of mending them. He was always there beside me, guiding me along. Years later, I wondered if he saw me as a "project." What would motivate someone to expend so much energy on someone so damaged? I wanted to be what he wanted me to be, but I also wanted to be something for me, too.

Having a baby at this time in our lives was not a good plan for anyone, but we could write it off as fate if we must find a way to come to terms with it. Neither of us was ready for parenthood, but it was what it was. A game changer, indeed.

Becoming a father at twenty-three was not on Johnny's to do list. He was brilliant, driven, ambitious, and determined to prove to himself and to the world that he was far more than the son of a cook and a waitress who owned their own little BBQ joint down on 6th Street. Perhaps these aspirations were delusions of grandeur, but he thought God had chosen him to heal the suffering of mankind. This noble ambition allowed no distractions such as fatherhood.

So things began to unravel. He had been like a God to me. After all, his omniscience had seen all and knew all, and he had guided me to higher ground. No doubt he was my savior. What form would his dreams take, and where would they take us? The answer swirled around me and separated me from my personal Jesus. He promised "to walk beside me, within me, and without me" when he gazed into my eyes and said his vows at St. Paul's Methodist Church on a cold and blustery January day in 1976. I really didn't think much about the last part, the 'without me' part, but later I understood that he always knew we would not maintain the level of symbiosis we once enjoyed. He knew that we would have to take different paths at some point, that I could not follow him like a puppy forever.

We didn't get married because I was pregnant. We were both way too unconventional to concern ourselves about what the world might think about anything we might do or fail to do. In fact, we had already planned the wedding at St. Paul's Methodist Church, arranged a minister, and rented the chocolate and peach colored tuxedos before the New Year's Dumas condom accident. His friend, Mike, was his best man, and my only friend, Ginia, stood by me. She worked at a florist shop while studying to be a nurse and made a beautiful bouquet for me to carry. When I walked down the aisle in my classic 70's wedding dress and puffy veil, I had no idea a little life, only days old, was percolating inside me. A few weeks after the wedding, I was late and went up to the grocery to get "the box with the stick". When the color turned pink, the reality of it did not register right away. I sat there on the toilet for at least ten minutes trying to process what that meant. The plates Beaneath my feet shifted, and it was a whole new world. One that I was totally unprepared to enter.

I loved my husband and mentor and loved the idea of being pregnant. Within the first day of the news, I stopped smoking and started eating, putting on a whopping eighty-seven pounds before it was over. My thin dancer body was stretched and torn with lacerated stretch marks unlike those ever seen before. I had not thought about the permanent consequences of all those late night milkshakes or endless buffets!

This was not Johnny's first child. Apparently, condoms were no match for his tremendous virility that had escaped twice now without even a break or a tear. He had a son with a girl named Earlene when they were in 10th grade and after much debate, they put him up for adoption. They were young, they grieved for their loss, and they accepted that it was the best thing considering their age and all. He mentioned it only once or twice with some degree of remorse and regret and seemed comfortable that it was the right thing to do. But he wasn't a kid anymore, and he had begrudgingly agreed to marry me when I proposed the idea, so this one was a keeper. There was nothing to debate. If he was too busy with his quest to be the great white doctor, then I would handle it myself. Little did I know at the time that I had never witnessed one single healthy bit of parenting, so I was clueless. I had all the mothering skill sets of a Tasmanian devil who are notorious for letting most of their offspring die soon after birth or akin to other horrible mothers who cannibalize or kill their young.

The summer before our son was born, we often returned to the park where we went on our first date. This time there was no guitar or singing. We would pack a bag with wieners and chips and charcoal and set up at one of the picnic table grilling stations. I sat silently and watched as Johnny squirted lighter fluid on the charcoal flames and read his anatomy and physiology book while our food sizzled. We did not talk about philosophy or religion or the stars and planets as we once did not that long ago, and his guitar had been retired to a corner of the closet. He was lost in his books, consumed by the idea of becoming a healer of men. I had never thought of him in that context. It seemed incongruous in a way because although I marveled at his brilliance, it never occurred to me that he would decide to actually use his gifts to do something concrete like medical school, like becoming a doctor.

We had many late-night conversations where my neediness and selfishness was in clear conflict with his delusions of grandeur and mission to save the world. Neither one of us had a realistic grasp of the choices and consequences that lay before us. I felt abandoned, he felt unsupported. Both of us had unrealistic expectations—I wanted him to work at the Harrington Cancer Center doing 9-5 cancer research with Dr. Perrimen who had promised him a job after graduation. What could be better than spending your day with T-cells and petri dishes and then get home every day in time to have a rich family life? He wanted to spend the next ten years in medical school and residency which would leave little if any time at all for anything else.

We fought like champions, and on a couple of occasions, it got physical. I would yell, he would push me, I would throw something, he would storm out. One night when I was about six months pregnant, he became so angry and frustrated at my inability to support him that he used his feet to kick me off the edge of the bed. The lesson: never keep an argument going past bedtime. It was a non-stop marathon clash of wills. Our vision of future failed to line up with one another, and we were clearly unable to get on the same path that headed in the same direction.

The honeymoon was clearly over, and I was alone again, naturally.

Landslide
Fleetwood Mac 1976

I was in my final semester at West Texas State University and beginning my student teaching with Tisha Lattimer, a colorful and artistic thespian, as my supervising teacher in a couple of weeks. Even though I was passionately in love with theatre, dance, and competition with the speech team, the only future in those fields that were realistic and accessible to me were in the area of education. I had never dreamed of being a teacher, but my love affair with the stage compelled me to stay close to it. Teaching was the only way I could make that happen and have a job that enabled financial independence. I could not see myself schlepping tacos at the burrito barn just so I could act and dance under the bright lights. I needed the security of a real job, and teaching would let me stay on stage, only this time with a cast of students standing there with me.

I gave birth on a Thursday and returned to class at WTSU first thing Monday morning. Johnny drove me in his revamped post office truck that was so formerly unique and quirky but now suddenly uncomfortable and bumpy. He had purchased it at a postal auction and had a friend with a body shop paint the whole thing brown and add wood panel detail. It looked kind of like the Scooby-Doo beach van minus the surf board, and the coolest thing was the wonky steering wheel on the right. A seat had to be added on the left where there was none, and it must not have been installed properly because it bounced around with every lump or bump in the road, so much that it actually detached and sent the person strapped into their seat rolling into the back cargo area. Good times.

My bottom was so sore and the stitches so swollen, I took a little pillow to sit on, but it did not help. I did not detach and go careening into the back; however, I experienced every bounce in the road with a new perspective even though I implored Johnny to go slower and slower. It was a long commute, nearly twenty miles each way which created a long day. A painfully long day.

Most new moms understand the importance of bonding and possess some instinctual clues about how to parent their young. The human race would not survive if this were not so. But for me, I had no clue what to do, no idea how to be a mother. How could I?

My own mother never modeled any positive parenting techniques and was oblivious to even my basic needs as a human being. She fed and clothed me and seemed to enjoy doing it much of the time, but it ended there. The rest was madness.

We named our first-born son Chaun which was pronounced like it was part of my dad's real name, Prachaun, so it was an Americanized version of a Thai name. Parents never think about the difficulty of some names. Everyone thought he said John or Shaun or Shan or something else instead of Chaun with the "CH" like Charlie whenever he would say his name. Blonde headed, blue eyed, and white as the driven snow, people must have thought I kidnapped him since we looked so very different.

Johnny passed his MCAT with high enough scores to have a good chance of getting accepted to med school somewhere, maybe even one of his top tier choices. We both still had another semester before we graduated, and I began student teaching in the spring—the last rite of passage before graduating. His focus was on applications and maintaining his 4.0 average, my focus in finishing up everything and getting a teaching job. Neither of us was focused on our parenthood.

Most days we left early and returned late, and baby Chaun was left with my mother and grandmother. We had three generations all living together at this time and had been in this living arrangement since we married because of school and the inability to work enough to get our own place. We planned to move during the summer as soon as I got a teaching job, so it was a temporary hell. In the meantime, I rarely had time for Chaun. I held him or gave him a bottle for maybe thirty minutes a day, but he was almost always fussy, and I would quickly pass him over to either my mom or grandmother. They seemed to know what to do with a colicky baby or at least they said they did, and it was certainly beyond my skill set.

My parents had sold the house on Royal Road around the time Johnny and I got married and moved in with my grandmother so they could travel frequently. There were many golf vacations and trips to visit the family in Thailand who would still speak to him. When Chaun was born, my mom and grams teamed up to become his primary caregivers.

People have a way of convincing themselves that something is okay even when they know it isn't if the consequences of admitting it would be too catastrophic. I needed their help so I could finish my degree and be self-sufficient. I did not have the resources to make other choices, so I thought to myself, "He's in no physical danger, and I will take him away from them before he gets old enough to suffer any emotional damage." Famous last words.

Things are never quite so clean and neat as we would like. Time passed quickly and soon I was in graduate school in Canyon, Johnny was in med school in Lubbock, Chaun was walking and talking, and we were 120 miles apart. I drove back and forth almost every weekend that year to try to keep our little family together. You can guess how that went.

When I refused to follow him to the Texas Tech medical school, I decided I would pursue a graduate degree as well. If he could do it, so could I. We were both equally ambitious and capable. So I moved out of my grandmother's for the sake of my sanity and because I was offered Johnny's old rock castle apartment for free by his parents. I just paid utilities, and I could manage that well enough with the job I had when I wasn't at school.

My classes that year began at 8:00 am. Research and Statistics, Guidance & Counseling, British Literature before the 19th Century. When I finished between 2:00 and 3:00, I went straight to work as a waitress at Gardski's Loft in Wellington Square. I worked until 10:30-11:30, went back to my dark empty castle-hovel, ate a bunch of mint chocolate chip ice cream straight out of the carton with a spoon, smoked a couple of cigarettes, did a little homework, and went to sleep around 1:30am only to get up at 6:30 the next morning to repeat the routine. By the time it was Friday night or Saturday morning and time to go to Lubbock, I would pick up Chaun from my grandmother's house and drive two hours to spend twenty-four hours with Johnny. Sometimes I would get Chaun if I had a day off, but that was rare, so I only had him with me on the weekends, and by then we were both love starved and fighting over which one of us would be ignored by Johnny first.

I probably could have secured a teaching job in Lubbock and followed him. That is what he wanted me to do, what he expected me to do. But I was angry that he chose medicine over family, and being so ill equipped to deal with a child on my own, I needed him to help me learn how to do it like he had taught me how to do everything else. That was not to be. His career took precedence, and I could tag along or stay behind and flounder about with my situation. I chose the latter.

I think the thing that was the deciding factor had more to do with my own career trajectory and less to do with my need for a parenting partner. I knew I was as smart if not more so than Johnny. I breezed through biology, government, economics and other classes we took together at ACC and beat him by several points in every class. What about graduate school for me? I had never planned to be a teacher. It was the fall back plan on my way to a PhD in psychology, mass comm, or literature studies. I was ambitious because my father's family all had terminal degrees, and I knew it was an expectation. I had let my father down in too many ways to count, but I was a superior student. It was the one thing I had always excelled at, even in the lowest depths of my drug induced, misery fueled life. I wanted to show him that I had worth. I wanted to show myself that I had worth.

So when he entered Texas Tech School of Medicine, I entered graduate school at West Texas State, and Chaun entered a relationship with my mother, his caregiver, the surrogate mom who sealed his fate. Somewhere in all this, I knew he was a casualty, that I was giving him up, passing him on to her while Johnny and I pursued our academic glory. I had no relationship with my family. I couldn't get access to my dad because my mother was always blocking the way. So I just ran in and out in a flash of speed with no time to stay more than a quick minute. Sometimes, Chaun would be there for days before I returned because of school and work and more school.

Years later I regretted the "drop and run" strategy because what goes around comes around, and my children would go on to repeat what I showed them. They would not understand how I could leave my child with someone I feared and loathed, and they would not understand that I had to turn and run away as quickly as possible for my own self-preservation. Fight or flee. I did my share of both, and nothing ever changed. I certainly spent years fighting before I decided that fleeing made a lot more sense. Every cell in my body screamed with a compulsive and desperate voice that demanded to be understood, to be heard, to be validated in some small way. Year after year I had stomped my feet, made my claims and proclamations and repeated them, repeated them, repeated them over and over again and all for nothing.

Johnny had his own brand of wisdom, and his insightfulness produced one of the most poignant and prolific truths I had ever been presented with. One weekend when I was with him in Lubbock, I complained about a day of particularly unreasonable irrationality from my mother regarding some moot point or trivial issue. He said something that was so powerful that it resonated with me for the rest of my life. He looked up from one of his behemoth sized texts, Dr. Pepper in one hand and a cigarette in the other and said, "Why do you do this to yourself? You are perpetuating your own misery."

"What are you talking about? She is the crazy one. She buys those damn peanut butter cups and feeds them to Chaun all through the day, so he is going to be diabetic or in a diabetic coma before he is five! She is the one who needs to stop and think about what she is doing," I responded with passionate conviction.

"You are trying to get something from her that she simply does not have to give. She just doesn't have it, doesn't even know what it is much less how to give it to you, so who is the foolish one?" he declared with the air of a sage or guru or something.

Usually, I continued to rant and rave to her, and then bring it home to rant and rave about her. But this hit me square between the eyes and I stopped talking.

He went on to say, "All your life you have wished for a mother who could give you what you needed, but she never even gave you any scraps or crumbs or anything. It's because she couldn't, not because she didn't want to. She is broken, too."

"It just sucks me in and swallows me up, and I can't be reasonable when she gets started," I offered.

"If you don't want to become her and be crazy and out of touch with what is real just like her, you need to look at her with different eyes. Don't just react to her from the heart. Accept that she can't give you what you seek. Find a way to get it for yourself. And then step back and see her for what she is—a damaged, pathetic, sick, mentally ill woman who is incapable of being a real mother to you," he said as he crushed his cigarette and turned back to his books. My weekend conjugal visits consisted of Saturday afternoons and Sunday mornings together before heading back to Amarillo, and most of that time he was studying and telling me to take Chaun to South Plains Mall or up to Maxi Park to feed the ducks so he could focus on school without distraction.

But sprinkled here and there, he made time to offer something substantial. And for a brief moment, there was clarity in his words. His assessment about my mother was spot on, lucid and irrefutable. But the heart will swell with such anguish that what the head knows is completely obliterated and obscured. In my head I knew he was right, but in my heart, it was something I could not accept.

"If I say it often enough and long enough, eventually she will hear me," I thought to myself.

"She will hear me and she will understand."

Love is a Battlefield
Pat Beanatar 1979

Three semesters and two summers later, I graduated with my Master's degree and accepted a teaching job in Lubbock so that Johnny and I could resume where we left off. It was exciting to be part of his life in medical school and have Chaun away from my mother. It was also nice to be out of Amarillo for the first time in my life. Although the two cities were only two hours apart and similar in most ways, it felt like a new world.

Chaun attended a nice little pre-school near our house, and it felt like a new chance to create a better life. While I was making chicken and spaghetti for his med school buddies to come over and gobble up as they did on regular basis, he was slipping away. Somehow, I had missed the memo that we were no longer on the same page, and I thought everything was going pretty well. I liked my school and had made a few friends. We attended all the fancy doctor parties and even got a babysitter for date night a couple of times a month. Sometimes we even went dancing at places like Tara's. I loved to dance, and disco was such a huge thing in the early 80's. Who could resist shaking their groove thang to the impressive sounds of Donna Summer? Family time took us took Maxi Park on Sunday afternoons to feed the ducks and have a picnic lunch before Johnny headed to the hospital or back to school for study group. Chaun and I wandered South Plains Mall or took long walks to get a burger at Sammies or some pizza at Shakey's. Like every disappointment or defeat, I took it with a good dose of Thai stoicism and resignation. There was no reason not to think his brutal schedule was temporary. But at the end of the school year, he surprised me with a confusing and disheartening request.

"The match results came in and I did not get my first choice at Vanderbilt, so it looks like I'm going to be going to El Paso. I'm beginning my residency in a few months and I really think that I need to focus on it. You and Chaun are a distraction, so I think you need to stay here," he announced one bright Saturday in May.

"I can't just stay here by myself without you. I want to come. I won't bother you or get in your way," I offered.

"It's just not what is best for any of us. If you can't be here alone, then maybe you need to go back to Amarillo to be closer to family who can help you out," he said with a cool air of emotional detachment.

"Are you kidding? I finally get away from all that crazy, make some friends, have a new start, and you think I should just quit my job and go back?" I asked in disbelief.

"Well, actually, I imagine you would be fine here, but you are the one telling me you can't do it. If you can't, then don't. You decide," he said as he walked away and headed for the door.

"Let's just talk about this and figure it out. I don't understand why you don't want me to come to El Paso. I'm excited and I have schools that are interested in me and have asked for follow-up interviews. I could help you, cook, and take care of things. I'll manage Chaun and keep him out of your way. It will be fine," I said with the sound of desperation coming up in my voice.

"There is nothing to say, Lily. I don't want you to come with me. That's the end of it."

So in the summer of 1981, Johnny began his residency at William Beaumont Army Medical Center and R.E Thomason Hospital in El Paso, Texas. When the graduating class went through their Match Day that spring, he was psyched about getting a surgery residency that was not so easy to get. It was probably because he finished third in his class of 128 med students, and that impressed schools as they made their picks. He was so into the program, he spent every waking moment doing something to be top of the pyramid which advanced only about 60% of the doctors who started the residency after the first year, thereby narrowing the field. Another 20% were eliminated at the end of the second year so that only 20% of those who started were afforded the opportunity to actually complete the program. It was rigorous and competitive, and I knew it would consume him in every way.

Fear has always been a force in my life even though I act brave and strong. My fear compelled me to seek a teaching job in Amarillo, and at the end of the summer after teaching summer school at Coronado High, I packed up the car and drove the two hour drive back to where I started.

It was a lonely year.

There were occasional trips to El Paso every few months, but he was always busy and distracted—never really there with me. Somehow I managed to talk him into letting me come to stay with him when school was out for the summer. I remember the conversation that led to the agreement. I was visiting spring break and left Chaun with my mom. I bought a black hat to go with my black and white dress and heels to make a very polished doctor's wife kind of ensemble. We went to dinner at a fancy restaurant where I ate my first artichoke with butter and dissected my first whole lobster. We went back to the apartment and ended up having sex on the floor in front of the fireplace. It was spicy stuff. Maybe we were going to find our way back to each other after all.

Little did I know at the time that the summer arrangement was actually a trial; I was being evaluated to see if he still had feelings for me. It was a side-by-side comparison with his girlfriend. During the year he had been there alone, he had embarked on a relationship with a nurse at the VA named Mimi. After stepping outside the boundaries of fidelity, he wanted to see how I measured up against her. I guess he wanted to give me one last chance to prove my worth.

Residency is three days on, three days off, rinse and repeat. Endlessly. So Johnny spent three nights at the hospital in the on-call sleep room, but no one ever really sleeps. I tried to stay perky about being alone at least half of the week, but I was lonely the whole week, even when he was right there. I took Chaun to the pool every day at our little apartment on Shadow Mountain Drive, and we met other widows and orphans. A lady named Christie came every day and talked to me while our kids floated around the pool in their floatie turtles and floaty fish. Her husband was a semi-professional baseball player for the El Paso Suns, so she was alone about as much as me if not more. We got really dark that summer; people didn't think so much about UV rays, carcinomas, or ozone layers in those days. I had reclaimed my mythology as princess mermaid and drifted aimlessly on top of the shimmering blue water with my tiny twinkling bikini covered in glittery, sparkly sequins like fish scales in the relentless sun.

Sometimes Chaun and I caught a bus and rode to the mall to walk around and have something to do. Everywhere we went, people tried to speak Spanish to me and wondered if I was the nanny or housekeeper with her little blonde-headed, blue eyed bosses son in tow.

On Johnny's days off, actually there were no real days off since he got called to come to the hospital on every day of the week, but on the days he was mostly available I would try to make good things for everyone to eat. One of the rituals I created was spaghetti and meatballs followed by a chocolate buttermilk sheet cake. It was a nice sit down dinner, and for a few minutes every week, we seemed like we were all okay. I liked watching him tie off stitches using catgut string and a coke bottle. He would do it right handed for a while, then switch and do it left handed. I couldn't even sew up a hole in a sock or replace a button if my life depended on it, so I was pretty impressed with his one handed suturing skills. Bravo Dr. Rolands, bravo. I still looked at him with the eyes of an enamored school-girl.

But it was apparent that we were hanging on to the last remnants of our relationship as the summer pressed on. Time alone together was time in silence. Chaun had chicken pox for the 4th of July, and they were so thick that he had them in his ears, his hair, his nose, and just about everywhere you can imagine. He was miserable for a few days, and then just looked much worse than he actually was. When I remember his sweet little face that summer, it was so pitiful because it was the last summer he had real joy in him. It was the beginning of his end, too. That childlike hope and happiness, the lightness of being, the silly-goofiness.

Granted, Chaun and I had never bonded the way a mother and

son were supposed to connect in the first months and years of their life together, but we had managed to muddle through somehow. But this was different now. Something shifted and when I looked at Johnny, I saw all I had given and sacrificed and lost. My terminal degree on hold and increasingly out of reach with each passing day. My years of teaching and being the breadwinner while he contributed absolutely nothing to our financial picture. My solo parenting since medical school had been a full-time job, and he had no time to be a father. In fact, he had never wanted to be a father in the first place and suggested that I get an abortion when I first announced my pregnancy. I had surrendered all of my dreams for him, and he did not even acknowledge my sacrifice or appreciate it.

Then I looked at Chaun, and I saw mini-Johnny. His mirror image, a full-time tiny person who constantly needed something. I didn't really resent him, it wasn't his fault. I just didn't have the mother instinct or intuitive wisdom needed to be a good parent. It was such an effort, such a difficult job. My temper had begun to come up over the summer, and I felt a familiar lack of control that I recognized as a bit of my mother crawling out of the deep places where sadness and anger live.

The first time I recognized pieces of my mother awakening in me, Chaun and I were having Cheerios and watching Sesame Street. It was towards the end of the summer and the end of my marriage, and I was painfully aware of the hardships ahead. Divorced, single-parent, lonely, over-worked, yadda yadda. He started complaining about wanting something else to eat.

"Chaun, just eat your Cheerios. There isn't anything else," I said with feelings of frustration coming up.

"I want donuts. Can I have a pop tart? Let's go get donuts. I don't want these," he whined as he stirred the spoon around in the cereal.

"Just stop it, okay? No donuts. Just eat and be quiet," I said in a louder, angrier voice. It was early, I was tired, and the coldness of the house was creeping up my spine.

"But, moommmm," as the demands and whining increased.

In a flash, I had seized the bowl and hurled it across the table, milk and Cheerios flying everywhere.

"Shut up, shut up, shut up! You are making me crazy!" I yelled as I saw the mess I had created and the anguish on his face.

And at that moment, I felt it. I knew it was true. Parts of my mother's out of control rage and insanity had been hiding inside me just waiting for an opportune moment to reveal itself. In that moment I knew I was a monster, too.

I cleaned everything up, apologized for the outburst, and we trudged out to the pool to bake in the hot El Paso sun. I squinted in the blinding brightness of the sun and spotted Chaun, tiny in the distance, floating on his turtle floatie, drifting on the blue water near the rope that signaled the deep end. I loved him and feared him. He had a power to reduce me to a crazy person, and I understood how my mother had always blamed me all her life for being nuts. It wasn't true, but it was real.

When Johnny came home from the hospital that night, I wanted to tell him about my new found cruelty and how it had frightened us both. I wanted to tell him that I needed his help, his guidance, his support. I wanted him to put his arms around me and hold me and tell me that it wasn't true...I wasn't like her. I needed him to tell me that he would be there for me. But I said nothing.

Later, I tried to figure out what pushed my buttons that day. I was tired and disappointed and lonely all the time. All I did was work, work, and then work some more. I taught high school all day and taught dance after school two days a week and worked at Sylvan tutoring SAT prep on Saturdays. I had just finished my Master's degree in record time with an average high enough to get into a doctoral program at Texas Tech, and I desperately wanted to complete my terminal degree. But I could not do anything except work and work some more, put my ambitions on hold, and forge bravely ahead. The two people I needed most were holding me back, breaking me down, crushing my dreams.

Comfortably Numb
Pink Floyd   1981

There was a numbness that permeated every part of me that felt like paralysis. My relationship with guilt had begun to grow to epic proportions, and now I felt guilty for a long list of things. I felt contrition for wanting to achieve something more and for wanting to use my intellectual gifts. What kinds of selfish people allow themselves to get obsessed with something like a Ph.D. when their children should be placed ahead of their ambitions? I wanted to do something I could be proud of so I could achieve some kind of redemption, and school was the only place where I could truly shine. I felt remorse for being a disappointment to my father, for leaving Chaun with my mom, for not loving Jesus as much as my Grams did, for all the things I did in the "dead years" following the loss of my baby. I felt guilt for losing not one, but two babies even though I had no power to save either. Even though my mind knew I was not at fault, my heart told me something else entirely.

There was the shame of knowing that I was probably responsible in some way for every male person who ever exploited or abused me, treated me like a disposable piece of meat, and then blamed me for it. I was weak and stupid to allow them to marginalize me and objectify me and then do nothing to defend myself. Maybe I deserved it—it definitely caused an erosion of my self worth that transcended any attempt to maintain even a shred of dignity. Maybe I gave off a "rape me" vibe. Maybe I was fatally pretty. Maybe I was just a bad person. In the end, everything was my fault. My dear, sweet mommy certainly never missed a chance to confirm it. And maybe she was right, "If you can't be a Thai princess, the only thing you can be is a Thai whore." Maybe Johnny was just now coming to terms with the disappointing reality that I was neither.

I wanted to be the kind of mother who did not place an evil curse or an injunction against joy on her children. I should have learned what not to do from watching my own mother. But there I was, playing the old messages I had recorded through the years, acting out the script she gave me. Being a mother should have been fulfilling. It should have been enough so that I did not need or want anything else. But my mind was filled with so many thoughts and no way to express them or develop them. It was like being at the pool, just floating aimlessly; looking up at the blue sky and watching clouds roll by. This weightless, emptiness compelled me to seek remedy, so I smoked a little pot and popped a few tranquilizers I had borrowed from my mother's own personal pharmacy in order to get through the days. Days that passed slowly and evaporated like vapor in the scorchin.

Writing had always provided some theraputic Beanefit in times of lonliness or distress. Over the years, I composed hundreds of poems, short stories, and material for longer pieces. Fellow writers who read my work at conferences, workshops, and other venues always said I was deliciously dark and reminiscent of Sylvia Plath or other wretched, tormented souls. Joan Didion was always the writer I hoped to emulate, but I could certainly see the Plath component to my writing. I was always better on paper than in person, so I penned several heartfelt letters to Johnny throughout that summer. They all ended up in the trash at one point or another. I knew he would be relectant to give full attention to something so silly, and it wouldn't change anything anyway. So eventually, the much dreaded "talk" had to happen. There was painful dialogue about the unsustainability of our relationship, about the different paths we had chosen, about seeking a divorce. When the summer came to an end, our marriage came to an end as well.

One Saturday night, the weekend before I planned to return to Amarillo for the new school year, one of Johnny's doctor friends from the hospital who had recently separated from his wife, had a birthday. Before I had time to think about it, we all found ourselves at a tittie bar near the airport called the Golden Lantern. I had never been to a place like that before and felt awkward at first with all the naked women bouncing about. Most were rather skanky looking with butterfly tattoos on their asses and other tacky business, but I remember one girl who had these crazy breasts that defied gravity. They were pretty big as far as boobs go, and they stuck straight out in front without any drooping or sagging for a good ten to twelve inches. They were shaped kind of like two giant eggplants or butternut squash. I could not wrap my mind around the physics of those boobs, and years later, I was still confused by the tricks they could do.

We stayed for an eternity, and I kept drinking Colorado Bulldogs to make it all a little more fun. By the time we returned to the apartment, we were both pretty wasted. We had not slept together more than a couple of times the whole summer and even that was cold and quick. It was goodbye sex, closure. But that night was something different— passion personified. In the kitchen. Involving spatulas. Spicy business. And then, as quickly as it began, it was over. Like a flame or grease fire that just flares up for a second and then disappears in a flash. Like that last pop or spray of sparks that happens right before the fire dies out. The next day, we did not speak about it or even acknowledge that anything had even happened. Before I left less than a week later, we mutually agreed to visit with lawyers to see about moving forward with the divorce.

But here is the irony. Life has a way of teaching you lessons and showing you how much you are not in control of your destiny. I had high hopes at the beginning of summer, but by the time I left, those hopes were dashed. I had accepted the finality with a deep sadness, but he was already gone. You can always tell when someone has checked out emotionally, and Johnny was long gone. It was just a matter of cleaning up the pieces and figuring out what to do next.

A few weeks later, I discovered I was pregnant.

Once in a Lifetime
Talking Heads 1982

Justin was born in May a few weeks before school was out. The year had been difficult with the unraveling of our marriage, but with new life, there seemed to be new hope. We made promises to stay together and make 'best effort' to survive as a family. I allowed myself to step back into the relationship, and all of the pregnancy hormones helped me feel closer to Johnny than ever. He responded in kind, but the true closeness I witnessed was actually between him and Chaun; I guess they felt a close connection that had always been broken with me. But baby Justin changed everything.

I felt like I too had been given a second chance when I discovered my pregnancy, and when I held him the first time, I felt the full range of feelings that mothers are supposed to feel. I never paused to consider how that might appear to Johnny or to Chaun, but later they confessed that they were despondent to see that I was indeed capable of this kind of love, but just not for them. I never thought about it as something I selected, something that I withheld from them and gave to Justin. In fact, I didn't even think about it at all. What happened happened, and that's just the way it was. I thought I loved them just as much, but they certainly didn't feel like it.

When Justin was born he had a small cleft lip that needed repair when he was only a few weeks old. Dr. Keller agreed to repair his lip as a professional courtesy since his dad was a physician, and that's how doctors all take care of each other and their families. We still had OR costs and anesthesia, but at least his surgeon fees were covered. I was so relieved and comforted by the idea of being part of something and not alone on this one. He performed minor surgery to close the gap which was small and did not even extend past the lip line. It could have been so much worse, and I was grateful that it did not continue up into his palate or extend further towards his nose. It was just a little piece of lip missing, but just enough to give him a scar for life. I remember thinking, "Is God punishing me by harming my child because of all of the things I have done to hurt other people?" I gladly would accept punishment with the resignation that comes with guilt, but the idea that my sins could translate into suffering for my children was too much to even consider. I started reading about generational karmic debt and spent a lot of sleepless nights trying to figure out how far back the curses went in our families. There's probably no reason to know since there's nothing anyone can do about it anyway. And it was more like a blessing than a curse. It brought me even closer to him, and I was grateful every single day that he survived the procedure without complication and was so sweet and good-natured through it all.

Children are resilient, so of course he bounced back and within a few weeks like it never happened. I put the little steri-strips on his lip that held all the stitches together and fed him an alternative bottle since he wasn't supposed to nurse like a normal baby. None of that mattered. To me he was perfect. To me he was the miracle baby that should not have happened. To me, he was here to save me and teach me how to love and how to be a better person.

He had monkey hair like I did when I was little. It's kind of an Asian thing with sharp stiff hair that stands straight up like a little monkey. Most Thai children have that hair, and now I had a child who was like me. When he looked at me with his big brown eyes, I felt like he trusted me, and thought I was everything to him. Nobody had ever looked at me that way. He looked like he loved me so much; it's hard to explain. Let it suffice to say that no one, not one single person in my entire life had ever looked upon me with such warmth. "So that's what it feels like to be loved," I thought, and the stone around my heart began to crumble and fall.

There is something so organic about love. Everything about them becomes so naturally symbiotic. The way their hair and breath and sweat smells. The feel of their skin up against yours. The sounds that they make, the way that they move, the rhythm that they set. You breathe it in until it absorbs into every cell, thriving, growing, at harmony with all that is you. That is how you love your children, and if you're lucky, that's the kind of love you share with your life partner.

It is difficult to say when or how the great thaw began, but Johnny saw it and so did Chaun. Make no mistake, I loved them both and wanted them to be happy and healthy even at my own expense. I had learned early on not to want much or expect anything or hope for things, so it was pretty easy to put their needs before mine. When I cooked something, I always made their plates first with the best pieces and most generous portions. I ate the ugly parts, the scraps, the mistakes, and the leftovers. Sometimes I lay awake at night and imagined how I would rescue everyone from a flood or a fire. I would sacrifice myself for them, and they would be eternally grateful and gaze at me with the same look of wonder and love that Justin had when he lifted his little face up to mine. But in reality, I had disappointed them both somehow, and their eyes held scorn and reproach and blame and pain and all these dark things that said over and over how much I had failed, how much I had let them down.

Johnny saw me as a traitor, someone who betrayed his best interests. When I failed to support his decision to go to medical school years before, he felt abandoned and never had the heart to forgive me. Chaun saw me as a deserter as well. Every time I would do the "drop and go" at my mother's house, he felt discarded and left behind. I think he longed for me and stood by the window watching me drive away to school, to work, to all the places that were more important than him.

So you can imagine how they must have felt when they saw Justin and I sharing such a powerful bond, such a strong connection that everything else fell away, and they were the outsiders, the outcasts. I didn't even think about it at the time. And if the thought passed by, I quickly dismissed it by telling myself that surely, they would understand that he was just a baby and of course I must be enamored by him because he needed me so much or something along those lines. But they saw it, and it was tough to watch.

Things change in an instant with no warning. Life has a funny way of surprising you when you least expect it. There is no way to be ready when it comes.

February 12, 1983 when Justin was only nine months old and Chaun was recently seven, when supper was done, the kids were asleep, and it was time to start getting ready for bed, Johnny took a suitcase from the closet which was already packed in advance, and headed for the door. I should have seen it coming, but I was blindsided. After all, we were on the brink of divorce when I became pregnant, so why would I think that having another baby would magically repair all that was broken in my marriage? It didn't. In fact, having Justin was the event that broke the dam and let the waters of discontent and disappointment flood our relationship.

"I am going to my dad's, and I'll talk to you soon," he said as he stacked his things in the back of his red Chevy Blazer.

"For how long? What are you doing? We haven't even talked about this," I managed to get out while I felt my anxiety and panic rising up from my stomach to my chest.

"I'm not coming back. I think we just need to move on, and you'll be happier without me. We haven't made anything happen here since I agreed to stay, and Justin isn't really a baby anymore. You'll be fine. You should call your lawyer, that Doug guy you were talking to before, since you'll hear from, my attorney before long," he said with a cold-blooded, calculated demeanor.

"I thought we were okay. We don't argue or fight. Please, don't do this. I need you here. Please don't go. I can't do this alone. I'm so sorry for anything." I pleaded through tears and snot streaming from my nose as a held on to his arm.

"Lily, let go. It is time. This isn't working and hasn't been alright in a long time. You know it. You know it is time for me to go," he said as he tried to get out the door with the last of his things.

"Noooo. No. No. Please. Please, I'm so scared. Please, please. Don't leave me," I begged as I crumbled to the floor and held on to his legs. I had seen my mother have similar histrionics and completely melt into a pool of blubbering, helpless slime. I had sworn I would be stronger, smarter, less helpless and crippled by life than her.

He reached down and took both of my hands and pulled them up and away so that I had to come off the floor. When I was to my knees and he was free from my grip, he quickly stepped away and went for the door, never looking back, never saying goodbye.

When he closed the door behind himself, I heard the click and just stared at the white wooden door. I felt like I was drowning and could not get my breath. At that moment, the world stopped. I did not know where Chaun was or Justin or if they were asleep or awakened by all of the drama. I just sat there on the floor, my face blackened with streams of mascara, all swollen and red and feverish, until the reality of the moment hit me like a shotgun blast to my chest. I doubled over, and a deep primal moan escaped me before sobs racked my body.

I don't remember how long I was on the floor feeling my life flowing from me like blood, and I don't remember what happened that night after his departure. One of my most disturbing characteristics as a person is that I have the uncanny ability to look past all the flaws and cracks and imperfections in both people and relationships and see only what I want to see, what I'm comfortable with. I guess I learned to do that early on when trying to make sense of my parents. If reality is just too horrible to accept, then it's entirely possible to adjust the focus knob on your vision controls and see something better. Something easier. So I saw our marriage as secure and solid even though Johnny never really made it back to me after the summer in El Paso. I think he was just watching the clock, doing the honorable thing and not abandoning a pregnant wife or one with an infant. As soon as Justin was walking and looking strong, his duty was over. I do know that my heart had never been broken quite like this before. The summer in El Paso forced me to accept our failed marriage, but there was something about being pregnant with his child and going through all of Justin's surgery together that brought me back to him and made me feel close again. I had been believing that all this was a second chance, perhaps even divine intervention. But now, I knew that the man who brought me back to life nearly ten years earlier had chosen to leave me. The man who taught me how to feel and how to be a real person, not some empty shell, was ready to make his exit. Maybe now, I would go back to being numb and empty like before.

"Maybe I will die because everything I am is because he made me, forged me in his own image," I thought to myself.

He had been my rescuer, my savior, my messiah. My perception of myself was so intrinsically tied to him that it was inconceivable to think I could survive without him nearby to define me. We were one. We had woven the threads of our lives together so that separating them was unimaginable.

But then there was Justin.

My sons were the real victims. I had no choice but to get up and get on. Isn't that what mothers do?

Time after Time
Cyndi Lauper 1983

There were so many times leading up to our divorce day in court when neither of us wanted to let go and go on. Johnny made an appearance the Christmas before our divorce was final. I had hired a fake Santa to bring the gifts to the kids. He was a very happy Santa with a jolly red nose and apple rosy cheeks. On the second helping of spiced eggnog, I noticed that he was already shit-faced. I guess he had a little too much holiday cheer.

That Christmas in 1983 was the one and only time in my whole life that my dad actually put his arms around me and hugged me. I always thought it was the restrained and reserved Asian thing or that maybe he thought it would make my mother jealous, but either way, I had never been hugged or even touched affectionately in any way. Ever. I remember how weird it was to hug this thin man in his scratchy wool jacket and allow myself to sob into his shoulder. But I was despondent and a little drunk, and I would have accepted a hug from the devil if he had been there that night. It was a moment of closeness that we had never had before and never had again.

Johnny showed up looking like he needed to be somewhere else, and the piercing reality that we were no longer a couple filled the house with a thick air of sadness and despair. After he had visited with the boys, we went away from the others and just sat side by side on the couch in the den in an eternity of silence. He reached for my hand, and I let him hold it while feeling like I was dangling over a cliff and that hand was the only thing saving me from certain death. I stood there with my fingers intertwined with his, trying to memorize every detail and sensation, knowing that it might be the last time his hand held mine. There really wasn't much either of us could say, so I turned and leaned into his shoulder where I found a familiar spot. It's strange how we come to find comfort in the smells and textures of another person. After about five minutes, he patted my hand and turned to face me to say he had better go. We had a few moments of awkwardness, and then he was gone.

My grandmother always said he was "all hat and no cattle." I think that was some Texan way of saying that he was an arrogant douchebag, but she never said tacky things like that and was about as country as one could get. Truth be told, he was indeed arrogant and thoroughly convinced that he always deserved something better. The idea of being traded in for a newer model with fewer stretch marks and a sweeter bit of sugar was simply too much to comprehend. In my view, people stayed together forever, no matter what. Look at my parents. They fought like dogs and cats almost every single day and seemed to have so much horrible baggage, yet they stayed together every miserable day. I understood that. You invest so much in another person. Time. Energy. Sacrifice. Heart. How could you just throw in the towel and begin again with someone else?

The muffled voices of the others were floating around the room as I felt the life drain out of me a little more with every breath. The boys were playing their new video games and did not give a thought to my absence. So I sat in the airless room and put a pillow over my face. I could wail like a wounded animal and nobody would have to know.

I collected wolves and surrounded myself with their images in southwestern framed art, a giant throw for the couch, t-shirts and jewelry, and even on the back of my favorite jean jacket. Whenever we went to Taos or Santa Fe, I always went on the hunt for wolves in the souvenir shops. They were my spirit animal. I knew their plaintive wail and felt connected in some intrinsic, mutually wounded way. There were so many times I just threw my head back and howled to the moon. It was raw and primitive from a deep ancient place. I was a wolf mother, deep in the solitary wilderness, grieving for the loss of her mate.

Can't Find My Way Home
Blind Faith 1984

February 12, 1984 was the one year anniversary of Johnny's departure, and I was still seeing Dr. Klingspeter on a weekly basis. Initially I had sought therapy because I was suicidal and had to go twice a week just to keep myself together enough to get to the next appointment. I would come home from my teaching job and lock myself in the bathroom, lie on the floor and curl up in a ball, rocking back and forth and crying until it felt like my insides were going to burst. Chaun was eight and Justin was almost two now, and frankly, I could not tell you what they were doing when I was losing my mind behind those locked doors. But it got better day by day, and by the end of summer, I was taking several kinds of antidepressants and mood elevators and saving my crazy episodes until after the kids were both asleep. I moved into a rental house right across the alley from my mother and grandmother's house, so Chaun went back and forth constantly. I'm not sure why I did that, but I guess I felt like I needed any and all the help I could get. I think it was kind of like being stranded at sea. Do you go to the island of cannibals and wild beasts, or do you stay in the middle of the ocean with no land in sight?

My impatience with Chaun grew into occasional bouts of exasperation when he acted out. Of course, he had a bundle of feelings that he didn't know how to handle. I was certainly not the person to show him how to manage himself, and my mother was the poster child for how to drown in your emotions. He was close to his dad, closer than he ever was to me. Even though Johnny was focused on his career, he made time to take Chaun fishing or to the park to throw a baseball or a Frisbee once in a while. They actually did things together whenever Johnny could find time, and love-starved Chaun waited for those moments like a hungry dog. If I had not been so caught up in my own misery, I might have seen his pain and tried to help. But grief makes you stupid and depression makes you empty, and consequently, you are simply unavailable to participate in all of the messy business of life.

Chaun was defiant and destructive because he really had no one when Johnny left. Their weekly time together was now almost non-existent as we struggled to establish a routine that fit into our consuming work schedules. To make matters completely dismal, he was surrounded by a bunch crazy women all fighting amongst themselves like banshees. So Chaun broke things, did reckless stunts on his bike, even caught the backyard on fire. And with each destructive act, I became angrier that he was making an already difficult situation even more unbearable. I would grab him by the arms and scream and rant. On the really bad days, I would throw things across the room or slap him on the back of the head and yank him around by his shirt. Clearly, we were both out of control and had no idea how to work through our suffering.

My baby Justin must have known something was wrong with his mother; he was always so sweet and so quiet and so good. He played by himself and watched TV but never talked. People asked me if he ever spoke, and I had to pause and think about whether he had ever said anything at all. We missed beautiful time together because of all of the chaos, but I was trying to find my way back to him. When I was close to the edge, I'd tell myself that Chaun had my mom and dad and grams who all lived together and formed this weird triumvirate of dysfunction.

But then I thought, "What would happen to Justin if I just checked out? Where would he go? Who would be there for him?" And then I would stop obsessing about the sweet release of death and focus on staying alive. I just didn't know how to be okay, how to be better.

I kept him close most of the time after that spring. We sat together when I was on the phone, we ate together, and he even had his spot on my giant sized waterbed where we slept. He would get his bottle and be asleep long before I could exhaust myself enough to pass out, but when I looked at him lying there so peaceful and perfect, I felt shame for being so weak and so selfish to even consider ending my life. I decided that it was Divine Intervention and God had sent him to me to keep me alive and make me stronger. To make me want to be a better human being. I just didn't know where to begin.

Voices Carry
Til Tuesday 1984

Seventeen months after Johnny left me and after many lengthy legal battles, negotiations, and expenses, D-Day finally arrived, and we were officially divorced. It was July and already a Texas scorcher when I pulled up to the Potter County courthouse. I turned off the car and sat there for a few minutes to summon enough courage to go inside and fidgeted in my purse for the little tube of Clinique lip gloss, pulling the little mirror on the visor down so I could see what a tragic mess looked like. The song, *Voices Carry* came on the radio, and I sang along while tears suddenly began to flow. When it was over, I lit a Marlboro Light 100 and inhaled deeply as the sobs subsided. I pulled down the little mirror again, fumbled for mascara in my bottomless pit of a purse, and brushed on a little dignity before going in.

The proceedings were surprisingly quick. We waited in different areas, then into the courtroom, a few words, and done. Just like that. He walked out without even looking up from the floor.

He had started dating the receptionist at the urgent care center where he worked a few months before the divorce was final. He always called it a "doc in a box", but he had to work there because his drinking had begun to affect his performance and the dreams of building his own practice were fading fast. DeeDee was a high school dropout with a GED and two kids from a previous marriage. I guess he liked how sweet and subservient she was. I'm sure she made him feel tall because when side by side, she was so painfully small. Small-minded but gooey sweet and mousey in that nurturing way that some men can't get enough of. I am sure that a narcissistic alcoholic like him really enjoyed having a meek handmaiden like her to stroke his ego and fetch his beers. In her defense, she may not have been a genius, but she was kind. Anyway, it's probably a bad idea to measure a person's success as a human being by how many college degrees they can hang on a wall. I just needed to believe that academic achievement was the alpha and the omega because it was the only truly good thing about me. The praise I received for being smart was the only validation I had ever received.

About the same time, around spring break, I started talking to a substitute teacher at my school named J.T. Surprisingly, I had survived thirteen months of loneliness, isolation, and despair, so I was ready to have someone else to talk to other than my therapist. He was a good listener and an even better talker which made the vacant spaces feel less empty. Boy could he spin a yarn, and his stories were never-ending. All sizes and shapes of stories, too. Glory days from high school and childhood, magical stories of wizards and ghosts, marathon stories of fights that lasted all night, and political stories of his radicalization. I had never met someone with so many tall tales, and I was ready to listen. After a few bourbons, he became quite the entertainer.

So I guess in a way, Johnny and I had both finally started to move on. Oddly enough, there was a day in mid-June, about a month before our court date, when he came by the house and wanted to talk. We drove up to Fleetwood Park which was across the street from the house where I lived the year I returned from Lubbock without him. It was spring and people were out walking their dogs, and kids were scattered across the playground. We rolled down the windows and sat in silence for a few minutes, the wind moving our hair, the sun behind us. He looked different somehow. Smaller. Things do look smaller when they are farther away.

"I want to talk about Dee Dee," he said as his opening line.

Hearing her name caused me to realize that I was in a very confined space with someone who had another woman in his life. I felt like all three of us were in the car. I could swear that I smelled her on his skin and on his breath.

Then he said, "Just say the word, and I will never see her again. Just tell me you really love me still, and we can make all this go away. I don't have to stay with her. You know, I care about her, but she'll never be you."

I was speechless. Did he not know the stages of grief I had passed through and how I had mourned the death of our marriage in a way that almost killed me? Did he not know the countless hours of counseling and medications and suicidal ideations that almost took me out of the game?

"I don't know what to say. I am different now. It's been fifteen months, but it feels like lifetimes," I said in a voice that was almost a whisper. My heart was beating faster.

"We can try if you want to. It doesn't have to be too late," he continued without really hearing what I had just said, without acknowledging my pain or validating what I had experienced.

"I don't have anything left in me. I am close to being the empty shell I was when we met. Remember that girl? The one who was numb and dead and had no emotions? I am trying to be present for the kids. You have no idea what we have all been through, or you wouldn't even ask." I started to feel that creeping anguish coming up from the dark place, sitting on top of my chest making it harder to get a breath and wrapping its fingers around my throat.

"I asked her to marry me, Lily. This is the last chance we will ever have to stop this thing that doesn't want us to be together, this destiny we don't have to accept. We can try to reclaim it, save it. This could be our last time together to talk like this and have this chance," he said with the same sage-like wisdom that I had always trusted.

"Everything that I am and think and feel and believe is all because of you. You made me who I am today, and I will always love you. But sometimes love is just not enough," I managed to say as I swallowed back the tears running down the back of my throat.

"I am so sorry, Lily. I am so sorry for all of it. I didn't believe you loved me. I saw you with Justin, and I just wanted you to look at me like that just once. To look at Chaun and me the way you looked at Justin with love in your eyes. To see your face with the light in it. I know now that you loved me, just in a different way. I'm so sorry. Please forgive me," as he began to cry louder and louder. Not a few tears, but sobs that wracked his whole body.

The grief was awake now and seizing me completely, so I cried too as we held hands and made messy, wet, snotty sorrow. When we were spent and weak from the emotional deluge, when we had wiped it all up with wipes from Justin's day care bag from the back seat, when we were empty and hollow again, I drove him back to my house to get his car.

"I can't tell you goodbye," he said as he closed the door and walked away.

I sat in my car, paralyzed, for what seemed like hours. Staring straight ahead as the sun hung low on the horizon and cast rays of the last light onto my face. But I had to pick up the kids and get supper and get ready for school the next morning. Life does go on, you know, with or without you.

Chapter 5

Free Bird
Lynyrd Skynyrd 1985

*W*ith the advent of MTV, everything changed. Music was always a great balm to soothe the spirit, and what better way to experience music than on the big screen. One of the first things I saw was David Lee Roth doing his cheerleader jumps in the bright red leather pants to his hit, *"Jump."* Dire Straits was another fabulous wonder with their *"Money for Nothing"* and *"Brothers in Arms."* The first time I ever heard that song was on an episode of the best show that ever existed in the history of television. It was a game changer. Michael Mann added a musical soundtrack of hip music in the background that played with the cheesy dialogue and adrenaline chase scenes. You can guess what I am talking about. Pink flamingos in the opening credits, splashes of sunny Miami with a slick soundtrack? Sonny Crockett and Tubbs. Fast cars in the fast lane. *Miami Vice*!

Forget about the 70's shows like *Mork and Mindy* and *The Brady Bunch*—this was some cool stuff. Don Johnson in his pastel t-shirt, white linen pants, and sockless feet in his fancy loafers. The whole show was a music and fashion extravaganza. It was so easy to get sucked into the idea of Miami, expensive cars, speedboats, high rollers, and all that. I think I was ripe for an escape, so with MTV and *Miami Vice*, my life was somehow better.

In part, it was J.T. who helped me finally pull myself back together. He was born in a podunk town near Amarillo and raised on a real ranch with horses and farm animals and Mexican laborers and the works. I had spent most of my life thus far being the quintessential hippie chick although I missed the true activism and political significance of the 60's movement by a couple of years. He was a boots and jeans Roy Rogers kind of guy—me, a braless Jane Fonda-Gloria Steinem loving liberal. We had absolutely nothing in common.

The first time we met, it was in the teacher's lounge where we were allowed to smoke. Hey, it was the 80's and the campaign against cigarettes had not fully come into being. I practically sprinted four doors down to the teacher's lounge to hotbox a cigarette mid-morning, at lunch, mid-afternoon, and sometimes after school. That and a pack of cinnamon gum got me through the day. J.T. was in there smoking it up during his planning period, and I asked to borrow his lighter. The rest is history.

He was about 6'4" with big bushy brown hair that looked like he had a battle with it every day and lost. I liked how he liked to hear his own voice and would go on and on about all kinds of things. He loved politics and philosophy and music, so we actually had a lot to talk about, but I got the feeling that although he knew a lot of things, he really didn't know a lot of things. He lived with his mother which should have been a red flag to any normal female, but there was nothing normal about me, and I was okay with that. His dad had leukemia when he was a junior in college, so being an only child, he dutifully came home to take care of him and never left.

It is unfortunate that so many times in life we have such great hopes and dreams for the future, then life throws us a curve and all of it just floats away or sinks to the bottom of the sea. Someone once said, "It's not what happens to you in life that matters, it is how you react to it." I think J.T. would have had a completely different life if his father had not become ill and died a couple of years later. Things like that change you and change your priorities.

So we began our journey together: two lonely, mismatched people with some crazy stories to tell. We were sort of like drowning victims who just had to cling to one another in hope one could stay afloat and save the other. He always said he was the rescuer trying to save poor little me, his drowning lady. Funny how I thought he needed my help just as much. And so we went on like that, floating in a sea of discontent.

I should have suspected the degree of his impairment when I noticed his little pillbox that was always in his pocket. At first, I didn't think much of it, but after a couple of months I asked.

"What is that?" pointing to the box that had fallen out of his pants that were crumpled up on the bedroom floor.

"It's my medicine." he replied nonchalantly.

"For what? What do you need medicine for?"

He poured another jigger of Dickel into his glass, swirled it around, and took a sip. "It's for when things get a little crazy," he remarked and smiled his little boy grin that was both mischievous and disconcerting at the same time. With that, we left it alone. But as time passed, I discovered that they were pills to take when he had panic attacks and needed to calm down enough to dig out his mother's phone number that was written on the bottom of the box with a marker. It was his phone number, since he lived at home with his mother. Why did he need medication and his own phone number? I couldn't imagine what could happen to him that would paralyze him so much that he couldn't call home for help. She always came to get him wherever he was and return to get his car after the episode had passed. These crippling anxiety attacks were so overpowering that he had a dissociative response and lost all touch with where he was, who he was, where to go, all of it. I had been reading a lot of psychology books for years now, but I had never seen anyone this crippled by their condition up close and personal. When my mom lost control and went straight to crazy town, I bet she could remember her name and phone number.

Well, crazy always finds crazy, so we were the perfect couple.

The first holiday season together, I was shocked at how much time he actually wanted to spend with his mother. We even left our New Year's party to get back to his house promptly at 11:30 so we could read some scripture from the Bible, open a bottle of bubbly, and watch Dick Clark's ball drop. I thought it was sweet to think of his mom being alone and all, but it was a yearly ritual year after year.

One of the things that helped to me get up and get on were those endlessly long stories. I never knew what percent was fact and how much was fiction, but it was a little bit entertaining or maybe I was just that lonely for adult companionship. I have often wondered how my life would have unfolded if I had any family or friends to run things by. I think just the process of saying it out loud when you are telling someone about it helps you hear how crazy what you're saying actually is in real life. Keeping all the debates and doubts in your head with all the internal dialogue conversations is quite frankly a little maddening.

A lot of his stories had to do with how others had mistreated him or did something unfair to him. Like his basketball coach who ruined his life by Beanching him because of some personal grievance. Poor little J.T. And that mean little kid named Bruce who tried to punch him in the face back in 1st grade but had to be taught a lesson instead. Poor little J.T. Or about how all the women he had ever been involved with were immoral, crazy bitches. Poor J.T. And another story about how he was stalked by the F.B.I because he was a member of the S.D.S. (Students for a Democratic Society) while in college at North Texas State in Denton. Poor J.T. So persecuted, so maligned.

My favorite story was about how he rid a house of ghosts and knew how to summon shape shifters from the other dimension. Too many Carlos Castaneda books if you ask me. He said he was a *brujo*, a male witch. I instantly thought of Uncle Arthur, the male warlock on *Bewitched*, so this all sounded batshit crazy. His stories were fascinating with graphic details about what it's like to fly above trees and perch on a roof.

"So, what kind of bird can you change into?" I asked with some degree of incredulity.

"A big black bird with a wingspan as wide as my arms," he replied without any clue that I was not entirely buying all this hocus-pocus and went on to say he got all these powers from his Blackfoot Indian ancestors.

"A giant grackle. Do you turn into a grackle?" I asked with some degree of amusement in all of it. The whole idea was actually pretty interesting.

"No. You would wet your pants in fear if you saw it because it is a bird not of this world," he said with such conviction and a tone that sounded like he was sharing a precious secret unlike any ever shared with another human being.

I should have been having Blockbuster movie night with the kids and popping some popcorn. That's what a good mother would have done. But I dropped them off at psycho Mom's house for her to babysit while I gave my precious time to this lunatic with a drinking problem and a magic obsession. I decided to read the books and developed quite an interest in all the shamanism and such.

And it's not as if I had never had any experience with magic myself. Quite the contrary. My dad had a friend who was a Thai witch. Make no mistake, Thai magic is extra spicy just like the food. In the desperate year following Johnny's departure, I summoned her to help me numerous times. There was even one particular time that had serious consequences.

She asked me my intention, and I asked for a binding spell that would tie Johnny and me together for all time. She gave me some homework in preparation of the casting.

I needed some of his hair, an item of clothing, a photo, and a piece of paper with his handwritten words on it.

"You gib me dees ting, I make hem lub you fo-eba n eba. No ting can break dees. Strong magic," she said in her strong Thai accent.

So when we came back together a few days later, she brought a paper pyramid with little cones rolled up to make each row. She placed the items I collected inside the cone and put little candles in all the cones surrounded the pyramid and lit each one of them. Then she lit incense and began chanting and a low, deep, guttural way that made chills run up my arms and neck and asked me to take thread and tie items together while saying magic words and phrases. A tiny stick was used to set the whole cone ablaze and after it had burned to almost ash, she sprinkled an equivalent of blessed water, and it was done. And what is done cannot be undone.

A few nights later, I was standing in the kitchen finishing the dishes when I thought I saw something pass behind me. I dismissed it, but after a few minutes had elapsed, I saw something dark like a shadow move quickly from the hall into one of the bedrooms. This continued for the next few hours until I finally got a better look. They were maybe three feet tall, dark, fast, and furry things that you could see straight through to the other side. Not human, not animal, these translucent beasties were something else entirely. I grabbed both kids and we all slept together in my giant waterbed behind locked doors.

The next day, I told my dad what I saw, thinking he would know what it was since it seemed pretty clear that his witch friend had brought all this activity into my house. He said they were little mischievous demon creatures that probably wouldn't hurt anyone, just pranksters. Somehow that did not make me feel any better.

"So what can I do to get them out of the house? They scare me, and I do not want to cohabitate with them," I said.

"Okay. Get big cook pot and put whole raw chicken in there and put in da front yard in front of da front door. Next, get big stick or golf club and beat at da pot. When you do dis, say- 'be gone, be gone, go now, go.' Say it over and over. That should do et," he said as he stared straight ahead at the PGA coverage on television. Jack Nicholson and

Arnold Palmer were playing. My dad was an avid golfer who played almost every day of his life. That is where he lived. But now, he was a ghostbuster, and I was comforted by that idea.

I don't know what the neighbors thought, but I did exactly what he said. I used Chaun's baseball bat and a chicken from Albertson's. I guess it worked because I didn't see the little beasties again, but that was the last time I messed around with spells and incantations—the spicy kind that Thai witches do.

So with this in mind, it is easy to understand why I didn't feel compelled to show J.T. the door when he started talking about shape shifting into a giant black bird. In fact, years later in the midst of an argument that was comprised of some rather nasty threats from both sides, he said, "Go home and look what I sent you."

I was picturing a steamy pile of poo on my doorstep or something along those lines, but it was actually quite a surprise. When I opened the door to my bedroom, there it was. Sitting on top of the bookcase headboard on my waterbed.

A big black bird.

Bridge of Sighs
Robin Trower 1985

Parents can really do a number on our heads. For JT, it was his mother who had no intention to directly harm her son, but inadvertently crippled him for life. When he was only a junior at North Texas State University in Denton, his father had the misfortune of being diagnosed with leukemia. What followed for the next two years required John to return home. His intention was to help his mother care for his terminally ill father; however, he never left. I have often wondered if he chose to stay with his mother to care for her because he thought she might not be okay without him. Another possibility is that his father asked him to take care of his mother when he was gone, and perhaps JT perceived that death bed request as an imperative to remain by his mother's side forever. Maybe that's what she wanted, and she asked him to stay. But whatever the reason, his dreams and aspirations for a future that he had full ownership of was officially over when he returned home that fall in 1971.

Sacrifice often breeds bitterness. It also creates martyrs.

I never fully understood how JT could surrender his independence and his life for another person. I think his mother knew that he was weak, and decided to use his father's death as an excuse to keep him under her wing. She told me many times, "JT is never going to marry. If that's what you want, then you better look somewhere else."

I thought she hated me. I knew that my divorce was an issue for her, and she often quoted the Bible to let me know that her son could not possibly marry a woman who was divorced. I also wondered how she was so certain that he would not choose me and create a life with me. But that was not meant to be. She was right. He would never marry. He was already married to her.

This love triangle went on for the next six years. Six years of spending New Year's with his mother. Six years of attending church with them to prove I was worthy of something. Six years of buying his whiskey, his clothes, his vacations with us, his entertainment on the weekends, everything. The substitute teaching gig that caused us to cross paths was not something he did on a regular basis. In fact, if he substituted once a week, that was all he could manage. Soon, even that became too much for him.

I always resented the fact that I had to drag myself out of bed every morning before the sun came up and scoop up my children and scurry off to school. I completed this routine in trecherous snowstorms, when they were sick, when I was ailing, and through the most difficult of times when I certainly did not feel like I had the strength to get to work and make it through a grueling day. I pictured him walking through his house in his comfy socks and cozy pajamas, puttering around the kitchen, making himself a cup of coffee, and enjoying a leisurely morning. Maybe that was all too much for him, and he went back to bed and snuggled under the covers, napping until he was so inclined to actually get up and get dressed. Meanwhile, his mother worked 9-5 as a bookkeeper at an Affiliated Foods Warehouse. I guess he did not feel too guilty about either one of us navigating on icy roads through snowstorms, grabbing fast food in efforts to get to work on time, and forcing ourselves to get up and get going when we certainly did not feel like it. It didn't seem fair, yet I stayed and kept doing it year after year for six long years.

Every year was filled with church, soccer, Cub Scouts, pot lucks, lessons, work, more church, and more work. Even though I never felt completely at home in my church, I did have relationships and regular involvement. From Vacation Bible School to helping in the nursery to working in the kitchen during Wednesday night suppers and to being a choir parent, I was there, trying my best to be the best I could be and ground my children in the love of Christ. Soccer was also a regular routine for the better part of eight years as I coached Justin's team. The Thunderbolts, come rain or shine, come mud or misery, were out on the field kicking the ball. I loved it that I was Queen Bee in charge of a little team of kids who all thought I knew what I was doing. Justin loved having his mom coach his team, so that was more than enough to motivate me to continue year after year. To fill in any gaps of time, there were drum lessons, fencing lessons, theatre camps, cub scouts, pine wood derby races, and other sports like baseball and basketball. But regardless of all the activities and commitments and wonderful times, there was still a hollow place, a longing. A longing for that sense of family that had been missing since Johnny left us. I wanted to be part of a family. Not just for the kids but for me as well.

So at the end of the sixth year, I decided it was time to make a move. Try something different and hopefully better. It was a bold move, and I didn't realize how much the odds were against me before I even began. It's never a good idea to issue an ultimatum or try to force someone's hand. If they don't come to it themselves, trying to make it happen will only make things worse.

All my life, I had wanted to leave Amarillo. There were too many ghosts. Too many good ole' boys. And too many bad old boyfriends. I applied for a job in San Antonio and tried to imagine what life would be like if we all moved there. I reassured him that I did not expect him to work or contribute financially in any way. I even went so far as to say that I did not expect him to marry me which I had been holding out for and dreaming of since the first months that we were together. I simply wanted to take him away from his situation and begin a life together in our own home in a new city. I was offered a job in Northside San Antonio ISD and decided that the best thing I could do would be to accept the job and encourage him to come with me. For some reason, I was confident that I could persuade him. He had nothing to lose and everything to gain.

As it got closer to the time for me to move, the argument escalated. He said he was not able to leave his mother, but I assured him we would keep close contact and visit frequently. I put a deposit down on a nice house near the school where I was teaching and even paid special attention to the kinds of amenities I thought he might enjoy. It was a pale yellow house with sliding doors in the back that opened to an enormous backyard and patio where he could plant a vegetable garden and sit outside to smoke. After six years, this seemed like a very logical and reasonable next step. I was wrong.

"So I'm going to ask you this and ask you to think about it one more time. This is important because we've been together for six years. It's time that we take the next step. Everything is set up, and you have so many more opportunities in San Antonio than you do here. There's no logical reason not to come with me. You don't even have to work," I went on to say.

"I've told you before that I'm not going. Why would you think I would change my mind? When people tell you something, you don't hear what they're saying or if you do hear what they're saying, you don't believe it. You think you can change it and make it be the way you want it to be. But the truth is really, that I have always been honest and told you that I'm staying right here, and I'm not going to marry you, and I'm not going to move in with you. I'm certainly not going to move all the way to San Antonio with you."

So that was the dilemma. It's not like he hadn't said that hundreds of times before over the course of the last six years. My mind simply refused to accept the answer. Somehow I thought if I kept asking, eventually he would accept my offer. Sooner or later he would see the light. And I think we both understood that he was probably never going to get a better offer.

That evening in a moment of clarity, I decided to craft a letter of resignation to the school in San Antonio where I had just accepted the teaching position. It was not something I wanted to do. I had always wanted to leave Amarillo, and this was my chance. But I wrote the letter anyway, and I even went so far as to call my school in Amarillo and ask them if they had hired someone else to replace me yet. I asked if I could have my job back, and they said yes. So now I had the option of going or staying, and they were both viable options that were still on the table. My parents thought I was going, Chaun and Justin thought we were going, and everybody was ready to make the move. I just wasn't sure I could do it alone.

I drove up to Belmar shopping center where the nearest post office box was located and sat in my car with the letter in hand. If I dropped it in the box, I was probably never getting out of Amarillo and the dream to build another life in a new place would be over. If I kept the letter, then that would be the final decision to be brave and fearless and just cut my losses and go. But I would be going alone. And the fact that JT had refused to come with me only metastasized his paralysis and his unwillingness to get more than a few minutes away from his mother. That should have been a clear signal that the ship had foundered, and there was no use trying to get it back in the water.

We had been arguing for years about my obsessive desire to have a daughter, and from time to time, the idea seemed to appeal to him. But the reality of his situation would call him back, and before we could entertain any real progress, he was back in the clutches of his dysfunctional relationship with his mom. Clearly, he needed a rescue.

So I sat there with the letter in my lap and my hands folded over it.

I closed my eyes and prayed.

What if I just stay but give up on the idea that JT will ever be able to make a life with me? What do I want most, even more than a marriage? What if I stay and just say to hell with it? He has had ample time and wants a baby and a life, but DonnaLou simply won't allow it. So what if I just stop taking my pills and see what happens? I could do it by myself. I had been raising Justin and Chaun alone for the last six years, and I had become more and more proficient at the whole parenting thing. I wanted to prove that I could be a perfect mother. I wanted a little girl that could wear pink tights and a little black leotard and practice her plies with me.

So I let go.

I let go of the envelope and listened as it dropped into the mailbox.

Done. A defining moment for sure.

I had let go of a future that might have been better and claimed one that was rooted in baby lust and fear of being alone. It was a selfish and weak deed laced with fear and filled with resignation. It was a betrayal of a man who was only a child. I had given him everything I had to give, but he had nothing for me. That should have been the catalyst for ending the hopelessly flawed relationship. But I just couldn't do it. I was familiar with dysfunction, even comfortable with it. The unknown was just too much to imagine with so many uncertainties that were beyond my control. I thought it would be too much to handle alone, but what I failed to see was that I had already been alone for a long, long time. In that moment, I gave up on finding Mr. Right and settled for Mr. Good Enough.

That was August 1, 1989. I was pregnant by Thanksgiving. My baby girl was on her way.

Under the Sea
1989

One of the best parts of being pregnant is permission to eat for two. I always had a love affair with food, and with Chaun, it was banana malts from Baskins Robbins that helped me pack on eighty pounds that never really left me completely. With Justin, it was bean burritos with green sauce and apple burritos from Taco Villa. This time, it was anything I could get my hands on: cheese fritters from Char-Kel, chocolate cake, pies from Marie Callender's, and anything made with lemons.

So here I was yet again, knocked up and going solo. The mermaid princess once more, adandoned by the Monkey God, left to bear the product of their love all alone. I had seen expectant couples on TV and how the fathers-to-be reached over to feel the baby kick or make trips to the store to get snacks like pickles and ice cream for the mother of their child and maybe even rub their feet and do all those sweet things that are supposed to be done. I wanted that. But Johnny never did those things for me because of the circumstances of those pregnancies, and I sure wasn't going to get those things now.

Having a child is so rooted in perpetuating the idea that it will somehow make you immortal. This precious child will carry forth pieces of you into the future that will live on forever. It is inspired by vanity, selfishness, fear, ego, and arrogance. But make no mistake. I wanted this baby so very much I could feel a palpable hunger that could not be quelled by anything short of a pink, wiggly, blubbering, cooing, smelly bundle of joy.

I guess I felt like it would be another chance to redeem myself. To prove to myself mostly but to others as well that I could be a devoted, awesome mother. That I had battled my demons and climbed out of hell to stand victorious over all the darkness of my past. I believed it would bring out the best in me and complete my happy family. Chaun had just completed a successful year with very little drama, and my darling little Justin had just started kindergarten, so I was ready for my little baby girl.

I knew from the first moment I saw the pregnancy stick that my daughter was on her way. There was no doubt. And there was even a prophecy to reinforce that truth. My sister's husband who was a pilot for Thai airlines was kind enough to do a Thai star chart for me years before. Other family members had said he was accurate and never made mistakes in his readings. What he said to me held a sobering authenticity to it, so I knew it was true.

We all gathered around my kitchen table while he rolled out the results that were on large pieces of paper that looked like blueprints. I thought it was interesting how he was so interested in the stars and had such proficiency with it while flying up in the sky all the time for his profession. He was destined to be in the sky and know the stars. He began, "It appears that your son Chaun and you have a break between you. It is almost as if your mother is his mother. It is fractured."

I listened intently and felt my heart flutter a bit inside my chest as he spoke what I already knew. He went on.

"Justin is the child you are closest to and it will always be so even though he will not live close to you. Many years will be spent apart with a great distance separating you although you will remain close since you are bound and share parts of the same soul."

"Can this be changed? I mean, can part be true and other parts be altered?" I asked with heaviness upon me at the mere thought of having any distance at all between us. At the time, he was only about three years old, so thinking about a separation caused a sick feeling and tightness in my chest.

"It is difficult to say. As I see it now, this will be your future. It is your destiny. I do not know what might be altered," he replied with an assured tone like a doctor explaining a diagnosis.

I felt the warmth of the hot cup of tea in my hands and took a sip. It was Constant Comment spicy orange and cinnamon, and I briefly considered a life without tea.

"There is more. You will have another child. It will be a daughter, "he said as he turned the chart and pointed to markings and numbers and symbols.

"She will always be close to you geographically speaking, but you will not get along very well, and there will be friction and disagreements," he replied.

I felt like he was telling me something I already knew would come to pass. I felt her close even though it would be a few more years before she became a reality.

"Is there anything else I should know?" I asked with a sense of hesitation since the news he had just shared was not all the best in every way.

"I see you until the age of sixty, and then there is nothing. I am not sure what that means. But I see nothing on the charts after that time."

"Could that mean I die at sixty?" I asked with a feeling of discomfort.

"Maybe. But I see nothing, and I don't know exactly what that could mean," he said with a finality that magnified my uneasiness. I thought about the distance coming between Justin and me. I thought about how the chasm between me and Chaun was concrete and irrefutable. But then I thought to myself, "I will have another baby. I will have my baby girl. A daughter. She will come."

So the first thing I did was create a list of names. I wanted something that was both Caucasian and Thai. In the book of baby names I had purchased before Justin was born, I wrote down all the names that had something to do with the ocean, my place of power. My love affair with the sea would resonate in my daughter, and it would become her power as well. I then took the names to my dad to see if there was anything that had Thai translations.

Of course, the first thing that came to mind was the magical mermaid princess from my childhood. Suvannamaccha, the beautiful Thai mermaid who loved deeply, sacrificed with grace, held fierce loyalty and courage, and possessed a spirit so much larger than life. Clearly, a name like that would be too much for any child to carry in a place where everyone had simple, country names like Billy Bob, Bobby Jo, Betty Sue, and of course Sara Lee.

My dad told me about his friend who was a local allergist from Bangkok who had a daughter and attempted the same thing I was trying to do—create an amalgamation of East and West. Her name was a Thai word meaning flower, and it was also a name in the baby book of names meaning "from the sea." It was perfect.

Maressa. My little mermaid.

Hang on Loosely
38 Special 1990

Years later when I reflected upon this time, it was so achingly apparent that my motivations were mostly selfish and that I had a rather Machiavellian notion that the end justifies the means. I was confident that I knew what was best, not only for me, but for everyone involved. I believed that if everyone would follow my lead, they would be much better off. I could fix them, fix everything… if they would just trust me and follow my lead. It was selfish, arrogant, and a hallmark quality of my codependency that drove me to make decisions that were not mine to make.

Since this time, I have come to learn that if you get things the wrong way by forcing them to happen when they wouldn't happen otherwise, it usually ends badly. There's a reason why we don't get some of the things we want. In the bigger plan, in the Universal order of things, it is simply not meant to be.

Every Easter, Donna would make a cake for JT. It was a good old-fashioned coconut cake with colored coconut and little malted Easter eggs on top. Sometimes she went all out and put little marshmallow bunnies on it, too. They would make a ham with all the fixins and go to St. Stephen's Methodist Church and sit in the pew that John T. Sr. had purchased with a little bronze colored plate with his name on it so everyone would sit on it and remember him forever. Needless to say, I was not included in the celebrations that year.

When I told JT that I was pregnant shortly after the new year, there was a real hullaballoo. A brouhaha if you will. He was terrified and acted accordingly as one in danger of losing their very life—or livelihood in his case. Donna would not believe it, would not have any part in it.

"Lily, you are a terrible person, you are a liar, I know something that makes all of your claims just a big fat lie."

"Why can't you be happy that you're going to be a grandmother," I offered as she went on to explain how JT could not possibly be the father of my baby.

"I tell you what Missy, JT had an accident, an injury, on the farm when he was a boy. When he was about twelve years old, he got kicked by a horse very hard in his testicles. The doctor told him that he could never have children. That horse made it so that JT is never going to be a father. If you are really pregnant, then I'm sure you don't even know who the father is. I'm sure that you are just trying to pin this on my son. He is innocent and is not the father of this child. I want you to stop calling here. I want you to stop coming over here. And I want you to leave my son alone. You hear me? Leave us alone."

I was so humiliated, so exasperated at her ridiculous words. It seemed completely irrational that she would act like this. Everyone knew how loyal and devoted I had been all of these years.

"I warned him all along that you were nothing but trouble. I told him to watch out for a woman like you. You were married and divorced. And it is adultery for him to carry on with someone like you. You cannot marry again in God's eyes, in the eyes of the church. And if you come over here again we're going to call the police. You are not fit to marry my son, and you are just a whore. Just like every girlfriend he's ever had. All of them just a bunch of whores who tried to ruin his life and take away all his opportunities to do anything with himself. His life would be so much better and so different if he had not gotten involved with all of these terrible women. So we know what you are, and you better leave us alone. You hear me?"

I heard it.

I made a few more phone calls, begging, pleading, imploring him to listen to reason. Asking him to trust that this was really happening. All he had to offer was a suggestion to end the pregnancy. He proclaimed himself to be such a God-fearing man, it seemed odd that he would suggest that I murder his unborn child.

Unlike many women who get pregnant to trap a husband, I no longer expected him to marry me and live happily ever after. Of course, there was a time, for years in fact, when I had hoped for that. I tried to be worthy. I tried to earn his affection and be the person he wanted me to be, but the reality was that I would never have been able to measure up; his expectations were unrealistic. From the beginning, I was always doomed to fail. I understood that now.

After over six years together, I decided that nothing would ever change. This was it. I had to go forward with what I needed to do to complete my life. Certainly I loved Chaun, but we really didn't have much of a relationship with my mother's self imposed surrogacy. And

Justin was absolutely everything to me. Everything except a little girl. And I couldn't be everything to him, either. We were lonely, and I thought a little sister would help to complete our little family and make us more complete and whole.

Months passed. The summer of 1990 was long and warm, and the 4th of July was exceptionally dry and hot. After driving around and looking for a place to do some fireworks, we found a big field with no houses nearby behind the Meadow Park area. The boys wanted to do bottle rockets and other pyrotechnics. I was only weeks away from my due date, but none of that would interfere with a little Independence Day fun. What I remember most about that night was the sheer speed at which fire can move.

We have only been there for maybe ten minutes when someone sparked a little ground fire. Within seconds it spread ten feet wide and three feet tall. The boys were screaming, kicking dirt on it, and running in circles around it. It took a moment for me to actually realize what was happening.

We had started a fire.

By the time the boys were back in the car, and we were tearing down the dirt road to get help, it looked like a conflagration with a wall of fire in the rearview mirror. In a panic, I decided the closest area to find a phone would be the hospital in the Meadow Park area. It was a short distance, maybe half a mile, but it seemed to take forever.

There is something hilarious about an extremely pregnant woman and two children running as fast as they could, screaming in a panic, asking for a phone to call the fire department. Of course, we pretended to just be passing by. And with of the chaos, we slipped away as soon as we heard the fire trucks coming. Unfortunately, no homes were destroyed by the fire. We later heard on the news that it had reached an area that spanned over a mile before it was contained. After that, we limited our celebrations to a few black jacks and a few sparklers in the back yard every 4th of July.

The night I went into labor, I had been at school all day. In fact, it was the first week of school. Back in those days teachers returned in the middle of August and students came towards the end or even after Labor Day in some districts. I had not even met my students yet since we were still doing back to school preparation.

After months of trying to contact JT, I finally gave up earlier that spring and had not seen him or spoken to him since February or March. But I couldn't help it, put all of my dignity aside and called him when I knew it was time. Of course, he didn't answer. So I called the neighbor lady teacher friend, Maureen, who had agreed to drive me to the hospital. The sad thing is that we weren't really even friends, and I didn't know her that well. The connection was that she just lived around the corner and was the ex-wife of JT's best friend. Somehow she got mixed up in it but didn't seem to mind helping out someone who was essentially alone.

After what seemed like an exceedingly difficult labor lasting nearly nine hours, my little girl was in my arms. She had these huge brown eyes unlike anything I had ever seen. She was so silent and alert; I have never seen a baby so composed. It was almost like she was a very old soul who had finally arrived and was contemplating the new environment.

My sweet Justin came into the room all smiles and excited to be a big six-year-old brother to this little strange looking creature.

The first thing he said was, "Can I touch it?"

My heart was full as I saw Justin carefully reach down to touch the baby's hair. He seemed genuinely amazed. Of course he was. He had such a sweet soul and kindness about him, and my heart swelled with love for him and my little girl.

Then Chaun awkwardly moved closer. I don't suppose he ever really felt like part of the group when Justin and I were together and now there was another child to take my love away. At the time, I didn't really understand how hurt and damaged he was. He was broken by his father's departure, by my own inability to deal with any of it, and the way I had always discarded him for more important things. I felt such love for him as I looked into his bright blue eyes, but I knew that my love was not enough to heal him. First school, then Justin, now this little pink prophet. All taking me away and leaving him alone to grieve or dwell with my mother and her madness.

The boys had both developed some kind of relationship with JT. He had been a regular fixture in Justin's life since he was eighteen months old and since Chaun was six. His withdrawal and absence now was even more acute to them. There were a few times when I could hear Justin crying alone in his bed at night. JT had always been around since he could remember, and now he was absent. It broke my heart and made me hate JT for being weak and cowardly, incapable of being a man, much less a father. We were all alone together.

So we all went home and resumed our routines. Our house that I had purchased within a couple of months after declining the San Antonio move, was located just around the corner from my childhood home on Royal Road. I bought it because I knew my dream of leaving Amarillo was once again on hold, and I was not going anywhere anytime soon. And because of the tall trees. When I was little, I often retreated into my large backyard because it was a safe haven away from my mother. I don't know what she did in the house all day, but I do know that I didn't want to be in there with her. My backyard had tall poplar trees, pretty mimosa trees with pink blossoms, a couple of towering elm trees, and the whole yard was encased with rows of purple iris. Wisteria draped over the fence so that it created a fairytale like retreat. Since that was my only place of peace growing up, I sought the same forest-like retreat in the first home I ever purchased.

The home I found which was right around the corner had three tall cottonwoods in the front yard that towered over the house. There were two large fruit trees that blossomed pink and purple every spring and a tremendous silver Ash that provided a canopy over the entire backyard. These trees, their enormity, and the foliage surrounding the house were exactly what I was searching for. Soon after I purchased the home, I'd drape little white sparkly lights around the front of the house and in a few of the trees. I kept these lights on which I'm sure might have displeased my neighbors, but I loved the way it always looked like sparkly stars surrounding my house in a magical way. The cottonwoods made a musical rustling noise as the wind moved the leaves that glittered like coins in the sun. Wisteria was always my favorite vine, so it soon covered the front porch area with long strands of purple blossoms. I collected wind chimes to accompany the sound of the leaves. It created the most peaceful place I had ever encountered, and I often sat on one of the Beanches in the yard and just listened. It was one of the few times that things seemed right with the world, and the turmoil within was quiet for a time.

About a week after I returned home from the hospital with my little sweetie, I looked out of my large picture window to see her father, JT, on a bicycle passing by. I sat down and kept looking out the window, and before long, there he was again. Over the next thirty minutes he passed back and forth several times. After a while, I walked out into the yard and as he saw me, he fell off his bike with his heavy body hitting the gravel-covered street like a big sack of flour.

Clearly he was flustered and embarrassed as I asked, "What are you doing here?"

He grappled for words and mumbled something unintelligible.

"Do you want to come in and meet her? Your daughter?" I asked as I studied how silly he looked with his tall socks and frumpy shorts. He actually didn't look familiar to me in the way someone should look, but it had been over six months since I had seen him and a lot can change in six months.

If there were ever an awkward first meeting between a father and a child, this must have been it. He didn't seem to know what to do as he stood over the bassinet with an alert but calm baby staring up in his direction.

"You can pick her up. Hold her," I suggested.

My feelings were a stew of mixed emotions as I watched this 6'4" child lift my daughter up and cradle her uncomfortably in his arms. After a minute or two, he replaced her in her bassinet and seemed completely overcome and confused.

"Can I get you a glass of water before you head home? It's hot out there, and you have a long way home," I said as I walked into the kitchen. He followed and stood there, uncertain about what to do or what to say. After he drank about half the glass, he set it down and opened his arms to me. It was like an invitation for a hug. My first impulse was to step back and turn away, but I paused and then moved towards him.

I didn't really feel anything as I stepped into his arms. It seemed unnatural and disingenuous. I thought to myself, "Why have I never noticed that he looks crumpled and broken? His head is so big... it bothers me a little. I must have been blindly in love because now I am seeing that he is not a real man in any healthy, normal sense of the term. He's a boy, an insecure little boy in a big odd body."

So with that hug, I opened the door to him and his presence in our lives. Later, years later, I wondered if he ever would have summoned the courage to knock on my door and request to see his child. I really don't think so. If I had not ventured out that early September day to invite him in, I think he would have stayed at a distance forever— constantly longing for us and continually denying us—thus remaining the dutiful son forever.

Bittersweet Symphony
The Verve 1994

I never found my love for him again after he abandoned me during my pregnancy. I guess I sort of loved him like a you love a family member, a family member that has behaved badly and disappointed everyone. Or like a family member that is impaired in some way but nobody wants to admit it or talk about it. But there we were. Raising this fuzzy headed little wonder.

Maressa was exactly what I had hoped for. She was perfect in every single way. Every moment with her filled me with such happiness. But in spite of the joy, the situation itself was difficult and awkward. Her father represented the antithesis of everything I believed to be true. The only common ground I could discover was that we were both Democrats, could talk politics, and liked much of the same music. I was amused that he had such wild and crazy hair that was never shaped quite right, wore his pants and socks pulled way up high like a nerd, sang *This is the End* just like Jim Morrison, and never missed a chance to tell me how much he actually looked like Jim Morrison. Mostly, I loved that he loved his daughter, even though it took a paternity suit to prove it. Were there hard feelings after the litigation was over? How could there not be? It was ugly and messy and did irreversible damage to our innocent little girl. I don't recall what motivated me to file a paternity suit against him in the first place, but I regretted it a thousand times over for a thousand different reasons. I guess it was that compulsion in me to demand justice—force people to own their actions and make everything as it should be. Problem is, they never do, and it never is. If I had left well enough alone, there could have been peace. After the test results, he responded in good measure with a custody battle that lasted for two years. I developed an ulcer and other manifestations of the constant stress, and it was rough on Maressa as well. I had not possessed the foresight to anticipate such an war with so many casualties. This was not what I wanted for her, being stuck in the middle of two feuding parents.

The custody battle took him straight to Crazy Town for sure. My neighbor, Mr. Reinkel, reported that he saw JT in the alley, fishing giant Hefty bags of my garbage out of the dumpster behind my house and putting them in his car. What could he have possibly been hoping to find? In a paranoid response, I developed the routine of putting my garbage bags in my car and driving around the neighborhood to find different places every week to throw away my trash. I felt guilty and humiliated for driving down alleys behind people's houses looking for dumpsters in places where nobody would see me do my dastardly dumping deed. This went on for almost two years, and at one point it became unsustainable. I had placed two large trash bags in the trunk of a rental car that I had for over a week while my SUV was in the shop for some major work. It was summer, and the Texas heat was unbearably hot. Almost a week passed when I noticed a foul odor coming from the car. After searching under the seats and all over the place, I realized the source of the stench was not actually in the car. As an afterthought, I decided I should check out the trunk. When I opened it, my brain could not process what I saw well enough to respond with anything except a gasp and a scream. There were thousands if not millions of maggots covering every inch of that trunk and swimming around all over the garbage bags I had forgotten to take to a secret location. It smelled like a decomposed body had been in that trunk for months. What does one do in a situation like this? This is what my life had come to, and nothing had prepared me to deal with it.

And then there were the mysterious yet troubling phone calls. They happened at odd hours day and night, and when I picked up the phone, I only heard what sounded like a train or sirens or other weird sounds. When he tired of harassing me on the phone, he decided to stalk me. On countless occasions he followed me whenever I left the house—to the grocery, to Blockbuster video, to Taco Villa, to the gas station. He would roll down his window and prop up his giant camcorder with VHS tape and start recording me as I walked into the store or put gas in my car. It should have been intimidating, but it was too ridiculous to be threatening.

When the dust settled, the realization that I would be sharing my child with this nearly forty-year-old man-child was a rude awakening. As with all parents who share custody, there was a profound undermining of one another's authority, and the result is most often the same. The child loses respect and trust for both rather than choosing which version of the truth to embrace at the expense of the other parent.

The years settled into a routine of visitations on alternate weekends and weeks away in the summer, but we made it through. We even managed to co-parent with some degree of civility. I was her Girl Scout leader, choir parent at church, dance teacher, and personal assistant. I provided tennis lessons, piano lessons, and cotillion. I coached her basketball team and t-ball team just as I had coached her brother's soccer team all those years. I wasn't even sporty and had never played any of these sports growing up, but I did it to be involved and to make that memory together. To etch my place at the top of their childhood memory chart.

Justin grew from the sweet little savior he had always been to a rock-star student and formidable talent. He played guitar and drums and performed in the local community theatre as well as in my dance recitals. He discovered golf during the summer between 8th and 9th grade year when my dad died and left him all of his golf clubs. Before long, he joined the varsity golf team and headed to Ross Rogers Golf Course every day after school to practice with Coach Grayson and his golfing buddies. It was a great fit and gave him something meaningful that would stay with him for the rest of his days. I remember going to the driving range on summer nights to hit a bucket of balls when I was a little girl, and now Justin was carrying on the tradition. In the following years, he took his clubs along on our annual vacation to California and played up and down the coast from La Jolla's Torrey Pines to Anaheim's Dad Miller's Golf Course. We even visited Pebble Beach, and although we couldn't afford the ridiculously cost prohibitive green fees there, he did manage to chip and put on a green while I pulled by the side of the road on 17 Mile Drive. To this day, I wish he could play the course and that I could come along in the cart to witness it. Clearly, that is one of those things you hope to do before your time runs out, and then it just does.

My dad spent so much time at the golf course, and now I understood. Justin found solice there, and I witnessed the peace and presence of being that happens as you're out there on the course. I felt it as I sat in the cart and watched him play. There is a kind of zen about it. When I imagine my dad in some version of heaven, it is a lush and endless golf course. He is chipping and putting, walking silently from green to green, looking as if everything is right with the world as the blue sky stretches infinitely above him. Now Justin had that same contentment and oneness with everything around him. I thought he was perfect. He was the real deal, the whole enchilada. Gorgeous, charismatic, brilliant, funny, kind, talented, and a great golfer to boot. I was the luckiest mother on the planet to have such exceptional children.

But Chaun was another story. Although he was also handsome, smart, and creative, he was unable to use any of his gifts. Maressa was barely walking when Chaun left home and never came back. Its strange how one event, one moment, can transform your life completely. Maybe it had been a storm brewing for years and just waiting for the tipping point to arrive. It seems like these things just come out of nowhere and just blindside you before you even see it coming. Chaun had a good freshman year in high school, our terrible fights had subsided, and it looked like he was on the right track- ski trips with friends, activities at church, good grades at school.

But in one day, everything just changed.

His dad came to see him on his fifteenth birthday, and he was belligerently drunk.

He said, "Boy, what's your name again? Do I know you boy?" as he stumbled around reeking of alcohol.

"Lily, who is this boy and why's he looking at me so crazy? You wanna punch me in the face, boy? You think you're big enough to take me down?" he went on as I tried to corral him and get him out of the front door.

I looked at Chaun's face, and it was broken like he had just gotten news that somebody died. I guess in a way, somebody *had* died and that day, he realized it for the first time. Something just snapped, and he was never the same.

Alcohol has a strange effect after continued daily abuse. The person with the addiction gradually slips away, loses their identity, and forgets who they are and the things that define them. Studies have been done to show how the brain of a lifelong alcoholic is visibly altered on an MRI or CT scan. Scientists who have studied these brains can see a discernable difference between their brain at twenty and their brain after years of drinking. They can also actually identify differences in the brains of healthy people and those with addiction. It changes a person. Not just their behavior, but their very essence- what makes them who they are.

Almost immediately, his acting out became so severe that I could not harness it or protect Justin or Maressa. He was consumed by a tornado of anger and pain. It's like he just caught fire and was standing there burning to the ground, and everything I tried to do to subdue it only made the flames grow hotter. It was a familiar fire, one that had consumed me in my youth. I understood its power.

I could not reach him, so I just let him go. In what seemed like moments, he had collected his things and moved into the garage apartment at my grandmother's house where my parents had moved a few years earlier. My mother was so far gone with her own brand of madness that they became a force that was not to be reckoned with. I had to keep things together and protect the youngest ones, the ones who still didn't know what Chaun knew. It didn't really occur to me at the time, but maybe there were other reasons for Chaun's inability to be okay. Perhaps he was impaired by something, a disability of sorts, some personality disorder that made it impossible for him to find peace or be at ease in his own skin. I wish I could have helped him, but I could barely manage my own life and was simply too ill-equipped to find the source of his malaise. What followed for Chaun placed him in the worst possible environment to be able to grow into a healthy, happy individual. My mother indulged his every teenage whim—all night parties with drugs and alcohol, endless supplies of Reese's Peanut Butter cups and Dr. Pepper as meal replacements, accessibility to guns and other weapons, and encouragement to share these wild adventures the same way she had quizzed me down about my similar, self-destructive escapades during my adolescence. When I threatened to have him sent away to a boy's school or a rehabilitation center, they would both fight back with a fierceness and ferocity that crushed any attempt to save him or rescue him from her grips. During the months that turned into years after he left, a kind of resignation set in that flooded me with guilt. It was like trying to save someone drowning. They clutch onto you and struggle and fight and kick and scream while they push you under and drag you to the bottom. Before you know it, you are both under water. I couldn't save him, so I let him go.

Losing Chaun was hard enough, but I worked so many hours a week that I did not have time to adequately grieve his absence. After the incident when Johnny took both Chaun and Justin on a ski weekend to Red River, NM and got so wasted that he let Chaun drive the car around the treacherous mountain roads, I told him I would call CPS and get his doctor's license revoked if he did not volunteer to take a 'fatherhood sabbatical' and leave us alone until he was sober. To sweeten the deal, I told him he would not have to pay any child support while he was working it all out, so of course he accepted the offer without hesitation. He never paid another penny. JT's mother didn't give him enough allowance to help out much with any significant child support for Maressa, so after teaching all day, I was forced to "moonlight." Teachers don't really make enough to support a family as single parents, so I always had multiple jobs. Maybe JT had no work ethic and was okay just taking money from his mother, but I had no one to help me. I wanted to provide a quality of life for my children that was comfortable and respectable, filled with not only necessities but also all of the perks from having a parent who was an educated professional from a family of diplomats.

Teaching was in my DNA, and my favorite job was a Tuesday night freshman comp class I taught as adjunct faculty at the local community college. I had always dreamed of transitioning into college academia when the opportunity presented itself, and the evening classes were a first step to that end. There was something very appealing about the idea of building a secure life by teaching students to build their ideas and ways of articulating those ideas. We explored ideas and perspectives and wrote about our conclusions. It was a challenge but one I enjoyed tremendously. All of the jobs that afforded us our yearly trek to Disneyland and the orthodontic bills and piano lessons and theatre camps were not so fulfilling. One desperate spring when all of the pipes ruptured under the house, I even delivered pizza for Domino's to pay the bills. I never felt like it was Beaneath me. In fact, I thought it was good to be in touch with the working class who struggle and work multiple jobs that all pay starvation wages. Everybody has a story. I remember this one old guy named William who was over seventy and schlepping pizzas because social security didn't send him enough each month to pay his rent and bills. Nobody should forget how these worker bees support the whole colony and yet fail to get the respect they deserve.

The hardships were eased by the joy and satisfaction I received from family life. Our routines and activities were fulfilling in ways I never imagined possible. When Justin and Maressa were happy, I was happy. We all enjoyed one another's company, and even though we all felt the acute absence of a father in the house, we managed quite nicely without one. My fierce independence and trooper spirit carried me through exhausting days and late nights at multiple jobs. It was all worth it, and I had no regrets about having another child. How she came to be was somewhat unethical and perhaps even immoral, but there was no doubt that I had so much to give, and she enriched all of our lives tenfold in return. I wanted to prove to myself that I could learn from mistakes and be the perfect mom, even if I had failed Chaun in just about every way imaginable. It was a second chance to get things right and have redemption. It was another chance to create the family we all dreamed of. These were the halcyon days.

Spice up Your Life
Spice Girls 1997

Summers were a great time to do fun things with the kids since I was off work from the first of June until late August. We were enthusiastic members at the Dolphin Swim Club, indulged in an annual trek to Disneyland and Southern California, and watched a lot of TV that we never had time to watch during the school year. For years, it was *Buffy the Vampire Slayer* that kept us glued to the sofa with munchies in hand.

It was also time to take advantage of the opportunity to make a little extra cash to pay for lifestyle upgrades. As a single mother on a teacher's salary with a negligible amount of assistance from anyone, the quality of life I wanted to afford my children was always a challenge to provide. It seemed like I was always trying to figure out how to increase our cash flow without asking for any handouts. I took a variety of additional summer jobs, always mindful of the kids' schedules and always attempting to minimize my time away.

Maressa attended an elite little parochial pre-K at St. Andrew's Episcopal school where she met a lovely little friend named Babs. What began as a temporary babysitting arrangement evolved into a nanny-like position that continued for the next decade.

Babs and her little sister, Mary, spent every free moment, holiday, and break when they were out of school in my care. Their dad, an art museum curator, brought them to my house at 8:00 am every morning, and they stayed till well past 6:00 pm. It wasn't long until they felt like extended family, surrogate daughters if you will. I even went to their house occasionally on the weekends when their parents had a special date night or event. I read bedtime chapters of *Harry Potter* or other chapter books while rocking in the great chair in their elegant bedrooms that transcended anything I could afford to do for Maressa. Their mother, Susanna, was a brilliant attorney at one of Amarillo's oldest and most prestigious law firms. She was the moneymaker, the power parent, the decision maker in their family, but her job did keep her away for long hours. That was fine with me because I liked having all three girls together. It was a good dynamic that created friendships that would last a lifetime. They had their safe place with me where they were encouraged to speak their mind, be fearless, discover their voice and strength, and be creative.

We had a busy schedule during those summers together. The girl's parents, liked to keep their daughters busy, so I became chauffeur for tennis lessons, violin lessons, swimming lessons, and other activities. Since I was a teacher for the vacation bible school at our church, we all spent a week there doing Jesus crafts, singing songs, and playing games. I was also den mother for their brownie group, so there were summer meetings with activities and overnight camping experiences. Babs suffered from some kind of social paralysis that included panic attacks that would happen randomly when in groups of people.

"Lily, can we go now? I'm not feeling well. My stomach hurts and I feel like I am going to faint," she whispered to me as we began another circle game with all of the little brownie scouts jumping up and down and screeching with glee. I certainly understood how she could feel like that.

"I think you are okay," I reassured her. "If you need to sit down, you can come over here and just sit here and watch awhile."

"I really don't think I can be here. Can we just go, please? I don't feel good. I can't breathe, " she implored with huge eyes that always looked absolutely terrified.

"Do you have your inhaler?" I asked as I led her to a chair at a table in a corner of the room away from the others. "Just sit this one out and watch. We'll be through soon, and we'll go home and change before going to the pool. You'll feel better in a minute," I reassured while trying not to minimize her discomfort or be dismissive.

Other times, I was confidant and advisor. As she became older, nine, ten eleven years old, we had many conversations about her life.

"My mom wants me to do such and such or have a play date with so and so, but I don't want to," she sometimes said.

"You really need to learn to talk to her. Be honest. Tell her what you're thinking. You are old enough now so that communication is really important. Especially with your parents," I advised.

"But she doesn't listen and I am scared to say anything," she went on.

"But you really need to advocate for yourself. How will she know what you need or want if you never tell her? How can she make good choices for you if you don't tell her the things she needs to know to make those choices? Help her. Talk to her. Just say what is on your mind. And if she doesn't listen, do not whine and cry. Just tell her how it makes you feel when she ignores your feelings. Use your words. They are powerful tools," I coached as she twirled her hair on her finger and considered what I was saying.

As time passed, she became stronger and braver and managed new situations with some reluctance, but she got through them without too much distress. Her sister was another story and came with her own set of issues.

Mary was a couple of years younger than Babs and Maressa, and was an adorable towheaded little cutie pie, only three years old when I first became the nanny. Her mom would tell me to be sure to "baste Mary with sunscreen frequently at the pool since she was so light complexioned" and it was all I could do not to smile as I pictured a plump little turkey getting basted for holiday dinner. She loved food, so I kept snacks like Otter Pops, chips and queso, Oscar Meyer wieners microwaved on a chopstick, and my famous homemade macaroni and cheese with about half a pound of Velveeta and a whole stick of butter in it. We also ate a lot of chocolate chip cookies with ice-cold milk as a regular treat. I never understood how Babs could eat all these foods and stay paper-thin. I probably should have chosen a leaner offering for my charges, maybe some fresh veggies or low-fat yogurt, but the other food made them happy and that, in turn, made me happy.

One of our annual traditions was the official "War of the Cottonwood Beetles." It was a savage bloodbath with fluorescent green blood. Cottonwood bores drill holes in their favorite soft wood trees and feed on the yummy sweet sap all winter only to emerge fat and sassy in the summer to fornicate indiscriminately and lay eggs in the ground for the next generation of nasty boogers. Loving my majestic trees that towered over the house and provided such tranquil rustling music as the sun made their leaves glimmer like a million gold coins, I could not let these foul vermin live. So we armed ourselves with spatulas, hockey sticks, golf clubs, and other weapons from our domestic arsenal and descended on the yard to search and destroy. Babs smashed them with bricks, Mary bludgeoned them to death with kitchen utensils, and Maressa and I captured them in plastic cups and doused them with BBQ lighter fluid, then tossed a match on them to watch them burn alive. No mercy. The crazy thing is the way these little beasts would shriek and scream when we torched them. And the most exciting part was when one of them would screech and then pop like popcorn, exploding into the summer sun. We were warriors and murdered maybe a hundred disgusting goo-filled creatures over the course of the summer.

We may have been ruthless exterminators, but we possessed a softer side, too.

Maressa's bedroom was like a Disney on crack princess-palooza extravaganza. The walls were pink and purple with the solar system on the ceiling. There was a hanging mosquito net surrounding the canopy bed with ribbons and glitter and ballet tulle. Empowerment came in many forms through the years, and they were convinced they had magic powers to do enchanted dances to summon rain and do witchy rituals they saw Willow and Tara do on *Buffy the Vampire Slayer*. And of course, I encouraged anything that might make them strong, fearless, and powerful women someday.

I loved those summers. We went to the country club almost every day to swim and eat chicken fingers with French fries that came in little paper boats. We did a lot of crazy things in the name of boredom or bonding. There were the late night sleepover toilet papering excursions when we all dressed like ninjas. And the holiday contests to see who had the best decorations were always a blast. If they bought illuminated deer; I bought two. When they added another baby deer; I added a nativity scene. Justin hoisted himself onto the roof to design impressive Christmas light configurations to compete with their festival of lights. It was endless and not just at Christmas. We decorated at Halloween, Valentine's Day, and even Thanksgiving. One year I had an entire life-sized scarecrow family with pumpkins and a bale of hay to create an autumn vibe, and they in turn strung a million orange colored lights all over their house and yard.

Making movies was a popular hobby for years. I would buy a fresh blank VHS tape and charge up the batteries on the good 'ole 10 lb. camcorder, and we would head to Medi Park or some other setting to make movies. One of the first was *Moulin Rouge*.

Of course, Maressa wanted to play the leading fabulous beauty played by Nicole Kidman in the film, and Babs took the role of the hapless suitor played by Ewan McGregor. That left the role of the little guy, Toulouse-Lautrec, to Mary. What a hoot to see Maressa singing "Diamonds are a Girl's Best Friend" while Mary affected a French accent for her sparse lines and Babs swaggered around with a mascara moustache wearing Justin's pants and suit coat that were three sizes too big.

My favorite home production had to be the *Buffy Musical*. Everyone had their own personal vampire stake and other Buffy paraphernalia. They knew the parts word for word, so it became a huge undertaking to do the musical numbers with dancing and complicated choreography as well as all the acting parts with dialogue. I had so much fun filming them, and they had the time of their lives doing it. Win-Win for everyone.

I liked doing things like that with Maressa and her friends. I choreographed a Spice Girls song and dance for the school talent show one year, and after that, I became the go to person when anybody needed to learn a dance for some reason. Since I did a dance recital twice a year with my classes at school, I had a lot of choreography just waiting to be re-purposed. But it wasn't all fun all of the time. There were times when something would present itself that needed attention. Little clues and hints that Babs and Mary might have their own challenges and that all of us were doing the best in less than ideal situations.

One of the most disconcerting moments during the carefree summers with the girls had begun with what I called, the "Mystery of the Disappearing Bedspread." It most certainly demonstrated some appropriate reaction, but looking back now, it's just weird and a little bit funny.

Maressa's room was a work of art. Pinks and purples, canopies and netting, castles and mermaids. But her favorite bedding was not colorful or Disney-fied. It was a white chenille bedspread with little decorative features sprinkled about. I noticed one day that there seemed to be fewer and fewer of the little puffy balls that looked like bunny rabbit tales. I had walked into Maressa's room without warning to witness Mary sitting sneakily and sheepishly on the bed. It was very suspicious. And then it hit me.

I hesitated, then sat down beside her.

"Do you know what has happened to the little fluffy balls here?" I said as I pointed to a couple of bare spots that were missing the embellishments. She suddenly looked full of shame. I was immediately curious. Why would sweet little Mary destroy the bedspread? What was going on here, I wondered.

"Mary, if you know what happened to them, please tell me. I promise I won't be mad. You can tell me. Did Maressa and Babs have anything to do with it?" I inquired.

"No. They didn't do anything," she said with a heavy dose of guilt in her words.

"Mary, did you do something with the little decorations on this blanket? It's okay. I know sometimes things just come apart easily and they were probably loose or dangling anyway, Right? Is that what happened?"

"No, Lily. I didn't pull them off," she murmured as I noticed that her words sounded muffled.

"Mary, please. Just tell me what's going on," I continued as I noticed that she had something in her mouth.

"Mary, what's in your mouth? Are you eating something in Maressa's bed? Remember, that makes her bed full of crumbs and that makes bugs come," I said.

She continued to hold whatever it was in her mouth. I stopped and thought about what she could be eating. Chips, a banana, what was it? Then it suddenly dawned on me.

"Here," I said as I held out my open hand in front of her face. "Just spit it out. It's okay."

After about a minute where I could tell that she was really debating about what to do, she leaned over and opened her mouth and out it came. A wet, disgusting looking little clump of white that looked like chewed up paper which, by the way, she was known to eat from time to time.

There it was. Mystery solved. Mary was eating the bedspread with the tiny white puffy balls.

"Thank you, Mary. Please promise me you won't do this anymore. I'm not mad or anything. I just don't want you to be sick. It's not good to chew on things like this," I said as she sat there looking really ashamed.

"Do you spit them out somewhere?" She begins to nod slightly, Are the other pieces in this room right now? Did you flush them down the toilet or something?" I asked as I tried to figure out what she had done with all of the chewed-up balls. Then I looked at her, and suddenly I just knew.

"Did you swallow all these little cotton puffs?" I proceeded as gently as possible.

Mary had a little nod affirming my speculation. She had swallowed them all. Maybe twenty total. Each one the size of quarter. At least it had been a slow snacking over a period of weeks, maybe even a few months.

Needless to say, that bedspread had seen its last days. I scooped it up and put it in my "Going to Goodwill" pile, and within a couple of days, Maressa had a beautiful new comforter for her bed. One with no edible parts on it.

We're Outta Here!
Ramones 1997

The death of nineteen-year-old Brian Deneke was a defining event in Amarillo and led to a lengthy court case that made national news. It didn't surprise me at all in light of the fact that I had seen first hand how intolerant and cruel our locals could be, and if you take into account my experience with the criminal behavior of some of Amarillo's most elite ruling class, it goes without saying that even murder could be forgiven if you have the right zip code or family connections.

There was a group of jocks at Tascosa High School who called themselves the White Hats and consisted mostly of white boys from middle and upper-class families in Southwest Amarillo. And much like the jock rapists from my youth, these guys could do no wrong. Their victims were never other kids from their own peer group; they were exclusively the ones who did not fit the white, conservative, Baptist, country club profile.

I couldn't avoid making the connection between their exploitation of minorities, females, and others who did not mesh with their status quo view of the world. It was fourteen-year old me in 1971, and now it was a new batch of home-grown terrorists who targeted the punk rocker demographic in 1997. Strange how the dynamic never changed. The mere sight of a spiked collar, leather vest, or Mohawk hairdo hurled them into a ravenous rage.

The night Brian Deneke died, I was with a group of students at the I-Hop on Western Street to enjoy a pre-cast party after wrapping up our fall dance recital at school earlier that evening. After the show, we headed over around 10:15 pm and got the big table in the back for our group of about ten students. Maressa was with me and only seven years old at the time. She had recently begun dancing in my recitals with a few kids from her dance class with Miss Bluejeans at ALT or in dances with my students who needed a cute little human prop for their choreography needs. That year, I did a generational piece with her as the child, a student in my dance class as the young adult, me as the middle aged person, and an elderly couple I recruited from the Senior Citizens of Amarillo line dancing group as the older couple. It was a profoundly moving performance that received a standing ovation.

I remember the I-Hop night manager, a skinny bespeckled guy in his late twenties with an unfortunate skin condition, called for everyone's attention and made the announcement that there had been an incident in the Western Plaza Mall parking lot across the street, and we would need to go directly to our car and not try to get a closer look because they had set up barricades. He said we would need to take the east exit behind the restaurant because sections of Western Street had been blocked off because it was a crime scene. I didn't think too much about it at the time and figured that it was a car accident or someone trying to break into a store at the mall. It was nearly 11:45 pm when we finally left, and there were way more police cars with lights flashing than I had anticipated. There were two policemen waving us along with flashlights as we climbed into our Ford Explorer and made our way home.

The next day it was all over the news. "17-year-old Tascosa jock uses his dad's Cadillac to run over punk rocker, killing him instantly."

Vehicular homicide. The prep was arrested at 6:00 am the following morning before we could grab our Pop Tarts and rush off to school.

Later that day as I continued to revisit the horror of that night at Western Plaza, I kept wondering what could have caused these young people to gather with such dark intentions. Before the murder happened, throngs of teens had already assembled in the parking lot and were escalating the conflict with verbal threats and drunken bravado. It goes without saying that alcohol was a factor for both sides, enhancing their superhuman and reckless courage. Two disparate groups, each with their raging hormones, mob mentality, and poorly functioning pre-frontal cortex. It's a wonder more didn't die. It was a recipe for disaster.

But then I remembered it was Amarillo. The toxic cocktail of privilege and poverty consumes everyone in this little town of 163,000 unfortunate souls. Sides are drawn, literally, to separate the rich and the poor, the white from the darker colors. In 1997, North and East were mostly low socio-economic minorities and South and West were more affluent and overwhelmingly white. It had always been that way. Even when I was little, I heard my grandmother talk about the drive through "Nigger Town" to get to the municipal golf course where my dad liked to play.

And where were the parents, the proverbial gatekeepers of the kingdom, on that fateful night? Many of Brian's friends were throw-always and orphans. And not unlike many of my students with similar homes, they self-parented because the adults were all absent, working, or impaired. They had to champion themselves, defend one another, build their own tribe. These faux families had one fatal flaw. They were children. Children who most often do not possess the resources they need to craft healthy, successful lives.

And what about all the jocks and preps, star athletes and straight-A students who crowded shoulder to shoulder inciting violence like spectators at a blood sport in some ancient coliseum? Where were their families while their children gathered to drink themselves stupid and wreak havoc without consequence? Were they at the country club having dinner, enjoying a night at the symphony, or hosting a backyard bar-b-que? Perhaps Mom knocked back a couple of Chardonnays and silently slipped away as Dad slapped junior on the back and reminded him to "put on that raincoat, son, if you're going to dip your pole in the pond. There's all kinds of nasty things you might catch from some of these girls these days," as he grabbed the keys to the Cadillac and headed out the door.

When Brian Deneke was murdered in the parking lot that night, and the perpetrator walked free with only probation and some modest monetary restitution, it clearly demonstrated the inequities inherent in our small community. What is the price of a human life? Apparently, it's only $10,000 since that was the amount of his fine. That and ten years probation.

The girl in the car with him who most likely screamed and covered her Mary Kay face as he sped up and hit the body with a blunt force trauma that tore Brian Deneke's collar bone right out of his shoulder, said the thing she remembered most was what he said right after the impact.

"I'm a ninja in my Caddy. I bet he liked that one."

Creep
Beck 1998

In retrospect, the 90's were my favorite decade. They weren't all sunshine and rainbows, but both of my children were with me and my life was filled with their energy and laughter and hope. Had I known that the time would come when I would long for those days, I would have stopped and listened and soaked it all in for a little longer—absorbing it into my bones so that it would always be a part of me to carry forward. They went by in a blur, but there were so many good memories along the way.

So I was busy, working, saving, planning, doing so many things that I thought I had to do. Vacations and lessons and activities and so many things that seemed so necessary at the time. And the drama with JT was always a distraction and sometimes a crisis, but it was a slow playing movie in the background that just kept looping over and over. In the forefront of it all was a full calendar of events.

In addition to teaching junior and senior English year after year, I built a dance program at my school. It was an elective that grew over the twelve plus years I grew it, and we converted the stage in the auditorium into a dance studio with mirrors on the back wall and portable ballet barres. When my babies were three or four, I found roles for them in our recitals that I produced in December and again in May. Full two hour shows with ten to twelve choreographed dance performances and a couple of guest dances. We hosted everything from sword tossing mariachi dancers to senior citizen line dancers to Christian mimes from the local evangelical church. It was so much work but oh so rewarding.

Gang-bangers donned ballet cups and tights to perform ballet pieces to Enya if I agreed to let them do a break dancing piece to 80's disco music. I cast Maressa in Spice Girls or Britney Spears dances, and we even crucified Justin on a giant wooden cross to the tune of the Joan Osborne song, *What If God Was One of Us?* At the time, it seemed like a great idea that was very visceral and evocative. He also did less provocative pieces like the soft-shoe with a cane and top hat and swing dance numbers with the girls in my class. He even did an ensemble piece to Van Morrison's *Moondance* where he had two or three rather spectacular lifts that he managed to execute quite well. I was constantly thinking of new ways to dazzle my audience and put together a great show. We always had a grand finale with balloon drops or fake snow coming down in chunky globs while dancing to Tori Amos' *Winter.* We were constantly selling gummy worms and M&M's to raise money to buy expensive costumes. It was a centerpiece of that entire decade.

And of course, there were the sports experiences that marked the 90's. I coached soccer, T-Ball, basketball, and other competitive teams so I could have the experience with my kid's teams. For eight seasons, I schlepped out to soccer practice a couple of times a week and spent every Saturday morning at a game come muddy rain or sizzling sunshine. The mighty Thunderbolts. Undefeated for three or four seasons, we were the badasses of the Panhandle Soccer Association leagues. And if that weren't enough, I coached the infamous 3rd grade girls team named the Smashing Pumpkins—a terribly inappropriate name for a group of six-year-old T-ballers with the misfortune of being assigned pumpkin orange jerseys. We smashed the ball, and we wore orange; therefore, Smashing Pumpkins stuck. Looking back, it was a silly team name that probably violated everyone's finer sensibilities. Many campaigned for Orange Crush as the team name. Very telling.

Church was also an important feature of my favorite decade. While I felt a little weird and out of place in Sunday school, I was always there—working in the nursery, volunteering as a Cherub Choir parent, or commandeering the kitchen and the breakfasts and potlucks. That's where I got all the incredible Methodist casserole recipes. Nobody does a lime jello-mold or a rice and broccoli bake like the Methodists.

I loved the music of the 90's—Radiohead, Nirvana, Pearl Jam, Green Day, and Talking Heads to mention a few. We played music trivia in the car, and there was always singing wherever we went. When Babs and Mary were with us in the summer, they loved to forward the CD player to Snoop Dogg and Dr. Dre every time I went into the Toot 'n Totum to pay for gas or grab a Diet Coke. I'd hear, "Hold up, hey…" as I approached the car, and I'd see three little white girls aged eight to ten bouncing up and down and getting their "gangsta" on. It was hilarious. On difficult days, I liked Dave Matthews' *Grey Street*. Music was a salve for a weary soul and an enhancement of the times that were already pretty good.

Every couple of years for about seven or eight years, I raised American Eskimo puppies—partly because we needed the money that we most certainly did, but mostly because Maressa and the girls, not to mention Justin, absolutely loved the puppies. Fuzzy, white snowballs with adorable puppy breath that they could hold and pet and play with endlessly. I thought that every kid should have that experience with baby puppies or kitties or something soft and snuggly. Pookie lived to be almost twenty and had two female companions through those years. One of them, Hootie, ran away in a thunderstorm, and we never saw her again. The other, Tabitha, died at age nine from complications after a litter of puppies. It was such a horrific experience that it ended the puppy days, but we still had Pookie, and he was quite a character.

I felt like I was a supermom by being so devoted to my children and trying to provide them with as many richly textured experiences as possible. Many years later I realized that my codependency was still alive and well, and I was essentially exploitative with my children, taking as much or more than I was giving—feeding off of them in unhealthy ways instead of having any boundaries or identity outside of my relationship with them. I should've maintained a private life outside of the one we shared, but I didn't. To make matters worse, my parenting of Chaun was an abysmal failure, severed, disconnected, broken. After moving into my mother's house shortly after the birthday incident with his drunken, dissociative father, he never came back. During those lost years, his life was so far removed from the seemingly idyllic life that Justin and Maressa enjoyed. I think we were all lonely and none of us had a clue how to be whole or healthy.

There are phases of development that people are supposed to pass through on their way to adulthood. One of the most important is the attachment phase. The evolutionary theory of attachment suggests that children come into the world biologically pre-programmed to form attachments with others because this will help them to survive.

Children typically form only one primary attachment, and that attachment figure functions as a secure base for exploring the world. In a sense, the attachment relationship acts as a prototype for all future social relationships. It goes without saying that my relationship with my mother was disrupted, thus my healthy development was thwarted. But my bonding with Chaun was also interrupted, and he was similarly ill equipped to face the world. Justin and Maressa fared much better, even developing attachments that perhaps went too far in the other direction. Bottom line, we were all lacking healthy development for one reason or another and trying to navigate through life with little direction, no compass, and little hope of finding our way.

Chapter 6

Round Here
The Counting Crows 2000

Everyone thought 2000 would bring some millennial meltdown at midnight, but for me, it was Justin's graduation and departure for college that ultimately proved too much for me. It was hard not to feel his absence with every breath and every step. Maressa was gone every other weekend and Wednesdays with her father, so I had new time on my hands that compelled me to stay even busier with more work and more commitments. Depression followed me like a shadow that was always right behind me.

Justin had a teacher his junior year, Dr. DeLarant, who was an eccentric academic of sorts. He spouted off quotes from literary texts and had a penchant for dressing up like Don Quixote. At one point, he played the role in the local community theatre production of *Man of La Mancha,* and the newspaper did a story on Amarillo's very own Renaissance man who was handy with a sword and an authentic seeker of windmills. With my penchant for strange intellectual types, of course I had to date him. Dr. D was handsome in a grizzled salt 'n pepper, nutty professor kind of way. He was truly quite erudite, espousing philosophical ideology and quoting the ancients, and I loved nothing more than spending time with men who were brilliant and quirky. Needless to say, we did not make it past a couple of evenings together. As it turns out, he had something that could best be described as a foot infatuation, and I cannot tell you more except to say that I did not get the kick out of it that he had hoped for. He was such a gentleman who attempted to get off on the right foot while I tried my best to toe the line, but toward the end, I had no choice but to stand up in defense of my ticklish tootsies, boots in hand, and be on my merry way. Nonetheless, he owned a vast intellect that was worthy of exploration.

This classical romantic high school humanities teacher possessed a passion for the liberal arts and a love for one liberal arts school in particular. St. John's College was the third oldest college in America and was ranked among the best institutions of higher learning in the country by *Newsweek* year after year. Their "Great Books of Western Civilization" curriculum with no grades, no competitive sports, and no fraternities or sororities was an intellectual's paradise. With twenty years of teaching English literature, composition, and rhetoric behind me, I salivated at the idea of ever becoming one of their esteemed tutors. Justin was equally infatuated. So that was that.

It was a 4 ½ hour drive to Santa Fe, New Mexico, and the magic of the high desert captured his interest right away. The school was nestled into the side of a hill, adobe buildings were staggered on different levels that absorbed the energy of their surroundings, and a pretty little meditation pond graced the main terrace. An amber wash covered the campus as it did the whole city of Santa Fe. I'm not sure why the light always had such a warm and inviting glow, but it was a perpetual pink and purple at dawn and dusk with air that was crisp and cool and always filled with pinon.

Over the next four years, I served on the Parents Advisory Board, published the *Parent's Papyrus*, hosted freshman dinners, attended numerous seminars, tried to keep paces with the student reading, and attempted to be as involved as any parent could be who lived 4.5 hours away and worked multiple jobs. The first year, we talked every day. I mailed boxes of monster cookies every week. I drove to Santa Fe or Justin drove to Amarillo at least once a month. But the second year, the phone calls lessened to twice a week, and visits stretched further apart, and by his junior year, he had met his future wife, Miss Jenny Bailey from Grants Pass, Oregon.

On the way home from the long weekends at St. John's, Maressa and I would turn up the CD player and listen to Rusted Root or Dave Matthews. One of the most iconic songs of the time was Adam Duritz's *Round Here*. We knew every word and would put our voices behind the plaintive words about people stuck in an oppressive place at the wrong time with the wrong people. We talked about getting out of Texas and moving west to the ocean, to the "Big Blue" as we so often called it. It was a seductive idea, one filled with hopes and dreams and imaginings about a place where nobody was lonely or outcast, where the sky and the water were always blue, where everyone was happy and free. It was a place in our hearts and minds where we would go just as soon as she turned eighteen and no inevitable custody battle would tear us apart—tear her apart. All we could do was talk about it. Where we would live… maybe we would bring Babs and Mary who were her primary companions through the years. Maybe they could come, and I could just cook my famous macaroni and cheese and make chips and queso and keep their beachside bungalow tidy while they became rich and famous and lived out their dreams in La La Land. We would go Ruby's on the pier in Huntington Beach every Sunday to eat dinner and enjoy the mini ice cream cones while sitting there over the water gazing out into the big blue. We would bring Justin out to finally golf at Pebble Beach and ride along in the cart looking for deer. We would shop at the resplendent Beverly Center and study the sky full of stars at the Griffith Observatory overlooking L.A. We would run slow motion down the beach with our long hair tumbling behind us like the girls on *Baywatch*. But for now, we would have to just wait. Wait and sing songs about getting out of this place.

Why did the world outside Amarillo, Texas call to us so profoundly? Maybe we were simply sad. Our lives had all had their share of disappointment, loneliness, and turmoil. Perhaps the distant shores promised something better, something more hopeful. There was a kind of romance about it. Everything was better in paradise, and we vacationed there every year like we were practicing for the day when we would come and never leave. We would be glorious. Me—fortunate and free. Maressa—fabulous and famous. And Justin would golf all day every day. Happy and complete as the world opened its arms to us, Maressa and I would finally become sisters of the sea. Beautiful mermaids with golden, glittery tales that sparkle and glimmer as we swim into the vast horizon.

When Justin and Maressa were growing up, I always tried to open the world up to them to whet their appetite and ensure that they would never be content in a box, confined by the limitations of a podunk town with their rigid boundaries like their rigid views. We traveled, not just to California, but to Europe as well. Educational tours allowed me to take my children on trips with a group of students who would travel during spring break to places like Paris and Rome and Florence. Justin and Maressa would be right there beside me soaking it all in. I think it was Mark Twain who once said, "Travel is fatal to prejudice, bigotry, and narrow-mindedness, and many of our people need it sorely on these accounts. Broad, wholesome, charitable views of men and things cannot be acquired by vegetating in one little corner of the earth all one's lifetime." Our journeys took us far from home, and we often spoke of one day escaping the confines of the Texas Panhandle with its myopic world views. So many people there accepted the limitations of their geography and politics and religion as if they were completely content in their little boxes. The world was bigger for us and calling to us, and we were brave enough to go. It was just a matter of time.

"You have to be fearless and unafraid of going out there and discovering your place in the world," I said as we sat on a train passing through Montreux, Switzerland on our way to Paris, the fog lying heavily on the waters of Lake Geneva at the foot of the Alps.

"It is a big world with so many opportunities to experience varied and richly textured experiences that will enhance the tapestry of your life," I would continue as we ascended the steps toward the Basilica of Sacré-Cœur de Montmartre and its sun washed travertine stone quarried in Château-Landon (Seine-et-Marne).

All of their lives, I tried to make their world bigger, open their minds wider, offer them more choices. I wanted them to become citizens of the world, steeped in diverse cultures, and globally astute.

"Someday, you will come back here and sit at this table and see all the twinkling lights and hear the clinking of crystal and be grateful that you have a good life, and you will share that with your partner and know you are blessed," I prophesied as we dined on the candlelit patios of a cafe in Florence.

I call these frozen moments. Snapshot moments. They are the precious moments in life where the mind records pictures and smells and feelings and sounds. They can be harvested forever, dredged up from the mud of memories to replay over and over with every detail in perfect place. For just a second, you are there, reliving that moment. I captured a frozen moment in that dimly lit far away courtyard. I remember the light in Justin's face, the eager anticipation for all that life was going to bring. His eyes were wet and filled with songs and laughter. His smile was easy and effortless with nothing tugging at the corners, pulling it down. Maressa was glowing and confident that nothing would ever come her way that would be too much for her. No misfortune. No sadness or lonliness. She had her family who loved her and in that moment, she was invincible.

So while the world would wait a while longer, Santa Fe would not, and Justin packed up his black Mustang and drove up the hill of our street and disappeared into the hills of New Mexico. My two sons were both gone now, but I still had Maressa. She needed me. She loved me. Most importantly, she trusted me. She thought I could do no wrong.

Everything in Its Right Place
Radiohead 2003

The Christmas holidays 2003 changed my life in profound ways. Justin brought Jenny home to Amarillo the same day finals were over at St. John's College, and Maressa and I had made cookies and other treats for days in preparation. Her parents lived in Oregon, so she was not returning home until summer. We were excited to have them since it was pretty lonely most of the time for just the two of us.

Suddenly, with no warning, I became critically ill.

I had never been so ill that I just checked out completely. I slipped into something that resembled a coma. I could not wake up, I could barely get to the bathroom with assistance, and I was unaware of what was happening around me. The fever spiked to 104 as I was rushed to the hospital.

As I lay in the emergency room, it was like a fog had descended and everything was surreal and disconnected. Doctors were baffled but knew it was severe enough to keep me and begin a battery of tests: first an MRI followed by extensive labs and x-rays. Time passed and nothing could be confirmed, but meningitis was suspected, so there were clusters of people jabbing needles in my back to draw fluid to see if that was the case. After more hours, they said there wasn't enough definitive evidence but that it did look like a type of encephalitis-meningococcal virus. They made speculations such as megalovirus compounded by other words I couldn't quite process, but let it suffice to say that I was one sick puppy.

They said the fluid in my spine was carrying viruses that were also affecting my brain and all central nervous system functions. That explained the brain fog, disorientation, and confusion even after the fever had resolved. Days passed and I was still disoriented and unable to get up and about. A week passed, then the ten-day milestone—still sick and weak and suffering from whole body aches and pains. The headache and accompanying nausea made it impossible to eat, and the only thing I was able to do was sleep and sleep some more.

The holidays ended, and Justin and Jenny returned to St. Johns. Then Maressa and I were left alone, with little support. It was tough to return to school and at first, I only went in for half days. JT came by to make sure she got to school and had some dinner in the evenings, but I struggled to be ambulatory and struggled to get strong enough to return to work full-time.

Mid January arrived, and I had been incapacitated for almost a month. I finally managed to return to school, twenty pounds thinner and pale as a ghost. I had to stop every few steps as I ascended the stairs by my classroom, room 202. The weirdest most disconcerting and absolutely unexplainable thing was that the right side of my face and neck were completely numb. It was such a strange sensation to be unable to feel anything at all. After several doctor visits, I was referred to an infectious disease specialist at the Amarillo Diagnostic Clinic who did a million more tests for everything from Lyme disease to lupus and Legionnaires. His conclusion was that I had suffered a super viral infection that was encephalitis-meningitis on steroids or something that had left me with nerve damage to my CNS with autoimmune markers. The illness had apparently damaged parts of my brain and body that would never recover.

It was four or five months before I regained complete sensory capacity. The fog had lifted, but the landscape somehow seemed different, unfamiliar. Recovery from a life-threatening illness is a slow process, and it is impossible to know if and when you have regained your former health and well-being. For me, I think my whole system was rebooted. I actually felt a bit fried, sort of like the light-headed dizziness you get from staying out in the sun too long on a hot day. There must have been some kind of nerve damage, but it felt more like brain damage or maybe like those movies where they bring someone back from the dead, but they are not quite right; they aren't themselves; something is different. It was such a strange sensation and a challenge to get accustomed to. It certainly allowed me to gain a new respect for health. I guess it's true, "Sometimes you have to lose something before you really appreciate it."

Grey Street
Dave Matthews 2004

Life has a funny way of showing you things and surprising you in the most ironic ways. The choices you make in a moment, right or left, stop or go, open or closed, can change your life forever. I remember the exact moment in time, the precise turning point when my life went off the rails.

I had somehow managed to make it to forty with the last decade or so being stable and responsible. No smoking, drinking, partying, nothing. Just work, church, sports, lessons, with occasional movies and trips to the mall and a yearly vacation for good measure. I kept my head down and devoted all my time to work and kids.

Maybe some things are just meant to happen. It's destiny or fate, written in the stars. Or maybe some people are just supposed to be together for whatever reason. Perhaps they are old souls who knew one another from previous lives. Regardless of the reason, we find the people that become the fabric of our lives, woven so intrinsically, so organically into our very being that there is no way to cut them out or remove them, even if we wanted to, even if we knew it would be for the best.

The first time I ever remember seeing Bean was at the annual production of the *Nutcracker.* He was leaning on a wall, looking terribly out of place and out of time, sporting a sweater vest that no one had worn since the 80's. I paused to reflect how strange this young man appeared. He could have been a ghost or something, I thought to myself as I dismissed him completely.

When the spring semester began at the college where I was adjunct faculty and taught freshmen comp, I saw him again. There were over 2,000 students, so it was entirely possible to never cross paths with all students unless they were actually in your class, but his friend was one of my students, so this odd duck sometimes waited outside the door after class. What an unusual pair. I was usually pretty 'spot on' when deciphering what a person was about, but not these two. They were walking contradictions with confusing signals that perplexed me. They were both pretty but strangely dressed with quirky mannerisms. I decided to go with bi or gay and dismissed it without further thought.

Towards the middle of the semester, I was in my classroom one evening packing up my briefcase and preparing to go home. It was late, and I had taught senior English all day and three hours of rhetoric and composition that evening, so naturally I was tired and eager to go. I felt eyes on me and looked up to see the same strange fellow at the door. His friend, Julian, was not there that evening, but before I could fully register what was happening or survey the situation, he was walking me to my car and asking about my class. It was a curious conversation that only lasted for minutes, but it stuck with me until the following week when he reappeared. Before long, his friend left alone and the evening walk to my car was routine. I discovered that he worked in the library in the computer center, so when I took my students there for their final research assignment that semester, we sat at his computer station and talked. The library job was his work-study position, and he was studying graphic design. By Christmas break, we agreed to meet for coffee or lunch or something. Maressa would be at her dad's for a chunk of the holiday, and Justin would not be home from school the entire time either. I had a new friend.

It was my eighth year as an adjunct at the college. The English department was comprised of four full-time tenured instructors and three or four adjunct instructors. Two of the tenured folks were older men, past seventy and nearing the end of their careers, so since I had seniority, excellent evaluations, and a reputable standing as adjunct staff, it was very likely that I would be able to assume any vacancy that might occur. I had been told that I was next in line, and that although the college was stepping away from offering tenure, they had promised to hire a full-time replacement for any impending retirements. They said they would not chop up the position and distribute it to the adjuncts in order to absorb the course load. I was set. This had always been my plan, and it was on track.

Bean was an unusual person, barely twenty, yet old beyond his years. The first thing that caught my attention was that he knew music from my generation that was a bit uncanny. He also knew a smidgen of politics, a crumb of psychology, a driblet of philosophy, and just enough about the world around him to appear savvy. None of that was very remarkable, but what he did know oceans about was the metaphysical world and all the intangible mysteries of the universe. The eyes he used to filter the world were fresh, different, and unique. It was like spending time with a young Carlos Castenada talking about diving into the abyss and discovering the nagual that reveals itself to us if we are seekers. A nagual is one who is good at talking, shape shifting, vision quests, and is like a witch or brujo sorcerer with an animal co-essence. Carlos Castaneda used the term "nagual" in his books to depict a person who has the skills to guide people to new areas of awareness and alternate realities just as valid as ours. I had read the books because of JT nearly ten or fifteen years before, but now I had discovered a wild shamanic guide to assist in navigating the abstract multi-dimensional journey.

When I was growing up with my Thai family who rejected all aspects of Western culture from food to religion to music, I became aware that there was more than one path to enlightenment. My father practiced transcendental meditation and was a monk in the Buddhist temple for a couple of years. Living in that environment increased my awareness of a whole level of consciousness beyond what most people in Western civilization practice in daily life. There was talk of reincarnation and Nirvana, and I opened my mind to a broader worldview of religion and spiritual evolution.

So Bean became the missing ingredient in my recipe for happiness.

In addition to the discovery that we were kindred spirits based on our unconventional ideas and perspectives, there was also a darker side. We were both orphans, both literally and metaphorically, and we had been forced to parent ourselves. Naturally, our attempts often led to disaster as we both had a history of delinquent behavior that included drugs, promiscuous sex, petty theft, and a variety of associated character flaws. We held anger, sadness, defiance, and despair close to us so no one would know how damaged we were. This recognition of the underbelly of our relationship drew us closer. My textbook co-dependency kicked in full force, and his opportunistic, exploitative nature responded in perfect synchronicity.

Bean had ambitions; he desperately wanted to be more than the wild child he had been. Countless "throwaways" had crossed my path through my years of teaching. They needed a mother or a mentor or a savior, and I think I became a teacher so I could help all the kids in all the ways my teachers could have helped me but didn't.

This was different.

I never thought of Bean in the same way I did the students I had helped through the years even though he was only a couple of years older than them. He was creepy yet intuitive, full of crap but surprisingly profound, fake but authentic. A walking paradox. And there was a quality about him that made me feel like I had known him a long time, maybe even reunited after a long absence or something. It was weird, but tangible. I came up with some crazy explanations for the familiarity. Maybe he was the reincarnated baby I lost when I was still a child myself. Perhaps we had been together in a previous life. Maybe he was my grandfather who died in 1973. Before coming to the conclusion that I was just reaching for a justification for this unnatural connection, allow me to revisit the ideas that swirled around me as I grew up in my very un-American, unconventional, unstable home.

"What going on in dis room? I'm hear some ting hit da wall. Is it problem?" my dad quietly inquired as he stood in the darkened doorway of my room with the hall light illuminating him from behind and making him glow like Jesus.

"I can't get to sleep because there's a cricket in here. I think it's in the closet, and it keeps chirping and chirping. Can you do something to make it stop? I had to throw some shoes to tell it to stop, but it didn't work" a nine-year-old Lily pleaded on hot summer night when the only noises were the evaporative cooler churning away and the cicadas in the trees as they settled in to get some sleep.

"Lily, don't ask me to kill da cricket because it bring good luck and also you not know if it really cricket or maybe your Uncle Thoy. Maybe he come back as cricket to help you and make lucky," my father explained as I suddenly saw it and chased it with a plastic cup so I could do a 'capture and release.' Later, after I had cornered it and summarily removed it to the comfort of the back porch, I passed by my dad on the way back to bed.

"Could Uncle Thoy come back as anything?" I asked with a tinge of doubt at the edges of my thoughts.

"Yes, I tink so," he replied as he scraped out the clods of mud from his golf shoes into a wastebasket. "Maybe cow or hummingbird or maybe monkey. My brodder alway like to talk monkey talk, so maybe he lib wid dem now."

So thinking my Uncle They could be a cricket or monkey prepared me to think that Bean might be my son or my grandfather Doc, or even my mother or sister in a previous life.

There was just enough uncertainty to make it plausible.

And like I always say, "Anything is possible."

The progression of our relationship only got weirder. One evening after we had been driving around together for about an hour, he asked if I would like to see a special place. In my head, the shrinking voice of reason said, "It's getting dark. Go home. This is not where you need to be."

But I heard my voice saying, "Sure, I guess so, but then I need to get home."

Suddenly, we were parked in what looked like an old neighborhood baseball field with a couple of bleachers and bases clearly marked with white spray paint. Darkness was approaching quickly, and he said, "This is where I like to come to see the stars come out. It's so dark in this spot with no street lights; you can really see the sky. I grew up a few blocks from here, and after my dad died when I was about nine, I would come here to sit and try to feel him close and talk to him up in the sky."

"I had special places, too where I would climb up into a tree or crawl inside some bushes by the side of my house to be alone and talk to myself mostly, but sometimes to my imaginary friend, Betty, and sometimes to God or to the tree itself. Kind of a Grandmother Willow moment or something," I explained.

"Okay, well let's try this one thing before we go. I'm going to put on a song, and I want you to recline your seat and roll down all the windows and try to feel the energy that comes from this place and the song and from me. I'd like to try to move your energy with my hands if that's okay. Can we try it?" he asked.

"Sure, but then we go," I reminded him.

The music began, and he turned it up to a moderately loud level. Radiohead. Soon his hands were moving on my arms and across my neck and head, then one hand on my stomach, then back to my third eye on my forehead. My dad told me to never let anyone touch my third eye—the space between my eyebrows. And the back of the head was another vulnerable spot to be protected. They were sacred, and they were the seat of the soul. If someone touched you there, they could steal it. Oddly, one of his hands was on my forehead and the other on my solar plexus.

Well, I guess that explains everything.

The music ended, and it was silent. His hands were gone, and

I opened my eyes. That was one of the weirdest feelings I ever felt. He started the car and drove me home without saying a word while Radiohead continued to play in the background, Thom Yorke's melancholy voice rising up from the car and wafting into the night

I think my dad was right. He was a thief, and he had stolen my soul.

Where Is My Mind
The Pixies 2004

Hubris is most often the tragic flaw in the tragic hero that causes the fall from grace, the disastrous downfall. Somehow, I managed to think that I could have it all—my children, my career, and my inappropriately young partner. Well, two out of three ain't bad, right?

Soon after Justin graduated from his college in New Mexico and married his sweetheart, Jenny, at an absolutely perfect ceremony at the Loretto Chapel in Santa Fe, Bean and I were unofficially a couple. We spent every free minute together and were seen around the college campus on a regular basis. People were beginning to talk about the forty something college professor and the twenty something student who worked in the library.

I had always been defiant about being "judged" by others and altering my behavior to comply with the moral prescriptions and dictates of those in our small Panhandle town of 160,000. It was a conservative community with a Baptist church on every corner and a megalithic monster church of evangelicals who influenced the attitudes and shaped the belief systems of the people there. The predator rapists of my youth had become Amarillo's most esteemed civic leaders and highly regarded businessmen, and they never missed a chance to press the flesh on Sundays. At least it wasn't my flesh. I don't think their church buddies would have believed any of it anyway, and I was too ashamed to ever tell. So it goes without saying, I had no respect for the opinions of these upstanding community citizens. In such a small town, they were all complicit in one way or another.

The worst part of it all was that Bean was closer in age to Maressa than he was to me. This uncomfortable proximity was a major point of contention for everyone, especially my children. Unfortunately, I could only see my own perspective which was blinded by the uncanny connection that was metastasizing daily. Bean had become a source to feed my obsessive-compulsive need for partnership with a kindred spirit. There was something comforting yet dangerous about him that compelled me to move closer when I should have stepped back. He was feral. And somehow, that wildness resonated in me, setting off all the bells and whistles that proclaimed my own savage soul. I had been dehumanized by years and years of neglect and misuse by JT and countless others over countless years so that I lost all self-respect and hope that I would ever have anything in my life except for my children. And make no mistake, their love and respect was everything to me. It kept me going, filled my life with purpose, and gave me something to celebrate daily. Their victories were my triumphs, and I tried my best to provide them with everything I could to grow them into interesting individuals who were independent thinkers and productive citizens of the world.

But then there was Bean.

Unruly dark curls of foolhardy hair dipped into iridescent green eyes. Eyes that churned like the green ocean. Like the cosmos. Green like the color of trees after a forest rain when the sun emerges and shimmers wet and sparkling. Although he was tall, he was wispy, light, and lean.

I watched him as he did his work in the computer lab at the library. The way he leaned over my students to help them with technical issues, his stealthy monitoring of the reference section, how he used his keys to unlock the copier so students could make copies. His hands moved in ways that were their own language. He was such an odd combination of wise ignorance and shy arrogance, always soft spoken with profound words spoken in awkward syntax. He seemed timeless and universal, perhaps an old soul like me.

It's funny how little things can make all the difference. The way someone smells, their skin, their breath. It's either a go or a no. I had declined interested prospects many times in the past because of stranger nuances. I didn't like the way they chewed their food or their hands always smelled like soap. I refused potential suitors based on the fact they were too white, too bald, too serious. Maybe they were too sane, thus too boring. But it frequently felt like a Seinfeld episode where they obsessed on one thing that became the deal-breaker. It was always silly, superficial, and inane, yet it was a thing. Enough of a thing that there was no possibility of moving forward. The politics had to be right, the religious beliefs needed to be in alignment, their backstory must be interesting yet provocative, and on and on.

Bean loved to tell a good story. His narratives were protracted beyond the curt, goal-oriented stories that Asian people tell. "Quick, to the point, okay, move on to the next thing!" No lingering and dawdling over details. "Cut to the chase. Get to the bottom line. Okay, and so what is the take-away from all this?" I would often think to myself as he launched into story mode. But I loved to hear him talk; it was soothing like a balm for a ragged spirit. And I understood what he was trying to tell me. I spoke his weird language, and he was eager to speak mine. I was fluent on so many levels. I could speak with an attitude that came from the hellscape I had lived through decades before. I also spoke wealth and culture, partly from being the granddaughter of an aristocratic Thai diplomat and also due to the eight-year stint as a doctor's wife. He wanted to know that world, and I was a ticket to a completely different kind of education.

Meanwhile, Justin and his new bride, were growing impatient and disgusted with what was unfolding in front of their eyes. I'm sure it was horrible to watch. After the initial shock of what was actually happening wore off, they were disheartened to the point that they decided to put as much distance as they could between them and the developing disaster. By spring, they had made arrangements to move to France for a year to teach and nurture their new marriage that had been disabled to a large degree by my disconcerting behavior.

I rationalized the whole thing by saying to myself, "They are adults, grown, college graduates, and not my responsibility. We should all be able to do what we want to do to be happy."

It was clear to everyone that I was racing toward a precipice, a point of no return. Obvious to everyone but me. I was still clinging to my own reality where I could indulge in an age-inappropriate relationship and maintain my lifestyle, relationships with my children, and career trajectory. I was still convinced that I could have it all, and everything would be okay.

Bean's living arrangements were nothing short of chaos, so after a series of unfortunate events, I agreed to let him stay at my house for a while. I had no long-term plan; I just knew I liked having him there. It wasn't the first time I had brought in a roommate for one reason or another. There had been Becky, a promising student who was transitioning into college and needed a place to escape an abusive home, who lived with us for a few months. There was Jill, a student attending WTSU from Michigan, who rented one of my four bedrooms one year when I was short on money and saw a way to add some additional income. So I told myself, "This is the same thing. I'm just helping a friend out while he gets his finances in order. Struggling college student. Everyone should be okay with that." I had purchased the home just months after I made the command decision to stay in Amarillo, making the best of my life with JT, and over the past fifteen years, it had become a very comfortable habitat.

But there were two main differences. He was not a female like the other roommates. And I had some kind of strange relationship with him that was headed in a questionable direction.

Johnny had been a kind of Woody Allen meets Mick Jagger hybrid while JT was more of a Jim Morrison-John Candy combo. Both were very interesting men, unusual-looking, oddly attractive. I was never really hung up on their looks; it was something else that made them appealing to me. It was always things like intellect, humor, musicality, vision.

But Bean was something else. I don't remember any physical attraction in the beginning, but there was definitely something else at play. He had the same birthday as my grandfather and somehow channeled that vibe. I felt like I had known him all of my life. Later, we encountered numerous metaphysical folks who all said he had been together for lifetimes and were old souls that had always traveled together. They said he had been my mother, my brother, and my wife at some point in time. Growing up with my father's talk of reincarnation and refusal to kill anything for fear it might be a dead relative made all this seem so much more plausible. I began to wonder what repurposed soul he might be.

So naturally, after he had been there less than a month, things did move in that direction and did take us to a completely different place both mentally and physically. When it took that turn, the bond that had held us together for almost a year transformed into something else entirely—something that neither of us knew how to handle. It was powerful and illogical and catastrophic and joyful all at the same time. It can best be described as being struck by lightning or being electrocuted.

When I was about eight or nine years old, there was a big Texas thunderstorm. In the Panhandle, the whole skylights up and thunder shakes all the windows and doors like an intruder trying to get in. I was in my kitchen one night during a storm and went to the icebox for a lemonade. That's what they called them in Texas before they were officially refrigerators. I had just washed my hands, and they were still wet. When I reached for the handle on the icebox, the ungrounded electrical current from the electrical storm sent a bolt of lightning through my hand and into my body. I will always remember that feeling like it was yesterday. I could not let go. My hand was held tight to the handle by the current passing through, so all I could do was keep holding the contact point as it rocked me back and forth with waves of current that traveled up my arm and down my right leg. After what seemed like long minutes and a certainty that if it ever stopped, my heart would be stopped, too, it threw me across the kitchen and into the wall about six or seven feet behind me. It utterly lifted my feet off the floor and threw me. When I opened my eyes, my whole body was tingling and vibrating like a million ants tap dancing just Beaneath my skin, and I swear I smelled something burning which I am pretty sure was me.

That electrocution experience was exactly how I felt when I touched Bean. I could not let go, even though I knew it would probably kill me. I still couldn't do it.

Float On
Modest Mouse 2004

When everything unraveled and started to go bad, it happened all at once. The college called me in and issued a stern warning. Within a couple of weeks, JT had discovered that Bean was living with me and Maressa and declared his intention to intervene. Either one of these encounters should have been threatening enough, serious enough to be a wake-up call. But like so many other times in my life, I just slept right through the alarm. And truly I was asleep in every sense of the word, oblivious to possible consequences, mindless in my determination to hold everything together.

"We asked you to come in today because we are having some recent concerns that need to be addressed. Out of courtesy to you, we want to hear from you and get to the truth of the matter," they said as we all gathered around a large wooden conference table in the English department's conference room.

"Please go on," I replied with a confident amount of collegiality.

"Numerous people have observed you with a young man who is a student here at the college. They have reported that your relationship with this person appears to be questionable in nature," Dr. Matthews went on. He had been the one who hired me nearly ten years earlier and had been a strong advocate and mentor through the years. I glanced at his face briefly, then down at the table where he folded his hands, one on top of the other.

"Can you tell us a little bit about what these folks may think they are seeing," he continued.

"I assume you are referencing the gentleman who is learning lab supervisor in the library. We are friends and carpool to school together. He lives close by, and I know his family," I offered with a conciliatory tone. I was shocked to hear what I was saying. The ability to lie in an impromptu fashion under these unfortunate circumstances surprised even me although I knew what an expert liar I could be. I learned that skill early on from my mother.

"So, you are saying that this student is a neighbor and friend only?" Meredith asked with a disbelieving look of consternation. She was a middle-aged professor that I envied tremendously because she had tenure and was set for life. I had been tapped to fill the next vacancy and now this. I felt like she was smirking behind her thick, black glasses. She was the only one on the hiring committee that was not excited to bring me on full time the following year when Dr. McGill retired.

"Yes, I am friends with his family," I countered although I had met his family and to say we were friends was far from the truth. They were as confused and baffled by our relationship as everyone else.

"Well, then, you just need to know that people are talking, and we are a small community college with a tight knit community. If there is anything untoward that is going on, it will undoubtedly come to light. I do not think that we, as a committee, can recommend you as planned for the upcoming vacancy unless repairs are made to this confusion or misunderstanding or whatever it is. We do not feel comfortable with that decision nor do we feel that it would be in the best interest of the college to offer the position to someone with questionable judgement. With that being said, you are under advisement to cease any contact with this individual, and we will revisit this in a couple of months to see what we are prepared to do about moving forward," he concluded as he toyed with a pen, turning it over and over, standing it upright, then laying it down again. I watched the pen as if it were a metaphor for situation. Stand up, stop going in circles, just stop twisting and turning and writhing in the wind. Dr. Matthews stood up and reached out his hand as if to say, "This handshake seals the deal and ends this ugly mess. You are lucky we didn't terminate you for your scandalous behavior. Shake my hand and stop being a foolish, old woman. You've flirted with a mid-life crisis, but fortunately there is time to avert disaster. Come to your senses and stop this ridiculous affair."

I shook his hand, nodded and said thank you as I left the room and walked down the long hallway of Ordman Hall. When I got to my car, I turned the key in the ignition and quickly drove away with Radiohead playing loudly, floating out the windows into the night air.

A week passed, and I still had not fully digested the warning given by Dr. Matthews. If I had been in my former mind, I would have been devastated and immediately in compliance with anything asked of me to secure my place in the world of academia that I had worked for, year after year for so long. It was my lifelong dream to transition over to the college full time after I had built a reputation and dazzled everyone as an adjunct for the past decade. We were talking about my whole career and the rest of my life. I simply pushed it aside to a dark corner of my brain and promised to do my best to show them that everything was fine, I was still the same awesome and devoted educator I had always been, and that Bean presented no true threat to my ability to be an expert instructor.

I was face down in the Kool-Aide. Reality was lost in some dense landscape far, far away in another galaxy, out of my reach, out of my mind. I was living in an alternative universe with my own version of the truth. When I think about what I lost at the college, I am ashamed of my ignorance and denial.

But what happened next was the thing that broke me, the thing that will torment me to the grave, or more precisely, the urn. When my children divvy up my remains and distribute them in whatever ceremonial fashion they see fit, I know that part of me will linger in the wind or the earth or the big blue sea, and those particles that were once a person named Lily Chaidee will dissolve into the stars, still holding onto the eternal sadness and regret—into the infinite universe, never letting go.

At the Bottom of Everything
Bright Eyes2004

Maressa was only thirteen when I met Bean and her life was inextricably changed forever. That is a critical time for a young girl dealing with adolescence and all the personal drama, insecurity, and confusion that accompany that age. It is a time when a child needs a guiding hand, a steady hand, to help her transition into the teens years and ultimately into adulthood. They need strong role models and an attentive parent that is present and available 24/7. Such a delicate time in her life, and I simply went missing one day. I abandoned her and forced her to become complicit in hiding what was really happening in her own home. I felt a little twinge of panic come up when I thought of her dad finding out, so I had to conceal it, alter it, make it something else. And she had to help me do it.

Throughout my life to this point, I had always had intolerance and harsh criticism for mothers who put their own love-life above their children's health and happiness. I railed at how selfish they were and how horrible they were to be so weak and stupid. Now I was that mother.

There is a moment in our lives when one little decision, turn left or turn right, stop or go, yes or no, changes everything—a defining moment that defines you as a person and seals your fate. That moment had arrived, and I was too out of control, deep in my own self-deception to recognize it when it came.

Bean liked to get in the car and drive around the neighborhood listening to music. It was like a soundtrack to our journey, and we would typically venture out for about an hour or so around dark. Other times, we took long walks around sunset, sometimes walking up to the elementary school park near the house. All of my children went there and played on that playground year after year. I had even attended that same school as a child. It should have been sacred grounds for me and my children to walk and talk and sit on the swings.

It belonged to them and to me, and now I had made it his space, too. And even more importantly, I should have been home, helping Maressa with homework, talking about her day, watching our favorite shows, supervising her piano practice, baking cookies together. But I was a ghost. Never really present, disappearing when she needed me, always absent. Essentially, I abandoned her at the most inopportune time imaginable.

One evening when I returned from one our walks, she seemed upset and said she had just gotten off the phone with her dad. We went into her bedroom and closed the door.

"Mom, this is getting really bad. My dad is going to find out what is happening here. He is starting to figure it out. I am scared of what he might do or what may happen," she pleaded.

"It's okay. I will handle him," I replied with little thought about the gravity of her words.

"You can't. He said he's going to call the police or make me come live with him or worse. Please, listen to me; you have to make Bean leave. Make him leave now. Please, Mom," she said as her voice was choked by sobs.

"Don't worry. It's going to be okay."

"It's not. Please, please. I am scared and I don't want to leave here. I don't want to go there. Please mom. He shouldn't be here. Just tell him to go," she pleaded as she sat on the bed with a look of terror on her face.

That should have broken my heart. That should have hit me with a powerful force that would wake me up. But I only wanted to deny the potential danger and believe that it could all work out for everyone. I just needed a little more time to make everything okay with everybody. Surely they would understand and come to accept it. I wanted to just keep going and keep everything calm and under control just like I had learned to do as a child when my mother would get her terrors, her episodes of madness. We were all good soldiers then, acting like everything was just as normal as could be, and showing no hint that we were crumbling or empty on the inside.

"Mom," she said with sheer desperation, "Are you listening? You have to do something. Now. It can't wait."

But I didn't get it. The big picture, the implications. I simply did not let it sink into that place inside of me where I should have reacted with a response triggered by imminent danger. The whole instinct to protect my young and fight for them was smothered by a feeling that was just white noise, blankness, denial, resistance, blindness, stupidity. If only…

"I will talk to your dad and make this okay. I will do it tomorrow, and it will be okay," I said with words that sounded broken even as I spoke them.

This was the moment that changed everything. The defining moment in one's life that shows them what they are made of. Are they truly what they think they are, or ruled by other darker forces like fear and obsession? I had worked so hard for so long to prove to myself and to everyone that I was not my crazy mother and that no part of her insanity lived in me, clung to me in dark spaces. And yet, here I was, being the one thing that I feared the most. The thing that was reprehensible and repulsive beyond all things. I was out of control and a destructive force to all those who loved me.

I had lost control of my ability to be a healthy, sane, nurturing parent.

I had become my mother.

And it was a tragedy by the textbook definition. Someone of high stature, well respected and trusted but deeply flawed and harboring a terrible weakness. They commit a disastrous deed followed by recognition of their mistake, a cathartic moment, but the epiphany comes too late, and they fall. They fall from that pedestal, from that high place, and they are destroyed along with many others who also perish because of their catastrophic deeds.

Everything comes at a price. Nothing is free. I knew this wisdom, yet I ignored it.

The price I paid to have Bean in my life was far greater than I ever imagined. And then there was that pivotal moment. The moment I should have put one foot in front of the other and marched right up to Bean and asked him to leave. The moment when I should have helped him collect his things and put them in his car and sent him away. What I wanted or how I felt should not have entered the equation. I was a mother. My child needed me. She warned me. She begged me. But I simply could not hear her or get to her in time.

It is one of life's great misfortunes that we never really recognize those life-changing moments when they are happening. And after it is too late, the tragedy plays in a loop, over and over, with every detail and sound and sensation—fresh, real, heartbreaking. Each one of us captured in time, acting it out, again and again. Only when we glance back do we see the poignancy of that moment and the endless consequences that change our lives forever. We slowly realize the magnitude of our mistakes, and it is too late to go back, rewind, and begin again—tabula rasa.

Something is hollow, empty, forsaken. Something is missing
Deep in a place that should be green and fertile—ripe with life
With lush forests that create canopies high above our heads
And lift us above tall trees into the pink and purple skies.

Look at me. Listen for a minute. I have something for you.
To make you see me, see what I possess. I bring these broken gifts,
Spiders and poison trickle through my fingers, up my arms, my neck
Their soft feet tickle as they race into my brain—too late to leave.

Arms that reach for you always empty, hold nothing in the night.
My love is toxic. And like Medusa, all who see me turn to stone
Their hearts burn to black in penal fires that consume me and
They die—like me. Our blue bodies crash through oceans of ice.

Now there is no mind or matter, only this feeling and this fire
Forsaken, we are nuclear and bloody lips speak lies like daggers
Words of devotion come in shattered breaths like broken glass
In a sad and silent place, we flow like holy water into one another.

My beautiful babies floated away to a distant place I can never reach
I grasped for them as they drifted deep in despair, now forever ghosts
My arms tried to cradle both them and you, but I failed so they fell
And with each moment, I can hear the sound of their hearts breaking.

Hold me tight, so tight I won't feel the hurt when the breath won't come
It's not too late to save yourself—swim to the surface—abandon this wreck
I am a pirate without treasure—I only have these pockets full of bones.
I'd give them all to you, but the weight would drag you and drown you.

We are criminal—you lie like me-steal like me—seek the dark like me
You are heart damaged—hollow and broken like an ancient sacred relic
Vacant like a pretty colored shell. We're only alive for a brief moment
When lambs kneel on bloody knees to worship at our deserted temple.

Tragically, I would drag my sacrificial offerings to your unholy altar
Blindly, I would look into your adamantine eyes and push the blade deep
I would do it all for you—if only it could set you free—save you
So you could be the one to finally see me, free me—save me at last.

Some people said it was a mid-life crisis. Others said I had always been crazy like my mother, so this was no surprise. I figured it must have been the years of abject isolation and lack of friends or any family except for my children. They were all I ever really had of value in my life, but we were all so painfully alone in our perfect little home. Or maybe the virus from the previous year that almost killed me had cooked my feverish brain.

But what foolish old woman sits around writing tragic love poems while her life burns to the ground?

There was no real explanation. My affinity for Sylvia Plath and understanding of her deliciously dark verse was quite fitting for the situation that was brewing. Sadly, while I was summoning my Plath and slouching towards Didion's Bethlehem, an apocalyptic storm was coming. Somehow, I failed to see it right there on the horizon. It was right there in front of me, if only I had the eyes to see.

I have been the victim, the rescuer, and the perpetrator at different times in my life. I have played the hero, the villain, and the martyr. And with each minute-tick, week-toc, month-tic, and year-toc that quietly slipped away in the distance, I made some good choices and some bad ones. I guess it's that way for everybody. But through it all, the timing was almost always catastrophically wrong. When the timing is wrong, and you see the dark clouds rolling in, you just have to call the game and go inside before the storm begins and you risk a certain death. You win a few; you lose a few. But I would always just stand there like the fool bird I've always been—Henny Penny alone in the rain, getting all wet, catching her death, and watching the sky come tumbling down.

Mr. Tamborine Man
Bob Dylan 2018

Years have passed, a dozen or more, and I continue to replay that moment over and over and over without end and reflect on my foolishness. I imagine who Maressa would have become if I had been there for her. There are a million pictures of her in my head—healthy, happy, hopeful—and they all haunt me. Searching her face in countless images, I memorize every trace of joy and every hint of wonder that no longer lives in her. Maybe she would have a house in the woods overlooking the ocean near Mulholland Drive, and we would meet up on the weekends to watch the huge blood-orange sun dissolve into the sea or go for some tea and treats.

I dream of the days when Justin was silly and weightless, living a life without limitations, planning a future that was filled with love and laughter. His sweet, hopeful voice echoes in my head from the years before I lost my halo. I wonder where he would be as distance stretches between us now. Maybe he would have a house by the college, and he would play golf at the Amarillo Country Club before heading over for Sunday dinner and evening walks with the whole family. We would go up to Olsen Park, and the grandkids would chase each other around the playground while we would sit in the swings and talk about our week. When I visit him nearly 2,000 miles away, his eyes remain distant and his words are laced with sadness and disappointment. The space between us never really dissolves as he manages his bitterness about how badly things turned out for two people who were inextricably linked and symbiotically connected once upon a long ago time in a faraway place.

Chaun lost his faith in me early on, but for Maressa and Justin, there was a time when I was everything to them, and they trusted me to be the one who was always there doing the right thing when nobody else would or could. There is nothing I can ever do to compensate for my failure to act. There is no excuse. There is no mercy. When I lost it all, I deserved it. It was the natural consequence of my actions, and I understand that now.

We are at the ocean. All of us. The kids are young again, laughing and running and splashing at the water's edge. It is almost dark, and we are dancing under the twilight canopy with our arms in the air and our faces to the sky as we disappear into the fog of time on that sunset beach that stretches beyond the reach of crazy sorrow. For a minute, our hearts are whole and hope is alive once again.

Fifty years later, I am still that stoic little Asian girl who never shows her feelings, who just stands there expressionless while life moves past her. I am still that fearful little girl who is numb and paralyzed by the chaos around her, not understanding the blurred lines between right and wrong, good and bad. Always seeing the villain inside the hero and the sometimes hoping for the angel inside the beast. Isolated. Alienated. Defiant.

I have wondered how my life would have been different if I had not been so detached from everyone and everything. If I had someone to actually bounce ideas off of, to consult and get perspective from. I needed friends or family who could be that voice of reason when I had none. Someone who would say, "Girl, have you lost your damn mind?" Or maybe, "What are you thinking? You want to do what? Tell me you are just kidding around because this is just plain crazy!"

But there was no one. I was always alone.

I had always planned to have my children close enough to participate actively in their adult lives. My children would bring their families over for cookouts, count fireflies on the patio, blow bubbles into the sky, make s'mores on the fire pit. I would have family, and I would have tenure. I'd do a little writing and publish a few things. I'd take trips with my children and their families to Disney World and the California beaches. I would die peacefully in my sleep with a book on my chest and Debussy or Bach playing softly in the background. My children would love me and respect me and my grandchildren would adore me. I had it all figured out quite nicely.

But, then there was Bean. And that changed everything.

The loss of a tenured position which I had worked for all my life was difficult to accept. My reputation, professional accomplishments, devotion to students, all of it, gone in an instant. But the worst loss was that of my children and my place in their lives.

Justin and Jenny spent a year teaching in France, most likely to escape the train wreck happening around them in Amarillo. It had been a very difficult time, I imagine. If I had to watch someone I love unravel and make a series of irrational decisions that were impossible to comprehend, it would be pretty hard to witness, and I wouldn't know what to do. Eventually, they chose graduate schools far away and moved to New England to begin a life with a distance that felt palpable- 1,948 miles to be exact. And I felt their absence with every breath. It was a loss too tremendous to fully absorb.

Chaun married around this same time and continued to do battle with the world around him. I think he was born in a mad season, with a terrible fear and loathing of everything he encountered. I didn't understand what he was going through when he was young, how he had such a hard time and struggled in so many ways. Even if I had known about it, I probably wouldn't have known how to help him. I still don't. He muddled through years in perpetual pajamas and in a fog of video games and depression. When I tried to encourage him to get some kind of training or go back to school, he frequently referenced his father and me by saying that we were overly educated and certainly no better for it, and that while we might be brilliant, we were also batshit crazy. He did not want to play that game. I had come to see that he had mental health issues like his father and his grandmother, but how do you help someone out of that chaos when you lack any real sense of direction yourself? It would be like the blind leading the blind. I had managed to always be high functioning while impaired, but I understand that not all people who struggle can hit that mark. Some days, just making it to the next one is a victory.

Both boys had a clear sense of how the world should be, how mothers should be, how everyone should be. Strange that they would have such a definitive view of life when I had always had a little more laissez faire attitude. Sure, I pushed for academic excellence and artistic development, but beyond that, I was always more tolerant of the varied hues and textures around me. I took them to the shelter on holidays and told them how the disenfranchised had really had a rough go and did not deserve judgment. I surrounded them with my students who were an assortment of unsavory stripes—gang-bangers, teen moms, addicts, you name it. All with the intention of showing them what it looked like to extend a hand and try to help people triumph over their hopeless resignation, cyclical dysfunction, and tragic endings—all without judgment or blame. Yet, somehow they developed an intolerance for foolishness and moral impropriety. They probably witnessed the enormous price extracted for such indulgences by observing their silly mother. Or perhaps they knew how close we all are to becoming that thing we fear the most. Maybe they felt the hot breath of the beast on their backs. Their father told me once that he felt like God and Satan were at war inside of him. He said he felt the epic battle being waged for his own soul. At the time I assumed he was speaking metaphorically, but addiction is indeed a curse, and surrendering to it is sort of like giving in to the beast and letting him devour your identity and shred your soul.

Maressa stayed with me for another fourteen years after Bean first entered our lives. Even though she stayed with her father the year after Bean was discovered, she returned. And although there was much anguish and chaos and craziness, she stayed. There were boys and parties and wild shenanigans, but I went along since I knew it was all my fault, and she stayed. I continued to serve her by doing everything for her and making her life as easy and effortless as possible so she would stay. We even left Amarillo when she started college so we could all be together in a place with more opportunity and brighter skies. We had always planned to go West to the big blue sea, but the move to Austin was at least an escape from the clutches of the Panhandle.

She and Bean were always too close in age to have anything but an awkward kind of sibling love for one another, and the blurred lines between them became dangerous from time to time. In a way, they both grew up together, and even though parts of their coming of age provided a great bonding experience, it was also a recipe for disaster and a ticking time bomb. Four and a half years after we all left Amarillo, she completed her college degree which was the milestone that gave her permission to begin a new life. It was a formidable challenge to find a job commensurate with her education, but she networked and hustled and scrounged up jobs and opportunities while remaining under-employed and dissatisfied. Since the summer she turned fifteen, she had been in a relationship with the man of her dreams. They shared a nice apartment, a little black cat, and talk of a happily ever after. But after a few tumultuous years, he turned out to be more than she could manage. He may have been kind, talented, smart, and handsome, but he was also an addict. So what could she do? He loved his alcohol and drugs more than he loved life and more than he loved her. She returned home again to get her moorings.

It was hard to imagine what the dynamics should look like at this point for the three of us—it felt like I was always in the middle of two people who both needed my time and attention. So instead of dividing the hours and minutes between them, it seemed like a better solution to simply combine forces and do everything together—dinners, movies, concerts, festivals, swimming, the gym, vacations, dance parties, grocery shopping, bookstores, museums, coffee shops, everything— the three of us. There wasn't much alone time for mother-daughter things nor was there much quality alone time with Bean. I guess we all should have known that our odd little triangle would not last forever.

It was great while it lasted, but about three years after Maressa returned home again and shortly after her 26th birthday, Bean finally crossed a line into territory that offered little chance of return. Somehow, while we probably should have seen it coming all along, I think everyone was still surprised. Once again, like so many years before, I tenaciously and impossibly tried to hold on to both of them and do damage control. And once again, I failed.

It's not easy for anyone to abandon a relationship. And for me, it's always been impossible to make that final exit. Bean and I had built a life over the years—a beautiful home, successful careers, strong partnerships, a secure future, common goals, and most importantly—a tentative trust. Our lives were knitted together into one tapestry that made it inconceivable to deconstruct. We had made it through quite a few rough patches and bumpy spots that tested our commitment to one another, yet we still managed to stand together somehow. So this was like surviving a tour of duty in a brutal war and then arriving home safely only to be hit by a bus. At some point, it's too late to leave, and there's too much to lose. Or maybe you already lost so much, you just need to hold on to what little is left and hope it's going to be enough.

It was like our own little # MeToo moment with a big serving of 'momentary lapse of judgment' and a side of 'collateral damage'. It is impossible to fully understand why any man would cross that sacred boundary of trust and voyage into darker territory. What if they were impaired when they acted out? Is there a cultural predisposition for an over abundance of machismo? What if they were raised by wolves who excused and enabled such behavior? Sure, there are varying degrees of misconduct, but they are all guilty of something stupid and impulsive and reckless and deserve at least some amount of trouble and shame.

Unfortunately, they are never the only ones to suffer. Why do they fail to hit the pause button long enough to consider the wide path of damage and long term consequences that will inevitably follow their inappropriate words or deeds? Maybe all men think they are entitled to express themselves carte blanche however they see fit and suffer from some kind of ego dysfunction that informs their actions and compels their misbehavior.

Yet, there is a larger question that looms. If love is unconditional, don't we find our way back from moments that shatter the trust by working toward discovery, accountability, reparations, and ultimately forgiveness?

It's not easy to abandon a child when they are in need—especially when someone they trust suddenly vanishes from their lives. It would have been easier if I could have demonstrated my love by running into a burning building to save any one of them or jumping into shark infested waters to rescue them. I would do it without hesitation. Mothers save their children before they save anyone else. That's just what they do. I wish I could have sacrificed myself to prove it to them.

But this was different. There were no raging infernos or circling sharks, and I couldn't prove my allegiance so easily. It was a muddled mess of people trying to stumble through an ongoing complicated maze compounded by an impulsive moment of insanity. Maybe we are all capable of fleeting bouts of delusion, but this was the ultimate fall from grace on so many levels. It was *family*—extended family, but family nonetheless. She was someone that was more like a sister than a stepdaughter and most importantly, there was a profound friendship between them that had grown for well over a decade.

Year after year, Bean and I were the caretakers, the problem-solvers, the rescuers, the support network, the financial backers, the compassionate listeners who always came through when she needed us. When something went off the rails, we were there to help get things back on track. It was a small way to achieve atonement for turning her world upside down when she was thirteen, and it was an expression of love and support that was important to us both.

She and I were certainly no strangers to betrayal or abandonment, but it was so much worse for her. Johnny broke Chaun's heart when he was seven, JT abandoned Justin when he was only six, and now Bean had torched his relationship with Maressa—who may have been a grown woman, but no less invested in their relationship. All of my children trusted men who put a dagger in their hearts. For me, my parents didn't really abandon me because they were never really there in the first place. In a way, that is better. But for her, she lost a trusted friend and extended family member, and with our tiny little family, it was an epic loss.

Perhaps the incident also provided the last chance Maressa and I would ever have to whip out our mermaid tails and head for the West coast where we would dive into the big blue to live happily ever after like we always said we would. In California, we could sip probiotic shakes and joyously dig our perfectly pedicured toes into the sand. That had always been our dream, and if we were ever going to make it happen, it seemed like now might be the time with the wind at our backs.

We are standing on the Huntington Beach pier, seagulls swirling and swooping around us as Maressa lifts French fries from Ruby's Diner into the air. She is small, six or seven, turning a toothless grin to the blue sky, her wild hair blowing in the wind. Justin stands nearby, maneuvering his ice cream cone and contemplating the waves. We are happy.

Actually, when I think about it, I realize that the mermaid dreams were my happy ending, not hers. She had no destiny or future or life apart from just being by my side. That was the script for my final chapter without regard for what would follow for her after a few more years passed, and I began my final decline. It was more about me and less about her, and the truth is that she needed to create her own path and identity, separate from mine. She needed to be free of me to enter the world and experience it as a self-sufficient, independent adult. Justin and Maressa had both been my happiness, but I should have learned how to be happy without holding them hostage. I know now that we are each responsible for our own happiness and should never be dependent on others to provide it.

Maybe this breach of trust was not the best impetus to catalyze change and end our strange little party of three, but in the long run, it was probably for the best. In the back of my mind, I knew at some point I would die and leave them both behind. Neither of them was equipped for that reality. Maressa needed her autonomy and permission to begin a life without me. Bean needed a reason to wake up and face the unresolved issues he carried that would require years of attention and analysis. I needed to redefine what my life might look like without any of them.

I had been unable to summon the kind of strength to stand alone more than a few times in my life. My therapist even told me that I was one of the most fearful people she had ever met. Often paralyzed by fear of so many things, my world held so many terrors, all shapes and sizes. Now my health problems all crowd together in the wings, just waiting to burst on to the stage. The impending loss of vision, the fluttering-sputtering-tattered-heart, the blood cells that get confused and launch their armies to attack me for no reason. All the inevitable infirmities. I always said I came from the shallow end of the gene pool, and now it was proving that to be true more than ever before. How could I become a burden on any of my children when I can no longer fend for myself and remain so fiercely independent? It wouldn't be fair. Bean had earned his rightful place as my caretaker, my helper, my eyes. After all I gave up for him, all I gave to him, and all he put me through—maybe it was an opportunity for redemption.

I have always been the drowning victim who frantically grasps on to anything and everything that might save them from going under. Save them from the monster that is always waiting for the right moment to wreak havoc and mayhem. In the chaos that ensued, I was forced to learn some strategies to stay afloat, even if actual swimming was never meant to be. I returned to Al-Anon after decades of absence. The first time I went was when I figured out that Johnny was an alcoholic, and it was there that I learned I was a classic textbook case of co-dependency. Now, I returned simply to get the support to reign in the destructive aspects of my dysfunctions. *God grant me the serenity to accept the things I cannot change…*

Maressa moved out and into her own apartment, and it was not long after that she met a guy, and the rest is history. Only the knight in shining armor that rescued her took her far away to his castle, across the deep blue sea, wider than our love, deeper than I could go to keep her. I'm not sure if it was simply time to cut the cord, leave the nest, and fly solo, or if it was Bean that made it impossible to stay. Either way, it was painfully certain that our time together had finally come to an end, and she could not have chosen a life farther away from home. Over 5,000 miles in fact, to become an expat in a place with a cold gray sea. This time, she did not stay. She was the one who let go.

I think Maressa came closest to understanding why I did what I did, how years of shame and guilt had eaten into my bones and created a twisted and deformed visage. But recognizing the elephant in the room didn't make it okay. Of course, everyone has reasons why they fail to be what they need to be for those they love, but the only thing that really matters is that they make bad choices and let everyone down in the process. For now, we manage to claim a week in the summer to reconnect, and I am happy that she has become such a strong woman, stronger than I could ever be. I guess at some point, most folks finally have to give up on people who can't ever seem to get their act together. I just never thought it would be me. It's crazy to think about how I always thought I was the responsible, hard-working, sane person in the family. Life is full of twists and turns, I guess.

God grant me the courage to change the things I can.

Justin continues to talk to me every Sunday afternoon and shows a kindness that speaks volumes about what goodness his heart holds. We share warmth and compassion for one another, but it is safer for him to keep a comfortable distance. When I visit for my week in Massachusetts with him and his family, I accompany him to the golf course and spend the day watching him from the cart, just like I did when he played in high school. Jenny is one of the most intelligent and caring people I have ever known. She is dedicated to Justin and their daughter who is bright, focused, and talented like her parents. They all play piano for me after dinner, and then we read together and discuss the books as darkness descends and the house falls silent. Grace is a dancer, and sometimes she puts on her little tutu, and we dance around the house together. We have special outings and stop for lobster rolls and then ice cream at Carter's and visit the beaches at Plum Island or Manchester-by-the-Sea. The day before I leave, we stop by Pirot's Bakery in Methuen for a Augietta pie to celebrate another summer visit until the next year rolls around. I always cry when it's time to leave and hug the girls tightly while trying to imprint the sensation so I can summon it at will throughout the long year apart. I hold Justin close, smell his hair, and try to capture a bit of that sweet and happy boy I lost all those years ago. Wherever I am, he is always nearby—palpable, present, smiling, yet out of reach.

Chaun moved close to Austin a few years back and came by to visit every couple of weeks. We were both optimistic about growing our relationship and getting to know each other better. But his demons kept him busy, and there were so many terrible things he brought along with him. He had been a cop in a small town near Amarillo where meth had taken over, and one afternoon on a call, the meth dealer opened the door with a shotgun and blasted his partner in the face. His partner survived, but I think there's something about standing there with bone fragments and a shower of bloody skin bits all over you that makes you rethink your priorities. Shortly after, he left the force and started planning his move. I didn't know how to help him, and there was little I could actually do. The years had done irreparable damage, and he did not really know me or trust me well enough to lean on me. And why would he? All of his life, I was too busy with something or someone to make the time to focus on his pain. Maybe it was better to just put it in the past and leave it there. And it did not help the situation that everyone he ever trusted—his father, my mother, even JT—they all vilified me and blamed me for everything which only helped feed his anger and resentment through the years. Timed passed, and his partner's wounds healed after numerous reconstructive surgeries, but Chaun's wounds were much more insidious and raw. After over three years of living near me in Austin, even Chaun decided to take his family and move 1,000 miles away to Colorado in search of his peace and blue skies.

It's hard to believe that I married Bean at the local Unitarian Church all those years ago; we mark our fifteenth anniversary this year. I've always believed marriage would make everything okay. I guess that's why I proposed to Johnny and later to JT. I thought getting married was the best thing two people could do and was the key to making it last forever. I had learned from the best. My parents failed to provide great role models for healthy relationships, yet somehow they survived together until the very end. Somehow that seems sort of inspirational in a sad kind of way. I think longevity is something commendable regardless of how you get there. And I bet all couples who spend thirty or forty years together have some really ugly, messed up stories to tell.

Through it all, Bean has continued to learn how to be a man and how to be a husband. In spite of his many failures along the way, he stayed, and he kept trying. I did, too. There did not appear to be any viable alternatives for either of us. It was a mutually Beaneficial union, championing one another's ambitions, planning survival strategies, and developing the same interests. It could have been the perfect marriage until closer inspection revealed the cracks and fissures that traversed the foundation. Maybe all the marriages that last are like that. Bones in the closet, secrets under the bed. We certainly had our share of these broken relics stashed all over the place.

How do people move on when they have built their world around someone and integrated them into the very fabric of their lives? The years allow them to metastasize and wrap around each other thus integrating and fusing into one being. To separate would most certainly kill them both. For me, all of the ghosts from the past crowd together and are always right there, sitting quietly beside me, standing behind me, following me from room to room, always watching their ever glorious queen of guilt.

All of the ghosts are frozen in time.

David is there. And Augie with baby Shane.

Students, many soon to be senior citizens themselves, are forever sixteen as they gather around. Becky twirls and dips with Thomas in their pas de deux for the spring dance recital in 1994. *Last time I heard, she had three or four kids and lived in a trailer somewhere in Idaho.* Michael stands and delivers his James Baldwin prose selection in his dark suit and skinny tie at the UIL state meet in 1982. *He died from AIDS about ten years later.* Mandy comes into the reception hall in her pretty wedding dress as I serve her guests slices of cake in 1990. *She divorced a few years later and works at the local Sam's Club.* Troy writes about using a dent puller to steal a Toyota and sing's Beck's *Loser* everyday when he comes to class. *He went to prison and was shot in his driveway a few years later.* Andie tells me she has no reason to wake up in the morning and is crippled with depression and occasional suicidal ideation. *She later gets tenure at the same college that turned its back on me after I married Bean.* Amie stands in front of the mirror backstage before our dance recital and declares that this will be the moment from her life that will be the high point and never forgotten. *Fifteen years later she messages me that she showed the dance recital tapes to her daughter and they remain a cherished moment for her.* All so endlessly young and hopeful. All frozen in time at age sixteen or seventeen.

And teachers I have worked with are still with me, too. Strange to think about little snippets of time when it seems like yesterday and everything is so perfectly clear. Nancy with the bad luck and amazing avocado dip. Jim, the crotchety old Latin teacher, coming to my Great Books seminar with his passion for wisdom and his beat up old briefcase. Sara, who brought lunch every week as we swapped recipes and shared meals. Jenny who went to the Crystal Confectionary and Adam's Rib with me after school on Fridays to play asteroids and drink pina coladas. Wally, the affable old golf coach who always had a smile and a kind word. Troy, the Beanevolent school counselor who took up a staff collection after my house was robbed. *Where are they now?*

And the friends of my children are also little ghosts who visit me. Justin's friends—Travis, Chad, Matt, Alex, Josh, and Daniel. All thirteen forever—playing video games, strumming guitars, sitting in the den watching X-Files with no lights on. Maressa's friends—Babs, Mary, Tiffany, Becca, and Emily. All ten years old forever and hugging our snowball puppies, jumping on the trampoline, running through the sprinklers and doing rain dances on the driveway under shimmering cottonwoods. Chaun's friends—Lando, Brandon, and Spencer doing bike tricks on home-made ramps, flirting with the girls, and planning their lives. All of them disappearing into the past and sitting with me in quiet moments.

My grandchildren are ghosts because of time and distance that makes them come to life and become corporeal only once a year when I visit them. Frozen moments capture four year old RaeRae sitting in her car seat in the back of my car, listening to Andrea Bocelli's *Time to Say Goodbye* with her eyes closed and her hands in the air like she is at a revival. I told her that she could feel the music come through her hands the same way people have Jesus come into them, and she lifted those little arms and raised her little hands with fingers wide open until she felt it happen. Then I summon five-year-old John, my only grandson, as he stands up with the band at Opie's Bar-B-Q on Sunday after church in Spicewood. He bounces his little body, taps his little foot, and lifts his little voice like a country angel. Next, is his sister Michelle who sits in the bubble bath at my house as we play music and sing along and play Name that Tune. She loves Taylor Swift and giggles and splashes as we sing. And then there is baby Grace in Boston who puts on her little ballet costume to dance and twirl with me until we are dizzy. Then we sing along to *Ho Hey*, her favorite Lumineers song as we are driving to Friendly's for ice cream. There is always music playing and joyful song when their ghosts come to visit. All of them, one by one, have disappeared into the fog of endless miles.

The memories are too real and too strong to bear, but I am a ghost hoarder. I have a penchant for holding on to things way past their expiration date. Things change, but I fight it. I want constancy. I need predictability. The same people in the same place doing the same things in the same way every day over and over and over forever and ever amen.

I'd like to tell you that we lived happily ever after. That when I lost everything, everything that mattered, it was worth it.

But I can't.

I *can* tell you that Bean fought the good fight, and sometimes he won, and sometimes he did not. His failures were epic, and there were always casualties and collateral damage. But I like to think he learned from them and learned things about himself and would never repeat them if given the chance.

Together, we established routines, focused on our work, completed household projects, and achieved a fragile kind of peace. And there are still things that bring delight. Food and films. Books and travel. Music and sleep.

I look forward to holidays and visits with the kids. Each one of my children became such a strange hybrid of strength and weakness, each with their own set of issues to manage. Chaun still struggles and sometimes surrenders but finds cold comfort in religion and nature and the peace they bring. Justin finally secured a tenure track position as a professor of philosophy at a small college and has managed his challenges with grace and dignity through hard work and determination. He is an attentive father and husband, an avid golfer, a great educator, and a moral man. Both of them fear the fading and unraveling that took their father, and they keep their fingers on the pulse of their physical and mental health. Maressa is a bright and beautiful woman, a talented writer, and steady worker with insightfulness beyond her years. She battles illness and anxiety but soldiers ahead, even on the dark days. I see my strength in her and am glad I had something she could use. Justin and Maressa both know how to do manage themselves and keep fighting and functioning, even if they sometimes feel the lonliness, the trembling like tiny earthquakes, and the bone chilling emptiness in the hollow place where I used to live.

Losing them has been my life's most crippling disappointment. When they left, I smiled and sent them on with prayers and wishes for happiness and health. I encouraged Justin to go where he needed to go for school and for jobs. I supported Maressa's decision to move abroad with her domestic partner and told her to enjoy every moment of the grand adventure. I told Chaun to go where he felt happy and at peace. But on the inside, I felt the landslide, the crumbling and collapsing of it all.

Some have said that you cannot change the past, so move forward and focus on making the future a better one. But I fail to see how any plan for the future could possibly compensate for what I have done in the past. I think some things are too big to ever accept or forgive. So when I think about living through years of infirmity and loneliness, I know I deserve whatever suffering comes my way. It will be atonement. It will be retribution for my sins. Sins that I can never be free of.

I think Justin and Maressa took a blade to the heart and writhed in pain while I just stood there watching in stupid awe. But Chaun did not feel a thing because we had never really connected as well as we should have, and he had suffered through so much already. Through the years, he looked on as a spectator, and after all the life-saving heroics had failed and everyone was gone, he stepped in a little closer. Moved closer with a heart full of bitterness and rage and fear. A heart swollen with hope and hunger. He did not have to stand in line behind the others for scraps and crumbs anymore. He could finally come closer and maybe get a little mother's milk to sooth his soul and heal himself. I guess what I had to offer wasn't enough in the end or maybe just too little too late, so eventually, he too decided to leave along with any chance we would ever really mend things or be a part of each other's lives.

But part of being a mother is letting them go, so I remind myself that it is only natural that they have ventured forth to build their own lives without me. It is as it should be. Children are not meant to stay with their parents forever.

But why did they all choose such far away places, and what about all the families that do manage to stay close? I guess some things are just not meant to be. Or maybe this is what happens when you *force* things that were not meant to be. Perhaps the universe is self-correcting and has a wicked sense of humor.

And what about the men I have loved? David lives a solitary life in the Panhandle while Augie is still married to Cyndie and living somewhere near an Indian reservation in Oklahoma. Johnny reinvented himself as the drummer in a rock 'n roll band that was always who he was in his heart, like that wild man playing in his Fruit of the Looms, cigarette dangling and drumsticks flying all those years ago and leaving his life as a doctor far behind him, buried in a faraway forgotten place. JT finally lost his mother and lives alone with Maressa's cat, Olive. It has made him into a kinder version of himself, and we talk regularly now. Conversations about our daughter, our cats, our jobs, our lives. He still believes that when trust is broken, you walk away and never look back. I don't understand that and could never make things that simple. It guarantees that he will spend his last days alone, sitting on the porch with a glass of whiskey, reflecting on a life unlived.

I have always liked to blame the alcohol for the ruin. It was easier than admitting the truth. I thought I could wish them back to wellness or love them back to life. Now my sons have manifested symptoms, and we all know alcohol is not the culprit. There is nothing I can do except say prayers and helplessly hope they will always be able to feel my love. Even if they are lost in the fog, I know the core parts of them will always be there.

And the wisdom to know the difference. Amen.

I think I know one thing: I am a trooper. The whole "trooper" thing began when Justin was ten or eleven and Maressa was about five. Our yearly vacation to Disneyland posed some issues when she got too big to push around in her stroller. We logged maybe fifteen to twenty miles per day walking the expansive grounds, and the first year she had to walk was brutal on the first day. Justin came up with the clever idea to incentivize her "walking without whining" campaign. She would receive the coveted trooper badge at the end of the trip if she would just put on her big girl panties and keep up. Miraculously, it worked! We made it through the next three days without any complaining or collapsing. It was genius. After that summer, we went on to award trooper badges to Babs and Mary and a host of other worthy recipients until we had a cadre of brave little troopers.

At least I like to think I am a trooper. That whenever the going gets rough, I get going. I can take a lickin' and keep on tickin.' Just like the Energizer bunny, nothing can stop me. I have coping skills and a giant toolbox of tricks and tips on how to cope with terrible things. I manage to stay busy and try to do good things. I survive. And sometimes, I even manage to find bits of contentment.

My children are all troopers, too, and for that, I am proud. They get knocked down, but they get up and get on and fight the good fight. That's really hard sometimes, but they summon the strength and just do it.

It is lonely now. Everyone is safely out of reach, and we are alone. It hasn't been easy for Bean to reinvent himself, but he understands now things he never knew before. Part of that could be the result of never missing a week of therapy since the incident nearly three years ago. He has been excavating in the ruins of his troubled life so that he has actually uncovered some nuggets of truth and wisdom to help him understand how he came to be and who he hopes to be one day. Both of us are still orphans, damaged yet determined to parent ourselves.

I hope to have my own identity for the first time in my life, but I don't know where to start. I still don't know where I begin and end and where the boundaries are for others. I always thought that absorbing the people you love in order to achieve some kind of symbiotic union was the best way to love someone, but I have discovered that we are all still alone regardless of how many people we consume. No one is immune from mistakes or bad choices, but as we move forward, we try to make sure that we never cause more harm. Hopefully, our future foibles and fumbles will only bring injury to ourselves and no one else. Our intentions are pure, but as we all know, sometimes things just don't go as we plan.

Bean and I find comfort with each other and live along side the sins of our past. We own them. Grieve with them. Pay attention to them. Take them out and weep for them from time to time. And then we sit together and breathe in the day and absorb the light and accept our failures. They are a part of who we are. But while they are part of us, they are not all we are—they do not define us completely. As each day arrives, we have new opportunities to do meaningful work and personal inventory. We hold hands and find little bits of peace here and there. We work long days and give much of our energy to our students and our schools. I guess we have common goals and common vision about what the future might look like. We help each other and take turns propping each other up or stepping in for the one who needs it most. We want what is best for each other and try to support each other to make that happen. We are a team. We are partners. I guess that's what love is... trying to help the other guy be the best version of themselves possible with as little suffering as possible. Helping them get up when they fall. Looking for the best in them and trying to forgive them when they are foolish or flawed. Believing they will always be there to respond and provide relief in rough patches and bumpy spots.

We are a work in progress. Bean takes long walks in the greenbelt near St. Edward's Loop every Saturday morning and records little videos for me since I am not well enough to accompany him. Waterfalls, glorious trees, crystal clear streams. They heal him. I enjoy my routines, hold my fat little Russian Blue in my lap, try to use the time I have left wisely. My health may be poor, but Bean doesn't seem to mind or fear it as much as he once did. We take our dinner to the couch and watch the world news, discuss our students, go to movies on the weekend, get bubble tea for a treat, and hang out in bookstores with any time leftover.

It is all the small things that make a life. So I guess we have that. And maybe things are as they should be with each of us learning how to be healed and whole.

Once a week I sit on the couch with Maddie, the emotional support dog, and contemplate distance and other troubling things.

Justin nearly 2,000 miles away. Maressa over 5,000 miles away. Chaun, about 1,000 and always an immeasurable distance away. My psychologist enters the room, and we begin.

We talk for a few minutes about things in the news that are so disconcerting. We speak of my impending blindness and my autoimmunity. We speak of my children and grand-children. We discuss my sadness. After almost thirty minutes of exploring the dark waters of my distress, she tells me, "It's time now. Let go of them."

"I don't know how," I reply. "I have always had a child with me since I was a teen-age mother. They are my life, my breath, my blood, my bones. I am nothing without them. I am invisible. I am without purpose, unmoored, untethered," I say as I fight back the torrent of tears.

"It is time to take care of yourself. Do what is best for you. They are grown adults. You are no longer responsible for them," she offers as I lean forward and clasp my hands in my lap.

"I don't know where to start. Truth is, they were my life, my identity, my anchor to keep me grounded in reality, in purpose, in life. The things I've done and failed to do. The ways I've hurt them. I can't forgive myself. There is no excuse to justify it. I feel so lost," I confess as I wipe away the inevitable wetness on my face.

"Lily, it's time to move on, don't you think?" positing what I think is a rhetorical question as she leans toward me with a tissue box extended with both hands.

I wipe away tears and blow my nose. There is a feeling of emptiness and loneliness that consumes me. I surrender to it.

"Lily, I want to invite you to come to the present. Be here in this moment. Step out of the past and walk toward the now. Tell me about right now," she says as she replaces the tissues and arranges on the table in front of me.

I pause, then take a deep inhalation and begin, "I am getting older every minute, but Bean never seems to age. I am circling sixty, and the indignities of aging are upon me, not to mention the fact that I am literally falling apart. But Bean is gloriously knee deep in his thirties, the prime of his life. Everything is in front of him, a wide-open road, while mine is mostly in the rear-view mirror. How can we reconcile that? I'm so uncertain about how we will navigate forward. We snuggle close every night until we go to sleep, but sometime during the night he scooches over to the edge of our enormous bed, and I know he is afraid of waking up with a cold arm wrapped around him in the morning. I was diagnosed with sleep apnea awhile back, and when I told him that I stopped breathing about ten to twelve times every hour through the night, I saw his face. I saw how his eyes turned away in quiet anguish until they found something else to fix upon so I couldn't see his apprehension. That's just one example. He doesn't want to think about me being sick, and he is still terrified of me dying because he says he connects it to his father's death when he was only nine years old. I try to joke about it and tell him that the way he drives, it's probably going to be him that's the first to go, but we both know the truth."

I can tell that the sun is getting lower in the sky because of the way the light filters through the window onto the floor. It always has warmer tones this time of day, right before dusk.

"That is one of many ways I am in decline and losing my vitality. It is certain that I am from the shallow end of the gene pool. Both of my parents died in their sixties and were plagued by numerous health conditions the last decade of their lives. It appears that I will suffer the same fate.

I get incapacitating flares several times a year from my auto-immune condition. They come at the most inopportune times, and I go down for the count, oblivious to the world, lost in a fever that will not let me go. I have never wanted to be a burden on my children when I am old or sick, but I have discovered that I hate to lean on Bean just as much. He is always there, patient, attentive. I think there must be some resentment behind all that. There has to be."

I reach for my bottle of water and take a sip, then return my hands to my lap where I pull at the little bits of skin on the sides of my fingers. I use my hands a lot when I talk, and when I am having difficulty reaching my words, I fidget with them a lot more. Still pink, torn, and tattered like they were when I first figured out the truths of this world all those years ago.

"That's not all. The scariest of all is the hereditary eye disease I found out about last summer. Retinal dystrophy will ultimately take my sight as it invades my central vision. Two years or ten years, who knows? The only thing for sure is that it will happen. I'm already unable to drive after dusk. But Bean is still there, reassuring and joking around about my blindness. He calls me "Batty" sometimes to joke about how blind I am and how cute it is, but it doesn't help. I make note that a bat implies not only "blind as a bat" but also "crazy". You know, "bats in the belfry" or "batshit crazy." He's probably right on both accounts. It's bad enough that I age faster and disproportionately to him, but this disability, this impending helplessness, I just don't think it's fair to either of us." I say with resolute certainty.

"It is not for you to decide what Bean should do. He seems committed to stay. Maybe it could even be a good experience for him to be the strong one if you become weak," she offers.

"He wants to be a good man. He tries to do the right things that good people do. No one ever showed him how or even thought about things like that when he was growing up. He's trying to learn, and even though he reverts to old ways and fails from time to time, he keeps trying. I love how he is always calm and composed, soft and gentle, but maybe that's not enough. I mean, he has been the single most destructive force in my life and my children's lives. I feel so guilty for allowing myself to be happy with him since it came at the cost of their happiness," I say with a sadness that hangs onto the edges of my words. For a second, my mind wanders down that endless stretch of sand.

I am walking beside my children on a beach, watching their babies scampering ahead, wild hair blowing in the wind, giggling, chasing the tide, and screeching with joy as the white foam tickles their toes.

"It should be his decision if he's up for what's coming or not. Maybe all of the challenges will provide him an opportunity to be selfless and devoted and cultivate positive qualities that will ultimately be very self-affirming and transformational. Maybe doing this for you is what he needs to be the person he wants to be and prove to himself that he can be that person. I want you to shift the focus a bit. Look at things from a different perspective. It is time for you to do some self-care. You need to begin now. With your declining health and uncertain career trajectory, you must plan for the future. Try to imagine who you are apart from Bean and apart from your children and give everyone permission to do what they feel they must do, including yourself," she offers with an unimaginable patience. I am back in the room, but the salty taste of the ocean lingers on my lips.

"But I don't do self-care. I am the one who takes care of everybody else. Imagine this. A little girl watches as her mother spirals out of control and is helpless to do anything to stop her or help her. The little girl grows up and marries men with mental health issues so she can have another opportunity to fix them. Anyway, it didn't work with her mom, and it didn't work with her partners. She was powerless and could only stand by and watch. I can't dive deep into my own health problems when anxiety over the others is always with me. I've gone to support groups and shared my story, but I grieve for all of us. I don't understand why mental health issues are so stigmatized. If you had a physical condition like diabetes or heart disease, it would evoke sympathy and compassion. But mental health issues don't get the same support. These are the illnesses that cause people to abandon you, or judge you, or fear you, or deny you equal status. No illness is a reason for shame or exile. I just want to know that the ones I care about are going to have what they need to be comfortable and secure and feel loved and supported. These thoughts consume me. I want everyone to be okay after I am gone."

"Let's try to come back to the idea that you must focus on yourself for now," she says as she shifts her weight and gives me her trademark lingering look.

"I feel like it might be too late to reimagine what my life might be. Maybe the tide is going out to sea, and I have to follow it," as I hear how my words might sound dramatic like my mother's frequent histrionic episodes.

She looks at her watch.

"You know, when I was in graduate school, my master's thesis was on transactional analysis, and I realized even then that I had played all the parts of the triangle already. Victim, rescuer, persecutor. So I'm not on the proverbial pity pot. I did this. I chose this. I created this mess."

As I look down at my hands, for a brief second I picture Lady MacBeth and Pontius Pilate and others with blood on their hands— all guilty of unforgivable atrocities. Then I begin to ponder when they began to look so old and wrinkly. I feel a tiny skin tag on the cuticle of my thumb and quickly tear it off. Pink, raw flesh reveals itself and begins to bleed.

I hide it by slipping my hand into the pocket of my sweater and continue, "Nobody wants to turn around and see a swath of bodies littering the road behind them. There shouldn't have to be collateral damage or any casualties along the way to achieving our happiness or attaining our peace. Why can't we just move along without leaving a path of destruction in our wake? It crushes me a little more every day to think about how I have failed to protect the ones I love. I've been trying to forgive myself for all kinds of things since I was a little girl. But this thing with my children. It's the most difficult."

For a moment, I can hear distant voices filled with joy as they laugh and sing and call to me. "Mom, watch me. Mom, mom," they urgently plead as they reveal their endless wonders and dazzle me with their blinding light. Justin's hair falls into his eyes as he throws his head back revealing a crooked smile and Maressa lifts her flawless face to the warm sun. For that moment, they are radiant, unbroken, and whole. For a moment, I am complete.

"Lily, it's time to work on yourself and prepare for the future. There is so much to do to be ready when these things happen with all your health issues and job uncertainties. Let Bean help as much as you can let him. Be present in the now. Holding on to the past is not going to make anything better because you can't do anything to change it," she says as she rises from the couch, the universal symbol that says our time is over.

"I just need for my children to know how much I regret the choices I made and the things I did that made their lives difficult or painful. I want them to see that they are everything to me. I just need to figure out a way to do something to make it better, to heal the hurt, to mend what is broken," I say with a heaviness of spirit. The sound of the surf rises in my ears.

"Your children have left you to live their lives. You have to let them go now," she repeats in a quiet but resolute voice.

The familiar crushing feeling returns to my chest like someone is squeezing me so hard I can't get my breath. I stand up and nod to signal some mutual closure and turn to open the door, quietly closing it behind me. I stiffly descend a few steps and head to my car, squeezing the keys tightly in my hand. An ocean of cars move like waves on the horizon as they make their way home on their evening commute. The air is brisk and filled with the promise of night.

So that's it. That's the story.

All I can say about it now is that time is savage. When moments pass, they are lost forever. When people leave you, they never come back. And if they do, it's never the same. After all the lessons life brings, sometimes it still doesn't make any sense. How you can love something so much it is like oxygen, yet you can't stop yourself from destroying it?

But this I know. Love is like lightning. Like being electrocuted. You grab these people you love and the light moves through you like fire. Like electric energy, and you can't tell where you stop and they begin. You can't tell if the power surge is making you stronger or killing you. You just hold on no matter what.

And I know this, too. I couldn't let them go. Not then and not now. It was never a choice. Not really.

Even if it killed me. Even if it killed them.

I couldn't let go.

If you have enjoyed this book, please leave a brief
review on Amazon or Goodreads or at your online
bookseller of choice.

OTHER ANAPHORA LITERARY PRESS TITLES

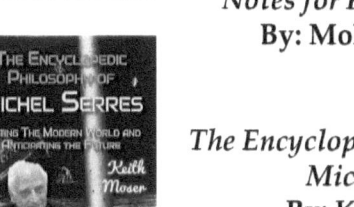

The History of British and American Author-Publishers
By: Anna Faktorovich

Notes for Further Research
By: Molly Kirschner

The Encyclopedic Philosophy of Michel Serres
By: Keith Moser

The Visit
By: Michael G. Casey

How to Be Happy
By: C. J. Jos

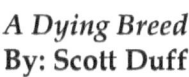

A Dying Breed
By: Scott Duff

Love in the Cretaceous
By: Howard W. Robertson

The Second of Seven
By: Jeremie Guy